THE CIRCLE'S CORNER

Jeffrey A. Ricken

Things are seldom what they seem;
skim milk masquerades as cream.
—William S. Gilbert,
H.M.S. Pinafore

EVAN DYLAN PRESS

Library of Congress Cataloging-in-Publication Data

ISBN 0-615-13493-9

Cover Design by Thomas Guerrero

Author photograph by Chuck Nguyen at
http://chucktography.smugmug.com

While *The Circle's Corner* contains historical characters and events, the book is a work of fiction. All fictional characters and all of the dialogue are from the writer's imagination.

Printed in the United States of America
At Publishers' Graphics

Dedicated to

Abbe

Wife, lover and friend,

From prologue to the end.

Acknowledgements

This novel would not have been realized without the generous, professional counsel and skills of the following people: patient advice and professional editing by Sally Noonan, guidance in writing support from Carol Eastman, expert photography by Chuck Nguyen, and innovative cover graphics by Thomas Guerrero. Preliminary reviews and encouragement provided by Phyllis Zapp and Sam Feldt. Finally, my grateful appreciation to my brother-in-law, Robert Axelrad, who gave his valuable time and inspiration to help me complete this *circle*.

PROLOGUE

How could seventeen-year-old Anna know that, within the hour, her innocence as a girl would violently end, and her nightmare begin? She always kept her appointments with Dr. Neugebauer. He was a fine doctor, and was kind to her during embarrassing, but necessary treatments. She had learned months earlier from the doctor during a routine examination that she would be unable to have children. He explained this was due to something called fibrosis of her Fallopian tubes. The condition, the doctor explained, was likely the result of a childhood fever she had.

She learned from Nurse Carlson about the research being done at this very clinic. Her doctor had success with other patients, over the last few years, in reestablishing the possibility of childbearing. Anna was elated. Being barely seventeen, she delighted in the hope of becoming a mother and wife. Most of all, she wished to fulfill her family's dream of the promise and hope of a new life someday for all of Anna's brothers and sisters. That she had not seen her parents for months was a constant worry. She had been advised that they were in a train accident, but they were in stable condition in a good hospital. The hospital was several hundred miles away, but they were to come here for further care any day now. Anna tried to get time off to visit them, but Dr. Neugebauer cautioned her that to terminate the treatments during her weekly sessions would risk her chances of future fertility. She was confused and anxious. She felt certain her parents would have been more overjoyed with her presenting them with a grandchild, than with a hospital visit.

Being seventeen, Anna was experiencing rapid growth and new urges and sensations. The focus of her attentions was on a supervisor at the firm. She knew Supervisor Graf barely noticed her interest in him. He was single, about five years her senior, and moved with an authority that was paternal, but always cordial and considerate. She felt this sensitivity was heartfelt and she interpreted it as meant for only her.

"Good day, Mr. Graf." She'd smile as she tried to hide her deeper feelings each morning when she saw him getting coffee at the factory station. He'd always smile back, even before he'd had his coffee. He acknowledged her by name, "Miss Anna," as if to be particularly familiar, despite knowing her last name, of course, from his employee records.

"Good day, Anna," Nurse Carlson said as she entered the examination room. Anna smiled at the kind nurse who helped her into her gown with the ties in the back that Anna couldn't quite reach.

"I heard from my brother, Carl, that he'd heard from a mutual friend, that my parents have been moved closer to here, and that they are walking now unassisted. That's a good sign, isn't it?" She wanted to see the nurse's reaction to this development.

"Of course it is, Anna," Nurse Carlson said. "Now let's get you into those stirrups. The doctor is in a hurry today. There we go, now just relax until he arrives." The nurse left the room.

Anna could hear steps in the clinic's halls. Today they were louder and more rapid than Dr. Neugebauer's. Nurses and doctors were talking just outside the exam room door. Anna even heard her name, and wondered what might be the matter.

The treatments were brief and predictable, involving the implantation of a gooey substance deep inside her. Initially, they gave her cramps for a few hours, although lately they were less severe. In fact, she mentioned to the doctor that her periods had ceased. He assured her this was a good sign. She wouldn't have to suffer with her monthly, painful periods any longer; the treatments mimicked a pregnancy, thereby weakening her monthly "friend." This reassured Anna. She had faith in Dr. Neugebauer and his treatments.

After what seemed like an unusually long time, Nurse Carlson returned. Her smile seemed strained, and her eyes glared hard at Anna. Their usual warmth was absent, her countenance cold. She even averted her eyes when Anna sought reassurance in the nurse's face.

"Dr. Neugebauer is delayed, but called ahead. His supervisor will treat you today. He likes things done his way, so let's accommodate him." Nurse Carlson looked everywhere as she moved about the room, but not at Anna. With Anna's ankles in the stirrups such a long time, her legs were beginning to go numb. Her feet were already lifeless, but she would be patient for her doctor. She considered protesting this new doctor treating her, but being just a teenager and raised to respect authority figures, she reconsidered.

"Good morning, young lady." The doctor pushed back his long, blond waves of hair. His sideburns hid his ears and the hair at the front waved across his smooth forehead and blended into the shorter hair at the temple on the left. He was tall, his features thick, as if chiseled from granite with a bold brow, square jawbone and prominent cheeks. His eyes were narrow with blond eyelashes. Anna thought that his blue eyes had a catlike quality. He must have just removed a hat; a red line crossed his forehead. He greeted her with a smile and a nod that seemed meant to comfort her. He didn't look at her, Anna thought, but through her. She felt a chill radiate from her chest. Her heart palpitated to all of her extremities. She wanted to vomit, but was unable. Yet, Anna responded politely.

She pretended not to be frightened. "Good morning, doctor. I hope Dr. Neugebauer is all right." He nodded. All was well with Dr. Neugebauer; a train delay was responsible for his absence. Dr. Grabel gestured to Nurse Carlson who, Anna thought, hesitated a moment, then attached ankle restraints. Anna was unable to move her legs from the stirrups. Why? The stirrups were already digging into her ankles. Anna's breathing accelerated; she felt warm, hot even. She turned to Nurse Carlson who was quietly closing the door behind her as she left, without addressing Anna.

His large hands were filling a glass syringe, like her doctor usually did. He tapped the syringe a few times, flicking his index finger against it. This medicine was not the gooey white milk she'd usually gotten from Dr. Neugebauer, but was clear with a yellow tint.

The doctor made no effort to instill the medication inside her. Instead, he had placed a tourniquet about her left upper arm. She tensed as he injected the medication directly into her vein. The fluid oozed into her, with warmth radiating from the site of injection. She felt less apprehensive. She noticed she was talking, but not to anyone directly. The doctor's hands began to look even larger. His handsome face became more contorted, almost grotesque, reminding her of a gargoyle she'd seen at a church when visiting the city with her parents many years earlier. Anna noticed the sweat on his brow and she could smell him. He smelled like schnapps, sweet like peppermint, and not like cologne. While he wore a white jacket, it wasn't buttoned up. Beneath it was a dark green shirt and matching pants with a brass belt buckle. He bent over her.

"Herbert, why are you taking my bicycle?" she asked her brother in the city park. "You must stop this now or I'll tell Mama. She'll get it back for me." The doctor smiled, knowing it was time to withdraw the needle. Anna's arms flailed all about as if trying to get her bicycle back from whoever Herbert was, but this didn't concern him.

With the snap of the bolt he delivered into the iron brace in the examination room door, the doctor removed his white jacket and slipped Anna's patient robe from her seventeen-year old figure. She'd resist no more. Her nightmare was to begin.

✳✳✳✳✳✳✳✳✳✳✳✳✳✳✳

An hour later, Anna lay unconscious on the examination table, her legs dangling from their restraints to the stirrups. Her figure was uncovered and her respiration shallow. Beads of perspiration shone on her abdomen. Her eyes were not quite closed and her mouth hung hideously agape to the left, her tongue not quite in her mouth, but rather to one side. Blood dripped from between her legs to the floor, clotting in a darkening pool of black, marking time. Anna's torso had lost its flesh tone and a grey pallor replaced it. Her exposed chest was blotched with blue patches. Her delicate fingers twitched, as if grasping for something, or someone.

He buttoned his jacket: olive green like his shirt and pants. He must get back home to the family. His driver should be waiting outside the clinic. His brass belt buckle was back in place. On it was engraved an eagle with stretched wings like the one on his cap, and more brass insignias shone on his uniform's epaulets. The red armband had the twisted cross of a swastika. The double lightning emblem on his collar instilled fear in his enemies for it confirmed he was of the SS, the select guard who'd taken a blood oath to defend and execute the will of the one, the leader, his Fuehrer, Adolph Hitler. There was a secret tattoo in his right armpit to commemorate the day of his oath with his troop's insignia: it was the shape of a human skull.

The Jewess would join the rest of her family tomorrow after her "shower" with Zyklon B cyanide gas. After her shower, the constantly working ovens would convert her contorted figure into flakes of white snow spewing with their horrific stench from the furnace's smoke stacks blowing gently toward Munich. Those living just outside the barbed wired camp would claim they were, indeed, snowflakes, this despite it being August.

Anna Bronfman would not be separated from her family any longer and, in fact, would be eternally intermingled with them in their final resting place on some Munich roof, sidewalk, or car fender.

****

Dr. Neugebauer's hand trembled as he added Polish vodka to his hot tea on the train. He was condemned to the front where he was needed more than at the Dachau concentration camp disposing of the Jewish problem. Hitler had ordered a quick sterilization method that was cheap, if not painful, to assure termination of the Jewish vermin from Europe once and for all. The SS didn't have the time or resources to gas and incinerate all of them. Bullets were for killing the Allied soldiers, not to be wasted on Jews. Looking out the window as the pine trees passed, he couldn't help his thoughts turning to Anna: she would not be able to have children; she would never see her next birthday. "God have mercy on Anna's soul," he thought. He looked at a picture of his wife, Gerlinda, and his two boys. He peered out the train's fogged window as he raced toward Germany's doom at a frozen Stalingrad. "God have mercy on my own."

CHAPTER 1

Wet Dream

Even if it wasn't the middle of the night, in the middle of a squall with thirty-foot seas, no one would have heard so much as a scream. Tassos Nikronos, a third generation sailor, was on watch from 0100 till 0600, when the new Filipino, Yuli from Luzon, would relieve him. Tassos had signed on for six months with the supertanker, *Hirotu*. Although raised on traditional Greek bouzouki music, he preferred American Rap and Hip Hop. He had gone so far as to shave his head like many of his favorite rap stars, but maintained a full, broad, black mustache like his father and grandfather did.

The storm was worse than forecast; trying to peer out the forward portholes was futile. All he could see were the instrument displays to his left, right, before and above him. The seas thrashed violently against *Hirotu's* double hull; sheets of rain attacked the windscreens around the steel deckhouse. The onrushing seawater flooded the portholes as if Tassos was in an aquarium, submerged like a fish. Tonight was making him nervous and the music wasn't diverting him.

On this voyage *Hirotu's* belly was full of Libyan low-sulfur crude. Its heft made *Hirotu's* bow penetrate deeper into the oncoming waves. When she heaved to port or starboard, she listed more than Tassos was comfortable with. He hated to admit fear, being the macho shipmate from Greece, but he wished he were asleep, drunk, or somewhere else.

He thought about the ship's destination; Galveston, Texas. From there it was a slow, cautious transit under the direction of a local pilot, up the forty-five-mile ship channel to Houston's refineries. The radar, its background screen green-tinted, sought traffic *blips*. Tonight, it was confused by the artifact caused by the rough waves making useless storm chatter interference. Under these conditions, if there was traffic he was supposed to see, the seas and rain conditions at this intensity obscured it.

The rain and seas swallowed the steel deckhouse, deafening his ears and, if there were any alarms on the radar or engine sensors, he realized he probably couldn't hear them. Fortunately, the monitors on *Hirotu* had warning lights he hoped would inform him of any traffic out there in the black torrent. With all hands asleep, Tassos was the sole helmsman on duty. He checked the autopilot and GPS for position and speed. All seemed well.

He blocked out the sea's foamy rushes at the ship with his Walkman and the urban poetry of rapper Dr. Dre. The welded joints of the deckhouse strained; their seams cried to hold themselves together in a painful whine. Sailors like Tassos worried about these *cries of the welds*, but they would never admit this to their fellow shipmates. A snap of a weld would weaken the entire framework of a ship, and if put to the test, under gale force conditions at sea like this, who knew what else would snap. Torsional forces on a fully laden supertanker were designed to be resisted *to a point*: a point determined by a computer program some nerd in an office decided *should* do the job. Tassos preferred video games to computers. The same people probably designed both.

The pilothouse was seven decks high above the tanker's main deck that, in turn, was eight decks above the water line. Tassos was alone. The wind speed indicator showed the winds clocking around to dead on their bow; there'd be a rough night ahead. He imagined *Hirotu* snapping in half every time the weld joints screamed. He visualized hundreds of thousands of barrels of Kaddafi's crude forming a liquid island in the Gulf of Mexico, washing up on the beach at Cozumel, Mexico, and the tourists getting darker than their sun tan lotion advertised they would. This amused him, briefly.

Tassos turned, thinking he heard something behind him. The second mate was asleep in the deck cabin directly behind the pilothouse and his door was closed. How could he hear anything in this steel chamber of crashing ocean waves and thundering sheets of rain? The storm hit them four hours earlier, and was a common weather pattern in these latitudes on the run from the Ivory Coast, transiting the Florida Straits to Houston's refineries. *Hirotu* was registered in Panama, as was common in international shipping, although her keel was laid in Yokohama, Japan and had never actually been in Panamanian waters.

Tassos rechecked the circuit breakers on his electrical panel to port to make certain all running lights on the bow, stern and deckhouse were operational. He checked his monitors and made his notes on the hour and half hour. All seemed in order, although he couldn't actually see anything ahead of the vessel. Where the display asked what he estimated his visibility was, he noted *null*.

Suddenly, the radar sounded a digital alarm and its panel flashed a red background warning of an imminent collision. Tassos didn't hear the alarm with the storm outside and the headphones on him. The flashing red screen alerted him. According to the radar, a large, vague mass lay twelve nautical miles ahead, thirteen degrees off the starboard bow. Tassos silenced the alarm and monitored what he saw. It was ill defined and stationary, and remained unaltered with each sweep of the scanner. There was no island charted anywhere near this sea lane. He adjusted the gain sensitivity on the radar panel and corrected for wave height. The mass disappeared. Scratching his head, he cursed the interference of the rain, waves, and storm that resulted in inconclusive information. Tassos checked the auxiliary radar screen for confirmation of the phantom *blip*. It was no longer there. He had to forcibly exhale three times to slow his heart.

He decided, after a moment of contemplation, whether to awaken the second mate. He decided it was *sea chatter* only, the result of enormous waves that the radio and weather fax were reporting. It was definitely not shipping traffic, or anything solid, that posed a threat. He noted the event and radar adjustments in the monitor's logs. "*Mallaca*," he cursed at the high tech radar scanner display, the universal Greek obscenity known by every tourist who didn't tip his Greek cab driver enough. Dr. Dre had his attention once again. The computer nerds needed to fix their radar scanners instead of working on video games. The two hundred and forty thousand ton, one hundred and forty million dollar *Hirotu*, ferrying fifty-five million dollars of Libyan liquid gold, was being helmed by a seventy-five dollar radar chip, backed up by a twenty-six year old Greek seaman from Rhodes who was listening to rap music in Force Four winds at sea with zero visibility. Tassos actually laughed out loud.

According to the GPS, they were now passing south of Puerto Rico's mid-section and in their assigned sea lane. Tassos knew that false blips were easily detected on this radar array. He wouldn't be fooled again.

The ship could have, in fact, steered itself the remainder of its preset course for Houston, through the Mona Straits, the Gulf of Mexico, the jetties of Galveston, and up the ship channel all the way to Houston under her own power and guidance. Only international agreements by politicians and ambassadors, all trained as lawyers, had determined that all ships must have a human *at the helm*, even under an autopilot linked guidance system. It just made good sense, even if it was a young, easily distracted man like Tassos.

The squall ended before dawn, when the first mate took the helm. He wore day whites with blue epaulets and shined shoes. Sahim was a Turk from Ankara.

Yuli, the cabin boy, arose from his berth. He was used to rough seas and the mess it made of his shaving kit. There was only one item he needed to be certain was there: a black, metal lunch-box. Everything in the cabin was on the floor, including his magazines and CDs. He couldn't see the lunch box. Yuli panicked. The ship's bell sounded meaning he was to be on duty. To hell with that. He could makeup an excuse later. He searched the cabin, tossing everything to one corner.

There it was, under the rug. He lifted it carefully and examined it thoroughly for dents or other damage to its seals. He exhaled a sigh of relief. He placed it in his locker and bolted the door. He wouldn't need it again until they anchored off Galveston and he did some *night fishing*.

****

After a quiet night at anchor off Galveston, the ship's radio advised that they had clearance to proceed towards the port. Captain Sorensen joined Sahim on board at 0830 hours holding a cup of tea prepared by the chef's steward, Yuli, who also made the Captain's berth each morning. They were slowing down now to enter the jetties of Galveston, and channel 16 on the VHF announced, "U.S. Pilot Vessel, *Texas Star*, to tanker *Hirotu*." With that, instructions for slowing *Hirotu* enough for the pilot launch, *Texas Star*, to align and match *Hirotu's* speed for the U.S. pilot to board. International maritime agreements dictated that a U.S. ship's pilot was required to take the helm of all ships in the channel.

Captain Sorensen slowed the ship to barely maintain rudder control and reached for his binoculars.

"What is that pilot boat doing? That idiot!" Captain Sorensen barked. "He should be on our starboard beam for boarding. He's heading for the bow." Both the Captain and crew members peered through the rain, which had moderated since passing through the storm back in the Caribbean Sea.

The pilot launch moved treacherously close before the bow of *Hirotu*. It idled in front of *Hirotu* long enough for the Captain to order emergency backing down of the engines even more, and dangerously close to losing steerage.

U.S. Maritime Pilot Jim McCarthy, a middle-aged, bearded, Navy veteran, was using his binoculars to examine the bow of

Hirotu. Folks in Galveston found there wasn't much that'd rile "Mac," but today he was truly shocked.

"Did ya see it?" Mac said.

"Did, but don't believe it." Kit said, keeping his eyes on *Hirotu's* bow with the binoculars.

"Book doesn't say what to do. Get the Polaroid." Mac said.

The yeoman on the launch with Mac was John Kit. The bow wave of the tanker bounced the *Texas Star*, and Kit braced himself on the bow pulpit. He held a radio on channel 16, giving Captain Sorensen what were probably the strangest orders he had ever issued an arriving vessel.

Kit could see that Mac clearly didn't intend to board alongside this tanker as they'd done a hundred times before over the last three years. Mac signaled Kit to start taking photos. He ran off a dozen photos of the bow of the ship.

Kit saw how close the ships were. In a panic, he ran aft along the rail and swung the wheel of the helm as fast as he could to help Mac avoid hitting the bow of *Hirotu.* Kit and Mac stared at each other when the photos were done. Mac barked more orders to Captain Sorensen. Kit brought the *Texas Star* alongside the starboard side of *Hirotu* where a staircase was hanging, attached to a gangway entrance, for the pilot to board.

Hirotu was a new class of supertanker and the shear of her bow floated over nine stories high above the waves. The pilot launch bobbled like a toy boat in a bathtub from the supertanker's bow waves. The *Texas Star* carefully paced the supertanker's speed and wake amidships, and Mac took the critical leap, boarding the waiting platform with a helping hand from a crew member standing by. Yuli grasped Mac's hand, safely helping him aboard with a, "welcome, sir." The pilot raced up the companionway to the bridge house and was greeted by a mystified Captain Sorensen and crew.

"Is all in order, sir?" the Captain asked, somewhat concerned after seeing the expression on the pilot's face. Mac reached into his pocket. His right hand trembled, but not from the cold. He handed the Captain a photo he had just taken of *Hirotu's* bow. There was an anchor on both sides of the forequarters of the bow. The starboard one, however, was obscured by something the Captain could not identify. It was shiny and white, with a red stripe. The fuzziness of the photo taken from a moving vessel made it too hard to discern.

"What do you make of it?" Sorensen asked. Mac handed the Captain the next photo, which was taken further away, giving a clearer perspective as to what obscured the anchor.

"Oh, my dear God!" exclaimed the Captain. He ordered Sahim to hail all frequencies and stand by. The first mate made the necessary frequency adjustments, and then looked to the Captain for further instructions. Tassos stared at the second photo. Sahim announced into the radio, "Pan, Pan, Pan. Tune to emergency frequency for details."

The second photo, much sharper, revealed a sailing vessel, a ketch, with its rigging wires and spars ensnared by the flukes of the starboard anchor of *Hirotu*. The keel was painted with maroon bottom paint, and the spade rudder looked intact. She was about fifteen meters or more in length, Sorensen estimated. Tassos hoped the vessel hadn't been snared on his watch. Why was this vessel at sea in heavily trafficked, international shipping lanes in such a storm?

"I will make the announcements via satellite radio to all vessels to be alert for potential survivors in our sea lane," the Captain said. Mac was silent, still looking at the last photo. His expression was grim.

"Will you search the sailboat for survivors, or should I have my crew do it?" the Captain inquired.

"You're in U.S. Coastal Waters and under U.S. authority, so this is a domestic matter. I'm notifying the FBI and Coast Guard. They'll notify our Justice Department if that vessel turns out to be under a foreign flag. Please post your U.S. Courtesy Flag. I'm in command of your ship from here on." Sorensen politely acknowledged McCarthy's orders and ordered the crew to take their commands from him. McCarthy ordered the engine settings and navigational headings, which he knew by heart. The pilot picked up his radio and hailed his pilot boat to notify Galveston Coast Guard of a maritime collision. He asked that the Guard's *Viking* search and rescue aircraft and Euro-copters be scrambled in thirty minutes for a grid search plotted by coordinates they'd get once McCarthy received the ship's logs showing *Hirotu's* course over the last few days. For now, a search team was needed to inspect the sailing vessel wreckage with an FBI forensics squad.

"Did you note the name on her transom?" a clearly shaken Captain Sorensen asked. Satisfied the supertanker was safely headed towards the Houston Ship channel marker, McCarthy hailed Kit aboard the *Texas Star* on their beam. He asked if he could make out the name of the sailboat hanging from *Hirotu*. Static ended the sentence, and the quiet alerted Mac that Kit was on the radio. He could hear Mac's heavy breathing before he answered. He knew they both had an unbelievable story to tell at the bar tonight. The front page of the Chronicle would probably have his photos for the evening edition. CNN might even interview them, if they were permitted to talk.

"Uh, Mac, Sir, you're not gonna believe this."

"Go ahead, Kit. What do ya think she's called?"

"I think it says *Wet Dream*."

Captain Sorensen looked puzzled. "What does this mean, *Wet Dream*, if you please?" Yuli, Tassos, and Sahim looked similarly puzzled.

McCarthy must have looked like an idiot trying to hide his smirk. Kit on *Texas Star* had no trouble breaking the tension he was feeling with a little laugh. Then his mood sobered and thought to himself, "*Wet Nightmare* would have been more like it."

CHAPTER 2

Fore!

The flight from Miami was late. I knew Eleanor and Rita would be angry with me. I left Alexa in her offices, after signing the documents she had prepared. I'd looked forward to seeing her impossibly heart-shaped face, with its regal cheekbones, and her waves of flaming red hair, and hazel eyes, but it was her smile that captivated me. She wore it when we were together and it brought sunshine to my heart.

"Here, here, and here," she pointed to each place for my scrawl. She had seemed satisfied looking over the volumes of patents and trademarks she had prepared.

"Have to keep the Board of Directors happy," I offered. Looking me in the eyes she reminded me, "You *are* the Board, Alan."

"Time for espresso?" she asked as she gathered the papers and began to walk down the hall to her office. I remembered our first encounter. Alexa Grey, beautiful attorney, wandered into my office over a year ago to introduce herself, and I become her primary client. Me, the owner and pharmaceutical developer of Triton Pharmaceuticals, Inc. She wore a black Armani suit that featured her figure, fine and fit, and her red coiffure, similarly fine. We were about the same age, me sixty-something, bald, but still fit, if I didn't look in the mirror; she was fifty-something. "We hadn't aged, just ripened," I told her.

No attorney and physician ever hit it off better. Co-workers and employees suspected we were lovers. We weren't. We'd never even kissed. Years of dating others without finding *the one* had made us cautious. We still shook hands, keeping our relationship professional. But, when our eyes met, I spent a moment too long fishing the depths of her hazel-colored eyes, trolling the hidden recesses of her mind.

We occasionally had a drink that wasn't under the pretense of a business meeting, but these were rare times. We spoke almost daily, but lived far apart. There was a familiarity we cherished that we hesitated to complicate.

"No, I can't have a moment's delay even for an espresso with you." I hated rejecting her, but I think she knew it had to be important for me to decline the invitation.

She smiled; she'd be visiting me, as we'd agreed, later in the week. There would be plenty more papers, contracts, with a chaser of flirting. She once joked after a few months of "working" together that she wondered if she was "prostituting" herself by billing me three hundred dollars an hour.

"Well, the girls on Biscayne Boulevard don't get that kind of hourly, so at least you must be very good."

"I give good contract," she quipped.

"The girls are waiting, aren't they?" she suggested. I nodded in agreement and picked up my satchel and a bag of gifts for the girls.

"I can just make the flight. Give me a lift?" We drove to Miami International and I was the last down the ramp to board. The cabin door closed behind me.

San Juan International Airport was packed with flights crisscrossing the Atlantic to reach obscure islands south of the Equator. The flight from Miami had hit turbulence, so I knew that the flight from San Juan would be even bumpier for the girls and me. I hired a taxi to run me over to the private end of the airport. There, the new fueling boy, Tito, had me fueled and checked when I got to Caribe Aviation's private terminal. My Cessna 182 was already pulled out from the tie-down slot and chains untied. I signed the gas voucher, customs manifest, and the flight plan I had filed by phone. Vanessa, the hostess at the lounge, brought Eleanor and Rita: my girls, two West Highland White Terriers, all spruced up from the groomer. They looked a little embarrassed by the pink silk ribbons about their necks, but were glad to see me, judging by their licks and leaps in my arms.

"They spotted you right away, Dr. Becker," as she pulled them from the lounge across the tarmac. My pride moderated when I noticed it was the treats in the bag I had for them that drew their snouts. I gave them each a treat and loaded them aboard the plane. I paid Vanessa for the puppy sitting and transport.

I revved the 182's engine after the checklist was done. The girls were latched into their harnesses behind me with ear headsets for sound protection. They enjoyed flying enormously. The flight would be less than forty-five minutes and the winds were a little lively. San Juan Tower cleared us for departure behind a 737, and we ascended cautiously with the crosswind until the aquamarine waters of Puerto Rico's lush coast fell behind. Condado Beach and its lavish hotels lining the strip were just beginning to illuminate their requisite florescent palm tree lights just off the starboard wing as I routed us for Culebra Island via Vieques Island. Having cleared San Juan International Airport's airspace, I set the plane's transponder beacon so any radar could identify me clearly. We headed for Harry S. Truman Airfield, U.S. Virgin Islands.

The girls licked their paws and each other, and then settled down for a brief snooze. The sun began to set as I spotted Vieques Island below. The U.S. Navy had used this barren island for shelling practice until the Puerto Ricans decided this was enough destruction and offense and got an injunction against it. Next was Culebra, the barely inhabited island belonging to the Virgins that was primarily a deep harbor surrounded by substantial hills. Seasoned sailors were familiar with it, for it served well as the best hurricane hole in the Caribbean. In approaching storms it could be counted on to protect vessels from menacing weather.

Just above my engine's cowl, St. Thomas came into view as I hailed the tower with my intentions to land. They advised of traffic about me both above and behind. I was diverted around the island until further clearance could be given. I kept the altitude to 5000 and toured the National Park that comprised most of the Island of St. John. Cinnamon Bay, Hawk's Nest Bay, and Trunk Bay were below with the unique underwater U.S. Park for snorkelers. I was cleared by the tower for landing and swung us back towards Red Hook, the west end on towards Truman Airfield. I checked my lights and did a few final chores on the landing checklist while above the mountaintop golf course at Mahogany Run.

I heard a spurt, then a sputter. The girls noticed it too. They stood on their forepaws as if asking me what I was fooling with that caused the change in engine whine.

Checking the instruments gave no clue as to the cause. I adjusted the mixture of the fuel. The cylinder head temperature was normal, and the fuel correctly routed from both tanks. I switched the valve on the engine tank; fuel seemed to be flowing in abundance, having no effect on the sputtering that was now more pronounced. "Pan, pan, pan," I alerted all listeners on the radio. I contacted Truman Tower. They asked if I wanted to declare an emergency for immediate clearance. I hesitated, hoping that the sputtering of my single engine was just a burp that would pass at any second.

"No emergency now, engine fluttering, but functioning. Will wait for landing clearance when available," I radioed, and they "Roger'd that" back at me. My heart fluttered like the engine, and I considered whether it was my pride that prevented me from declaring the emergency. I was living my worst nightmare, but couldn't wake myself. Sweat soaked my clothes. I glided the single engine, sick as it sounded, and my altitude maintained 3500. I could see some late duffers on the golf course, when the sound of wind rushing by the plane's airframe overtook the sound of a now silent engine. Was I really awake? Maybe, if I just let go of the steering yoke, I'd wake up.

The girls stood on their hind legs thinking we were on the ground since the engine had ceased its whine. The nose dropped perilously to earth until I pulled the yoke back in my lap. This slowed the wings to almost a stall as I increased the angle of attack of the airfoil. We buffeted a bit, which alerted the girls that we might have just hit the runway for the landing. We were still 3,000 feet above the sea.

I hailed the tower. They gave me immediate instructions to land on runway one three zero left. I "roger'd" that and repeated the instructions after my "Mayday" cleared the airport's control space of all aircraft not already on final. The tower advised me of my new transponder frequency, and I dialed in the Mayday codes they instructed. At least they'd find our bodies, I thought, if the Emergency Locator Beacon in the tail section wasn't enough.

The sun was almost gone, and our altitude was my biggest concern. I was flying a sinking crate, and I was scared. I feared death had become our co-pilot. There was a group of hills I had to clear to reach the airport from this direction, and the 182's engine didn't have the juice to lift us over them. It sounded like it was in the throes of its final death rattle. Was there water condensation in the fuel tanks or some tiny piece of particulate matter clogging the fuel injectors? There was no time for a diagnosis; just barely enough for rash decisions and remedies. I had taken all of my pills before takeoff; this had to really be happening. Decisions needed to be made since I figured we were about 1200 feet above sea level. I reached back and tightened the tethers holding the girls in place, and they licked my hand.

"Truman Tower...Cessna RS22467 Mayday, Mayday, Mayday. Declaring an emergency. Total engine failure. Pilot and two canines on board. Cannot reach runway designated and will make emergency landing, Mahogany Run golf course."

"Roger that, Cessna RS22467. Sending emergency assistance. Winds south southwest at 15, steady. Good luck, Captain." I turned on the landing lights which I really needed now that darkness made the landing much more perilous. To tell the altitude, I'd only see the grassy fairway at the last twenty feet when the loom of my landing beams caught the ground, not before. We descended quietly, except for the rattle of the airframe and winds rushing past us. I hoped all the palm trees had lamps in them around the course, but I knew from playing there that they didn't. I lined the aircraft up for a potential final and dropped the flaps when I saw what I hoped was a smooth fairway. This wasn't going to be a pretty landing; the wheels would probably rip off. I could only hope the nose gear wouldn't fail upon touchdown and would allow some time to slow on the soft grass without causing us to nose over. I didn't want to think about any holes in the fairway, let alone a sand trap. At two hundred feet, I slowed the plane for a final touchdown. Trees suddenly appeared like black shadows ahead and I swerved left, then right. Each swerve caused us to lose more altitude; altitude we didn't have to spare. A particularly large sand trap guarded the otherwise broad fairway. Airspeed was minimal at 53 knots; I dared not slow it much more or we'd stall and spiral to the ground. I had to gain a few more feet to clear the group of palms dead ahead before we were on the fairway. I pulled perilously back just an inch on the yoke when the buffeting began warning me that the wings were about to fail converting the Cessna to a Chevrolet. *Not airworthy*, we'd drop like the crate of gas-filled aluminum that we were.

The wheels must have touched the palm fronds I wanted to glide over, for the nose of the plane dipped and ripping noises now mixed with the sound of air rushing by the windows. I opened the door on my left a crack in case it crushed tighter on impact, locking us in a smoke-filled cabin.

My heart was thumping and my hands seemed to be plastered with fear on the grips of the yoke. I turned the fuel switch off since we weren't using fuel anyway. Hopefully, it would minimize the spread of fuel after impact. The yoke and ailerons hardly had control with the slow airspeed. We dropped into a black hole and the headlights quit. Now I couldn't see anything out the front windscreen. I lowered the flaps, but the servomotors failed to complete the process. The electrical failure was total, but the circuit breakers indicated all was well.

"Well, I did my job," I joked to myself. I completed emergency procedures 101 with flying colors, but all hands were lost upon crashing. Serious again, I hoped I had aligned us with the fairway and planned the slope vector of the final descent accurately. I no longer had visual, and the yoke had almost nothing to do with our flying attitude. I prayed what was below would be forgiving. I thought of Alexa. She'd read about this in the papers tomorrow, if no one called her first. I hoped the headline would read "Pilot Makes Emergency Landing on Golf Course" instead of "Tragedy on Mahogany Run." I rubbed the girls' fur on the scruff of their necks a final time without taking my eyes off the bleakness ahead.

Guessing that the ground was only inches below, I pulled the yoke back into my lap. Just then the airframe shattered, the tires bounced, and the fuselage impacted the sloped, grassy fairway a second, then a third time. We lunged hard against our seatbelts. I felt for the foot brakes, knowing I had to stop this right away before the wheels came off. I recalled flight school, and realized how dangerous that would be in the damp grass. The nose would dig into the ground from the forward momentum.

There was no learning curve for emergency landings, so I used my best judgment to stop us. I gingerly toed on the foot brakes, until I felt that the plane, in its slogging rush through the grassy field, wanted to nose down, and then I lifted off the brakes. I tried turning the right rudder to get the nose wheel to turn a bit to help slow us down. It threatened to break away, and I stopped urging it to do so. The forward speed was too fast; the fairway had to end. Trees must be ahead: great for providing shade, bad for onrushing airplanes. The girls bounced violently about, but their tethers held. Eleanor threw up her biscuits, literally; I didn't have to see it; I smelled it. Then the smell of gasoline entered the cockpit. Would this be our future incinerator?

The plane lurched to the right when the nose gear came off and the engine compartment dropped to the ground. I saw flames from the right wing tank and knew it would blow. Our time was limited. The loss of nose gear was a blessing, for it became our ultimate brake. Then, our trip ended. I didn't see the tree in the dark, but felt it when we stopped. The engine suddenly moved closer to my legs and the cockpit became shorter. Hot smoke filled the cabin; I couldn't breathe. My charred hands felt for the girls' snap releases on their tethers. They made no sound; were they still alive? They could have flown out the side windows or been crushed. I found some fuel-soaked fur. I freed her and put her on my lap while I fished in the smoke for the other. She barked and then coughed. Thank God, but the one on my lap wasn't moving.

With a blackened White Westie's body in each arm, I would have to kick the cockpit door open. I was beginning to black out from smoke in my lungs. The gasoline vapors prevented any inhalation. I didn't want my lungs exploding in the heat coming off the right wing. I knew I had only enough conscious time left for one sharp kick. If I failed, we'd all barbeque. I kicked spastically with my whole body in a convulsive thrust, hoping there was oxygen on the other side of the door, freeing us from this oven. Both girls were lifeless in my arms.

The cockpit door flew off. We fell to the ground, and Eleanor ran away. Rita remained motionless. We had only a few moments. I could hear sirens on the grounds of the golf course; their headlights intermittently probed the darkness from the rolling hills and trees that obscured them.

Smoke shut my eyes. When I tried to stand, I hit my head on the left wing. I wished the wings had broken away along with their gasoline tanks. I didn't really know in which direction I was moving; my head must have split open: blood clotted in my smoke-burnt eyes. I managed to crawl, with Rita still in my arms, away from the fiery blaze. Being the only source of light and intense heat, it oriented my fading consciousness just enough to limp away.

The wing tanks erupted, blowing Rita and me to the ground. The furnace – my plane – created a wall of heat. My eyes were seared and the heat pressed my face against my skull. My eyes filled with water mixed with blood. My throat was a funnel of smoke and dust. Mucous, laced with blood, bubbled from my nostrils. I heard Rita gasp.

Then blackness.

****

At Miami International's private terminal, Yuli, a young Filipino from Luzon, formerly a cabin boy and chef's assistant on *Hirotu*, now passing as a Cubano fuel attendant named Tito, hummed a familiar Beatle's song. A sedan came by the private terminal's service entrance at the back of the building, where no one noticed the pick-up in the darkness. The diminutive, dark complexioned youth jumped in. "All you need is love, da da dah da da..." The blue sedan churned up the gravel on the road. He nodded to the driver to take him to the other side of the airport for commercial passengers. The driver handed him a passport. He would be a Malaysian this time.

CHAPTER 3

You Are Who You Eat

"Please, come now," the voice said.
"But where are we going?" I said.
"It's time for your shower."
The hand was not Mother's, not Father's. I entered the large room, naked. It was full of steam; no, it was smoke. I couldn't breathe. There was a hideous yellow gas, in a shower!
"Tell someone to shut it off!" I screamed. I was howling, and the room echoed. A hand reached to me from the smoke: Mother. I reached to her. She smiled, and although we kept walking toward each other, our hands never touched. The smoke engulfed her. I screamed, "Mother!"
Then I sat up and heard the mega cruise ship's horn.
I was in my sailboat, *Vanity Fare*. I awoke, shaking in a pool of sweat, trying to remember why I was injured. I could barely move. Then the girls came to my side at the berth. Their fur looked charred and smoke-damaged, but they were alive and licking. I needed my medications, and noticed the bathroom had several new ones from the ER.
I lived on the hook in Charlotte Amalie Harbor, St. Thomas, where the cruise ships' horns prevented sleeping past sunrise most mornings. The docks and ships were already blasting Calypso music, juicing up the tourists for shopping. The coffee in the cleanest mug smelled of not-so-fresh cream, but I downed it anyway. Fetching groceries by dingy in my condition was a challenge. I reviewed the lengthy documents I needed for the NTSB and FAA hearings about the plane crash. Initial discussions with the authorities from their Miami offices went smoothly, though Alexa was more circumspect being the attorney at my depositions.
"That was it!" I thought aloud. I had to meet her when she flew in today. Where and when my groggy, sputtering memory couldn't

quite recall, and I couldn't even remember if I'd written it down. My beard was becoming full and graying, though not, admittedly, prematurely. The accident had shaken my cerebral hard drive a bit, so it was difficult to distinguish reality from the imagined this early in the morning. The fact that I was on narcotics for pain didn't help the old operating system either.

I was shirtless as the tourists looked down on me; it was the uniform of the islands. My skin had simmered to a deep, dark pre-malignant tan. Sunblock was for tourists and snowbirds; my skin was proudly desiccated and leathering in keeping with my native appearance. My bald scalp hurt when exposed to excessive sun, so I generally sported a hat, except now the bandage and stitches made a hat unnecessary. I looked more like Captain Marshmallow than Captain Becker. The tourists probably assumed I was a drunk recovering from tying one on at one of the pier's numerous bars.

Many live-aboards, like myself, wore sandals, but, after years of barefoot walking on burning sand and baked decks covered in layers of sea salt, a person might have difficulty knowing whether I was actually shod or not. My hair was not trimmed, but I had more of a fringe than a hairdo anyway. Alexa suggested that the part in my hair was simply wider than most. I told her I was growing my eyebrows extra long in order to one day comb them back over the void.

I had to admit it. I was middle-aged, and *middle* was probably more behind than ahead of me. I offset this inequity, I rationalized, by having more gut in my bow than butt in my stern. In fact, I could see the golden years ahead. On the other hand, from the people I knew enjoying their twilight years, these seemed more *rusty* than *golden.* I was certainly stiff most places in the morning, and not in a good way.

My injuries prevented all but cautious walking. I remembered where and when I was to meet Alexa: at 1300 hours, on the rear deck of the Wharf restaurant in Christianstead, St. Croix. The weather channel advised of fair weather with winds ten to fifteen knots out of the southeast. That would put the sail on *Vanity Fare* at three hours, in my present state of rehab.

The girls cried for me from below. Their medications constipated them. This eliminated the need for me to carry them on deck in the middle of the night, as I usually did, to allow them to use the poop deck for what it was really named for. While Eleanor suffered mostly smoke damage to her bronchi and fared well, Rita had been unconscious after the wreck from smoke poisoning and asphyxia. I managed to bring her around with CPR, clamping her snout with my burnt hand and breathing for her until she coughed a welcomed breath on her own. She suffered more trauma than Eleanor, emotionally, being the more sensitive of the two.

As for Alexa, she went into panic mode. I had her phoned from the ambulance, and the EMT's assured her that I looked worse than my injuries actually were, and would recover after some sewing, splinting, and spackling.

I thought about her, en route to the ER in Charlotte Amalie. This lady was a far more prized catch than I. She always dressed more like a woman than an attorney for me, or so I fantasized. Being an awful judge of people, especially females, especially females I was fond of, especially Alexa, well, perhaps my assessment of her feelings was way off. I didn't care. When we were together, I was happy. She seemed to enjoy the time, not to mention the billable hours I was paying her. I could afford it. I wasn't willing to risk jeopardizing our relationship, business, or fantasized romance, in any event, to explore deepening it.

I reflected on our first lunch together in the Coconut Grove section of Miami. We were a little intoxicated from the rum punches and each other. She'd been a Kansas country farm girl, a Four H winner with a prized honey-colored lamb, and a good student at Kansas State University. She moved to New Haven to become a contract lawyer, giving up the sheep for a Yale sheepskin. At the time, I was at Columbia in the M.D.-PhD. Program, seeking to become a pharmacologist-microbiologist.

Over our first lunch, it was hard to keep to business. I managed to answer her obvious inquiries about what I actually did.

"I take toxins from one bacterium and feed it to another bacterium to see who wins the battle." I oversimplified.

"Sounds fascinating," she lied.

"About as exciting as contract law."

"No, really. What does a micro-pharmacologist do?" she asked.

"Have you ever heard of Ciguatera?" I asked. She shook her head.

"How about Manchineel poisoning?" Her red hair bobbed when she shook her head. "What's your billable rate?" I asked, changing the direction of the questioning.

"Three hundred and you are not my client," She left the yet off the last quip, and we both knew it. "Lunch is on me," she said.

"Several years back, while vacationing on St. John, I sat under a Manchineel tree. It's a common and attractive shade tree found on tropical islands all over the eastern Caribbean. Rumor had it that the Rockefellers, who owned most of St. John at one time, had planted them along the beaches. It is likely this was done to discourage nosey visitors from discovering their covert sugar mills for rum production. They probably produced their own profitable sugar cane rum made sweeter by the eighteenth amendment legislation on Capitol Hill called Prohibition."

Alexa swallowed a bite of her pecan-crusted salmon. I continued.

"A native warned me that Manchineel trees have poisonous sap that burns and scars skin. The sap is abundant and runs free, particularly after a rainfall. It lies just beneath the thin crust of its sweet bark. The bark is the only part of the tree that is not poisonous. Any unsuspecting intruder who unwisely seeks shade or shelter under its large, graceful leaves will soon learn its secret; the sap is a highly potent acid, like nitric acid. Contact with skin causes immediate pain. The sufferer naturally attempts to wipe the stinging syrup off, but only spreads it, not only leaving him in agonizing pain, but also ulcerated and ultimately scarred permanently wherever the skin was exposed to it. There have been reports of campers on our beaches using its wood for campfires, and the wood is equally noxious. It can cause death by poison gas and asphyxiation to those inhaling it. Eating its sweet smelling apple-like fruit is also fatal."

Alexa was grasping both of her exposed arms together as if I was telling a ghost story. She pressed me for what must be more to the tale. I had another swig of rum punch. She looked up and studied the tree above us that was suddenly suspect to her.

"Banyan tree." I offered. "Completely harmless."

"You're a lot of fun on a first date, I bet," she quipped.

"Is this a date?" I inquired.

"Business meeting of professional neighbors," she answered.

"I became fascinated at *why* this tree needed such protection. I mean, why does a tree develop a defense against mammals? Trees don't normally need defenses from mammalian predators. If a mammal steals a fruit, nature generally likes this method of spreading the seed inside the sweet fruit, when the critter deposits it, along with some handy fertilizer, back to the earth for propagation of the plant's progeny. Why does the mammal die if it eats Manchineel fruit? Sounds a little self-defeating for being *fruitful and multiplying*, and all that biblical encouragement."

Alexa seemed amused.

"The bark was the key. I discovered that this tree grows particularly well in the semi-fresh, semi-salty mixture of brackish water of the mangroves of many islands. The bark contains many carbohydrates and proteins that might be of value to animals. The only animals that might benefit were fish! I considered the possibility that if the Manchineel grew in mangrove swamps and these mangroves are best known as spawning grounds for almost all fish, both fresh and salt water varieties, the critical question arose: Could the peeling bark of the Manchineel tree provide nourishment to spawning sea life nibbling it under the water?"

"Why not?" she asked. "Are you the first to figure this out?"

"Maybe, maybe not. I'd like to think so, and the journals don't show any such information has been published. I haven't published my theory either, though."

"You need to copyright this if it's the basis for what I think you're leading up to."

I continued. "Away from coral reefs, fish are unable to feed on the living matter of the coral where most reef fish get their protein and carbohydrates. There is a special time in the lives of fish they need to leave the cozy food of the reefs and seek shallow mangroves."

Alexa chimed in, "Off to Motel 6 for a one night stand, followed by a trip to maternity to lay their caviar in the warm, sheltered mangrove waters." She looked at me for confirmation that she was dead on, and my smile led to hers.

"Since reef foods are not available during gestation time, they developed a taste for what was available," I said.

"Manchineel bark, I'll bet." Alexa was sure she was right again.

"Perhaps they became vegetarian as they awaited birthing and got their fast food at the roots of the peeling Manchineels."

Alexa was truly engrossed, bored to death, or snookered on the rum in the heat in Coconut Grove.

"So, what's the purpose of the poisonous sap, you ask?" She nodded. "Roots, I hypothesized, needed their bark-skin to insulate them in the unfriendly saline waters this unusual tree tried successfully to grow in. Hence, a water insoluble, gooey sap that proliferates and effuses as the sweet bark the fish eat is peeled. On land, while the tourists don't remove the bark, the sun's heat does indeed peel the bark revealing the acidic venom beneath which drips on unsuspecting tourists."

"Let me guess," she interrupted. "You found the antidote to Manchineel sap poison?" poison?"

"Good guess, but the antidote is in every botany textbook the world over: It's seawater! *Saltwater neutralizes its toxicity*!

Freshwater doesn't. That's why the fish can eat the peeled bark underwater without dying while spawning in the mangroves. The semi-salty, semi-fresh water mixture of the mangroves indeed weakens the Manchineel sap from poisoning the fish, but upon their getting a small dose of it with their bark diet, it actually *disinfects* their intestines from certain impurities.

"That's only half the story, I'll bet," she said. She reasoned out loud, "You don't make a living in pharmaceuticals unless you've found something that this Manchineel poison goop is good for," she asserted, like the smart lawyer I knew she must be. I'd have to be careful not to placate her, I thought, or I'll truly bore her like so many suitors must have already.

"Right on, counselor!" I said and she laughed. She seemed satisfied that she managed to stay with the narrative.

"Two years pass and I am on an airplane en route to a pharmacologist's conference in Vienna. Seated next to me is a young man who reveals, after several vodka tonics, that he was once a commercial pilot and used to fly the Miami–St. Thomas route. We naturally reminisced about this or that favorite beach and golf course and restaurants. After learning I was a doctor involved in pharmaceutical research, he confessed to me he suffered with a medical condition. He could no longer fly due to *Ciguatera poisoning*, which he contracted on the islands. I was already somewhat familiar with Ciguatera, a toxin associated with fish. Native Caribbean islanders say it primarily affects tourists who don't know which types of fish are safe to eat. The poison is the result of algae, one with a long Latin name, that the fish eats. Accidentally, the algae actually produce the toxin, but *fish are not killed by the toxin*. People who eat the fish, in whose intestines this particular algae resides, succumb to the toxin's effects." Alexa nodded her understanding. I knew her next question.

"And this toxin has something to do with Manchineel poison sap, I'm certain. I hope we'll get the surprise ending before I succumb to alcohol toxicity." She polished off her third rum punch. I noticed she was no longer eating her salmon.

"I'll skip the rest of the fish if you don't mind. You really are a charmer at lunch," she joked, "Don't get out much with the opposite sex, I surmise." We smiled what we now call our own "understanding what the other is thinking" smile.

We broke our trance and I headed for the runway with my tale.

"Cooking, unfortunately, does not kill Ciguatera toxin, even after the fish is long dead. The toxin endures in the fish's gut and ultimately takes up residence in the unsuspecting tourist's intestines. The victim initially notices indigestion, fever, chills, aches and pains in their joints, or even, perhaps, convulsions. After the acute symptoms subside, which they almost always do, most victims recover, though some have reported lifelong relapses. Some report recurrent bouts of numbness in the arms and legs, the inability to taste food, partial episodes of blindness and intermittent seizures. The course is generally not fatal, but the victims often wish it was. Obviously, this pilot's commercial license was revoked with good reason. He was bitter and I empathized."

"You have an epilogue, don't you, about how you put two and two together and discovered something?" she said.

"I was beginning to make the connection between why some fish affected only tourists; the islanders seemed to know which fish were dangerous to eat. There is no lab test for Ciguatera. It was the lore of islands and islanders whose tribes, the Arawaks and Caribs, learned *survival of the fittest* by passing down the secrets of survival. Island fishermen knew that it was mainly the larger grouper fish that had Ciguatera. This was their secret lore passed down from generations, though the reasons were not fully understood. They simply knew that smaller fish meant long life."

"Bigger isn't always better, is it, doctor?" She giggled. "The larger ones were larger because they lived longer, probably been exposed and infected with Ciguatera, and yet, survived it. The smaller ones probably didn't have the toxin due to their youth, so the odds alone reduced their chances of exposure to it." She searched my eyes for validation and I didn't even try to elude them for she was good.

"True, but no Nobel yet. The tourists demand bigger and bigger fish for dining, and why should islanders discourage this? Symptoms don't show up for a week so they'll long since be gone and never make the connection with the island restaurants. The islanders won't eat the larger fish, so why waste the good catch that a tourist will pay for by the pound? *It is the islands, mon*! Furthermore, not *all* large grouper contained the toxin. More importantly, why don't younger, smaller groupers get Ciguatera earlier in life? The answer: remember where they were born?" Alexa leaned forward suddenly and took over.

"You already said the answer," she said. "*In the mangroves*, feeding off the nutritious bark of the Manchineel trees, limited only by that nasty sap of the tree that proliferates so well underwater and which they unavoidably nibble as well. The baby groupers are disinfected from the nasty algae that carry the toxin of Ciguatera, with this poisonous Manchineel sap coating, in low, seawater-diluted doses. The partially weakened sap burns and disinfects the algae right out their colons when accidentally ingested."

She was ready to ask the next logical question. "Okay, so the smaller groupers are disinfected at an early stage in their diets by the sap. Why not the larger ones?"

"The Ciguatera toxic algae can infest them from the seawater they reside in later in life long after their spawning is over, that's the key! Let's think like a fish. Don't laugh," I said.

She didn't. I smiled though.

"Here's what the mature fish thinks: I have learned about the spawning grounds in the mangroves, about eating that sweet bark of the Manchineel tree when I was a kid fish." I paused and stared at her sunburned cheekbones that no longer needed makeup. Alexa considered the challenge and jumped in.

"If I'm a fish, I know I liked the sweet baby food that was the Manchineel bark, but hated the syrup it exposed in the tree which burned my tongue. Do fish have tongues?" She didn't wait for my response.

"As hungry as I am," she took over now, talking as if she were a young fish with her lips pursed in a pseudo-fish toned voice, "I'm never eating that spicy, spinachy stuff that burned my mouth, again. So I guess I'm vulnerable to contracting Ciguatera the more I live in waters that apparently have Ciguatera-producing toxins of the algae. I assume Ciguatera algae like warm, Caribbean waters, so that's why we snowbirds never hear of it. Right?" I nodded and let her finish the puzzle. "Since the older fish are only there to either lay eggs or inseminate someone's roe, and they are older and wiser parents who used to eat the Manchineel tree bark as baby food, they do their business, sire their young, allow their progeny to get their sap vaccines against Ciguatera, *but do not partake of it themselves*! They remember their nasty-tasting formula from birth, but due to their larger size, have enough meat on them to avoid eating any more spicy, sappy Manchineel bark. They ultimately pick up the disease from lack of disinfection by Manchineel sap and, therefore, carry Ciguatera. Then they pass it on to visiting airline pilots who carry it in their guts, but don't carry any more passengers. Newborn baby fish are starving since they have no food reserves or nursing mothers so they *must* eat the bark, it's medicinal, if not diluted sap and, therefore, are Ciguatera immunized."

She smiled a self-satisfied grin as if she'd just won a major court victory. She didn't let me interrupt. "That's it, isn't it? You made the connection by being in the right places, learning the pieces of information you needed and saw the possible cause and effect. Ta da! You're a genius! And a successful micro-pharmacologist. Your firm, Triton Pharmaceuticals, manufactures and markets Manchineel sap extract for the treatment of Ciguatera poisoning and probably has patents worth millions with international licensing agreements multiplying that figure exponentially. The royalties should reap millions; I assume you've patented your findings. Yet, your office looks so modest from the doorway. I thought you were bottling aspirin in there. Are you famous in your profession?"

"I hate to burst your bubble, but I don't make a penny on it. I give it away to any island or nation in warm, equatorial latitudes that needs it. I front all of the costs of collection, purification, and distribution through a non-profit firm offshore in the Caymans. I lose money on the project each year and do not permit anyone else from profiting from the formula. You see, while we might enjoy the mental exercise we just tossed about, the sad reality is that the victims of Ciguatera are often young and reside in third world nations who cannot afford pharmaceutical manufacturers' prices for a cure." I was certain this final revelation would deter the attorney opposite me. "This business luncheon was kind, but I'm afraid you're probably bored and thought I'd be a good prospect as a client. Sorry to disappoint you. I'll pick up the check."

Alexa sipped the last of her punch and dabbed at her lips with her napkin. Raising her eyes she drew her face mere inches from mine and said, "On the contrary, Dr. Becker. Now you just got interesting." My heart soared, and it showed, shamelessly.

****

From the Wharf Tavern's balcony we could see *Vanity Fare* rocking on her mooring in Christianstead Harbor, St. Croix. Alexa had flown in to meet me on short notice after she was notified about my unhappy landing at Mahogany Run. She planned to stay at the Buccaneer Hotel, as she usually did when I summoned her.

The rum punches reminded me of our first meeting at Coconut Grove and the scarf she wore reminded me that, even though an attorney, she never looked too businesslike. She hugged each of the girls in her arms, and then gave each a kiss. They wiggled, barked, and jumped at the sight of her. I kept my wiggles and jumps on the inside. The girls then lay on the patio to complete their siesta with one eye on duty for scraps of food that might fall off the table.

Alexa was to bring some deeds of trust and other personal documents I asked her to create to organize certain matters in my estate should I not be around to manage them. These instruments, trusts, and contracts took weeks for her to write. Since I had no heirs in the form of children or wives, the legal matters were more of a formality to assure my company's survival. Trusted employees and volunteers would be taken care of with detailed guidance to assure the firm would continue its work.

The ease with which these meetings went belied their real intent. I simply needed an excuse to see Alexa again, to get me anchored after floating on the hook in St. Thomas Harbor for so long. My injuries restrained my ability to move about, but also gave me more time to think of Alexa. Of course, all of our business could have been conducted by fax, email and snail mail, but today I really needed her.

"Alan, you look better than when I saw you last week at the ER. Dr. Crowley said you have a concussion. Navigating *Vanity Fare* over here must have been painful. I could have flown into St. Thomas." She marveled at my gauze turban.

"I read in the papers about the details they learned in the airplane investigation. Not much more than we already knew. How you rescued the girls and managed to barely get away with your life, how you made an impossible forced landing in the dark without an engine was the amazing part they said. Were the reporters over-dramatizing? The girls must be traumatized. Wouldn't blame them if they wouldn't fly with you again." She opened her attaché case and found some dog biscuits, which the girls chomped down. Then she put the usual pile of files on the table. The waiter brought fruit punches, rolls, and the menu.

"I'm fine, really. Aching here and there, but remarkably fine. I made the Miami papers?" My curiosity amazed her. She nodded that I was now something of a flyer's legend being the first to land a Cessna at St. Thomas' only golf course. "It was the ninth fairway, by the way, if you were curious." I opened her copy of the paper and read that I had nosed down into the sand trap after the dogleg right. Would have hit the water trap if I hadn't veered to the right as I apparently did.

"Heard from NTSB and FAA authorities yet?" she asked, sipping the fruit juice.

"Gave them the initial details at the hospital after my suturing and dressings. Hearing is to follow next week after initial inquiries are completed and the wreckage studied. Wreck's over at the old submarine base, quarantined and guarded. Insurance company adjustors already taping my every word. I don't want to sign anything while I'm under the influence, so I had all forms directed to you. The girls seem fine. They had nightmares the first few nights, but are getting better."

"How could this have happened, Alan? I was really worried when I got your call from the ambulance. You pooh-poohed so much of it to cushion my shock. Imagine how I felt when I saw you that night at the emergency room? You underestimate me. I can take the truth. There's thick skin here and I need to know you're okay. Okay?" She clenched my hand for emphasis and our eyes met – with inquiries of their own, I fantasized. She leveled a look at me that transcended the attorney-client relationship as if she were peering over bifocals. It put me in my place and I loved it.

"Thank you for coming," I held her hand in mine.

"As for the cause of the engine flame out, I haven't a clue. I'll know more after the wreckage has been examined. Wish I could have had a sample of what was in the fuel tanks. Sure seemed the fuel supply was the problem. I contacted the private terminal back in Miami where I departed from and kept the plane. They didn't have any records of fuel contamination problems with their customers. I'm sure NTSB is already getting their fuel logs and service records."

I thought there was a twinkle in Alexa's eyes as if she really wasn't hearing my words so much as just being happy to be with a *vertical* me rather than identifying a *horizontal* me on a cold slab at the coroner's. I realized that things had substantially changed in the world, specifically, *my world*. I needed to adapt, anticipate, and switch to proactive mode. Unfortunately, I was without an ally in my circle of trusted associates.

The role might fall to Alexa if she would consent. I couldn't tell her everything and certainly didn't want to unwittingly underestimate the undercurrents I felt coming into play and the menace they posed. By association and, possibly, by participation, she might engender similar risks. I probed, testing her trust on blind faith, for I knew her analytical mind would obligate her to delve far deeper into the facts than I could permit. I felt guilty roping her into this without fully briefing her on all the facts and threats. I knew I'd be opening a Pandora's box of inquiries if I started the story of the whole affair. Better we trust each other, for it would allow me to control *her risks* by her ignorance of what it was I was doing. This consoled me somewhat, so I proceeded.

"I need a non-legal favor," I said flatly. She almost choked. She put down her drink and touched her napkin to her lips. Then she checked to see if I was serious.

"You chose your words carefully. 'Non-legal', huh? Let's see; that either means the favor involves matters not pertaining to my expertise and what I'm paid to do."

I let her go on.

"Or...the favor involves activities that might be considered non- or *il*-legal. That would be a euphemism for criminal, would it not?" There was that look again: like she was peering over invisible bifocals.

"Does it matter which?" I asked. "Well, if you have to know it's one, but not the other, okay?" I was being a little too cute, but I didn't want her asking any more questions; not right now.

She thought about her answer a moment and her hazel eyes returned to confront me directly.

"I guess it's only a matter of whether or not I should bill you for the services? If it's truly illegal, I could bill you double or triple for the risk factor. But, do I really want to record what could land me in an island slammer? By the way, did you know Harry Houdini was challenged to escape from an island prison in Tortola just a few miles from here in the British Virgin Isles? The prison was so old and decrepit, and the locks were so rusted and difficult to operate, even when he keyed and picked them, Houdini himself couldn't unlock the primitive padlocks. I wonder if they serve drinks with little umbrellas in there. On the other hand, if it's a little, how does one put it, "grey", what you want me to do, it would be as a friend, I suppose, and would be unbecoming for a friend to charge another friend for a favor so; the answer is, *of course*. If you're going to jail for *reckless endangerment of the public and incompetence as a pilot*, I guess we could get adjoining cells."

"And don't forget all those billables for handling my, excuse me, our criminal appeals," I reminded her.

I clasped her hands in mine. The girls smelled some conch fritters coming out of the kitchen and stood up.

"Thank you, Alexa. Now, for the caper."

"Can I ask what it is?" she asked, serious again.

"It's a box." I indicated with my index finger that it was under the table. She glanced under the table in an exaggerated furtive manner as if she were Mata Hari. It was a small, grey, metal file cabinet with a lock on the front and a handle on top. Using my foot, I slid it closer to her, slowly so that the noise of it was not too conspicuous to diners nearby. She peeked under the table and gave me a wink and a thumb's up.

"I don't hear any ticking," she said with a smile in a secret agent-like hushed voice. "Do you know what's inside the box?" she asked

"Yes."

"Do I get twenty questions?"

"No."

"What do I do with it?"

"Put it in the safe of the Buccaneer Hotel."

"And when I leave there for Miami tomorrow?"

"Go to the safe to pick it up."

"And when I get it?"

"You won't."

"How can I get it if you say I won't?"

"It won't be there."

"And that's because...?"

"It will have been removed."

"And you know this because...."

"I'm smart."

"The hotel will be very surprised and apologetic."

"They'll be very apologetic, and you can raise a fuss and file a claim."

"But you didn't say they'd be surprised." I didn't respond. "One more thing." I knew the next query.

"The name at the top of the label. Who is MR. GASTHAUS?"

Again, I didn't respond. I smiled. She knew question time was over. She took her attaché case and, leading the girls, I carried the file cabinet for her to her car. I placed it on the passenger seat as she buckled up. Her quizzical expression amused me. Not knowing everything really annoyed her. She would do as I asked, and let her trust for the man she thought she knew and admired guide her, albeit, in the dark. She must have wondered if my accident had something to do with my strange request or, perhaps, the drugs adding to post traumatic stress disorder, were affecting my behavior.

As she engaged the gears she said, "I'll see you next week. Safe sailing back home. I'll miss you."

"I'll miss you, too, Alexa." We'd arrived at another level of trust in our relationship, even if it was blind trust.

I smiled and waved, but my gut trembled at my trespass of affections. Even the girls stared at me quizzically.

After I weighed *Vanity Fare's* anchor and set the sails to catch a breeze back to St. Thomas, the girls and I sat in the cockpit. It was time for a codeine cocktail as the pain in my head began again. I set the autopilot and linked it to a vector for Charlotte Amalie Harbor with an alarm on the radar one mile out. I was hoping to snooze a little. Taking a break at the back door of the restaurant, a Rastafarian with beaded dreadlocks smoked ganga rolled into a brown cigarette. When he noted Alexa's departure, he wiped his hands on a dishtowel and took off his apron. Once she was out of sight, he jumped on his scooter in the alleyway and followed her.

As the codeine kicked in, I climbed into the hammock hanging from the mizzen boom on the aft deck. The girls curled up between my legs; Jimmy Buffet sang on the stereo as I thought to myself, *"It is time. The past is the prologue. The circle is being readied for completion and I am in the vortex of its whirlwind about to blow in from long ago and far away."*

CHAPTER 4

Uneven Keel

"What do you mean you lost it? How far could it go? Go back and find it. It's that or your badge!" With that, Houston Station Chief Derek Sweeney of the FBI slammed down the phone. Twenty-three years with the Bureau and he'd lost patience with incompetence. This case was high priority, direct from Washington. A former college wrestler, Sweeney managed to maintain a semblance of an athlete's build with his broad shoulders. They had to compete, however, with his ever-threatening paunch: the result of the sedentary lifestyle of the administrator of the Houston division. At the moment, his team was not making him happy because something very important had been lost and he didn't want to hear about anything from anyone until the "damned thing was found."

FBI headquarters in Houston was called in to investigate this sailboat-tanker encounter. That's what they were calling it. The Bureau's books didn't describe encounters, he mused. Crashes, rammings, illegal boardings, illegal salvages, piracy, seizures, trespasses and, of course, murders, lynchings, keel haulings, enslavements and kidnappings; but no *encounters*. The affair of *Hirotu* and the sailing vessel that his station, with his full team of seventeen special field agents, was to investigate for potential criminal mischief was tentatively labeled an *encounter on the high seas*. Sweeney wrote this at the heading of his file documents where *type of violation* needed to be justified, so he wrote *maritime encounter*.

Ensnarement or *rigging entanglement* would be more accurate, but he couldn't be more specific than maritime encounter for now. This was one for the record books. He was waiting for Washington to clarify jurisdictional issues. He had briefed the team on what the

Coast Guard and Homeland Security at the ship channel had told him. Back in his office, he looked at the photos of the *Wet Dream* hanging from, and being dwarfed by, the supertanker, *Hirotu*. He could imagine the expression on the pilot's face when he first saw this wreckage. Waiting at his office door was special agent Hobson, Kelly to her friends, but she had few friends at the FBI in Houston.

"What d' ya got?" barked Sweeney. Sweeney had not lost his Brooklyn accent after all these years with the Bureau and certainly called attention to that fact whenever among Texans, socially or professionally. He did not tone down his loud voice for agent Hobson, but treated her like any other agent. He didn't particularly like the locker room talk, or her nickname, *Hotson*. She was always professional. She had straight, auburn hair cut short and businesslike, some would say boyish. The less kind occasionally suggested *butch*. At only five foot three, her thin extremities, narrow hips, and boyish figure wouldn't intimidate anyone. But her striking green eyes that fixed a commanding stare upon anyone caught a suspect's attention, and more than one of her partners, as well.

"The sailboat is registered in George Town, Grand Cayman, to a Monsieur Champignon of Zurich. Interpol reports him "no known record" on their database, and the Swiss authorities haven't even a record of his birth. As you know, our search of the vessel found nothing, including no sign of a crew, no sign of mischief, no signs of distress signaling on their radios, emergency beacons, and the life raft was intact. No blood trace below or topsides, and the cabin was dry and battened down. The sails were not raised, but that would be consistent with the storm conditions, and the engine's ignition was in the *off* position."

"You're telling me what's in the Coast Guard report from yesterday. What have you found in the twenty-four hours since then?" the Captain asked. He was always a little rough on his newest assignees. Privately, he thought Hobson, with a little more experience, would turn out to be his best field agent, despite being the only female in this men's club of both the FBI and Texas. She had a knack for details, patience, persistence, and most importantly, insight, feminine or otherwise. He appreciated that from having lived with his wife of thirty years and he respected Hobson for her pure intelligence in assessing people and the meanings behind the facts. Besides, she wasn't bad to look at, although she certainly kept it professional in an office with so much testosterone flowing. What had his boss, Captain Arlene Stokes, always reminded him when he joined the Bureau? "Beware of middle-aged married men, away from their wives, with weapons."

Hobson remained a cool agent with a matter-of-fact attitude that could keep up with the team. She was single, unattached as far as anyone knew. Her cohorts on the team would deny it, but when she used her head in her quiet way, it saved the know-it-all guys an awful lot of legwork. Secretly, they often solicited her input on cases she wasn't even working on. She never threw it back in their faces when they pumped her for her insights.

On the other hand, her absence from their locker room kept her from bonding with the other team members. She missed a lot of inside jokes and quips about this person or that case. Most of the females at the Bureau favored the computer work for background checks, intel research, surveillance, and the like. She was the only female field agent currently staffed in Houston and never complained at all about much of anything. Her performance reports were A-1, but Sweeney knew she'd never been tested in close quarters where brawn might be needed. She'd never had to even draw her weapon though her marksmanship scores were aces.

"This event we're dealing with..." Hobson started.

"Encounter," Sweeney corrected.

"Sir, this initial investigation is uncovering more questions than answers," Hobson continued. Sweeney lost his train of thought for a moment. She reminded him of another Kelly, his daughter, who'd left home during college; he hadn't heard from her in two years. It drove a wedge into his marriage; neither he nor Isabel ever understood why she disappeared. Sweeney assumed it was drugs and a bad boyfriend. The college heard nothing from her again either, not even a request for a transcript. Despite his access to FBI resources, not a computer or a credit card trace or a bad check red flag could pick up her trail. Hobson gave him a father-daughter relationship in some ways and filled a paternal void. He broke his lock on his agent's eyes and returned to her report.

"The sailboat is about fifty feet, built in Clearwater, Florida and has Cayman registry. The owner appears to be Swiss, from Zurich, but without a birth certificate as yet from the Swiss office of records. The hull ID number matches a vessel christened *Mushroom*, not *Wet Dream*. Generally, when a yacht changes names, it must be registered with the home port, in this case, the Cayman's. They already have it so registered, but show the owner as its original owner with no prior title. They must do an international search for title in case this vessel was reported stolen or had its title documents somehow encumbered on financial or criminal grounds.

"The ID number engraved into the inner liner of the hull didn't appear to be altered and had no signs of tampering. I checked and verified the documentation papers which show Monsieur Champignon as the original owner, but instead of using the usual French-Swiss form of address of Monsieur they used Herr, which would be German-Swiss." Hobson brought the documentation papers around to Sweeney and placed them on his desk.

"You see the discrepancies: here, and here." She pointed them out. Sweeney didn't understand the documentation protocols as well as Hobson apparently did. He was puzzled by other issues.

"How do you know so much about French and German titles anyway?" Sweeney asked, a little upset at not seeing the relevance of this, but grateful Hobson did.

"French mother, German father," she said. "I know the *Hobson* is misleading. When the folks immigrated stateside after World War Two, Deutsch was not so fashionable. Hochstein became Hobson, a little more British and more correct for the times, if one wanted a job." Sweeney seemed to recall this family history when her file first crossed his desk. He thought of her as a "Franc with Kraut," but kept the joke to himself. He didn't know her sense of humor well enough, and she wasn't from Brooklyn.

Hobson considered the phrasing of her next question. She'd overheard the chief's phone conversation in the doorway to his office and didn't want to appear like she was prying, which was, of course, exactly what she was doing. It was her job and her nature. She'd always been a snoop and knew it was rude. Yet, it helped her grow up *in the know* with the guys she competed with. It gave her the edge that she couldn't get in the locker rooms. Even in little league baseball, she could talk her way onto the field by knowing how the game was played and which pitcher for the other team had a sore elbow and which base stealers her team needed to beware of. She discovered that she could learn a lot by overhearing conversations, comments, and opinions from those who least suspected an innocent looking girl was cataloging every nuance.

She asked, "Is there anything you need to tell me about the case? I could use all the help I can get. This case, excuse the expression, as we used to say back in Sweetwater, is a *booger*. I'm getting more questions than answers and the few answers I have aren't giving me any cause to think this is going to be simply a collision at sea." Sweeney contemplated whether she could be trusted and whether he should be mad that she'd overheard the phone conversation from Galveston. Results are what mattered and he needed Hobson sharp and on a long leash. She'd keep details from the newspapers, which might prove embarrassing to the Bureau and him.

"Well, the fact is, something related to the case just popped up. Agent Fielding, who's been attached to our team on this, just phoned to inform me that the Coast Guard dissembled the entire vessel for Homeland security protocols: scanning for weapons, toxins, WMDs, and IEDs. It seems that a part is missing. That's all, I'm sorry, but I'm sure one of a million parts lying in an airplane hangar at Scholes

Airfield could disappear. It'll turn up with a little overtime on their part. I don't want this leaking to anyone, Hobson."

He knew she was the best at keeping secrets. In fact, she was the only one he could share the story of his stressed marriage and missing daughter with. Hobson and he could eat lunch over their desk and have an intelligent conversation, even after he cleared his mind about what distressed him in his own family. Hobson respected her relationship with the chief and, although they were old school and new school, it didn't mean they couldn't work as a team together complementing each other's expertise.

"What exactly went missing, Captain?" She knew she was lighting his short fuse, but needed to know since it was *her* case, on *her* desk, and would reflect *her* record with the Bureau.

"Just the keel, I think he said. Part of the ship, I guess, I never knew what it was for, but couldn't go far under that security. It was supposed to be delivered by flatbed over to Homeland for a security scan and sniff. Sweeney looked at Hobson for her take on it since he didn't think it meant much.

"One doesn't *lose* a keel," Hobson said. The Chief nodded, but started to smell fish.

"It's big, huh?" Sweeney saw Hobson's wheels whirring, crunching numbers he'd never begin to fathom.

"A keel? Let's see, for a thirty ton sailing yacht, ketch rigged, two meter draft for the islands a keel would weigh about 8,000 pounds. Captain, you're telling me four tons of lead keel have vanished and no one noticed?" Her freckled, dimpled cheeks flushed like when she had a glass of wine after work.

"What do you think a missing keel means?" the Captain asked, letting her show off more of her nautical knowledge.

"Keels stabilize a boat. Look here," she said, showing the Captain the original Polaroids of *Wet Dream* as it hung ungracefully from *Hirotu's* anchor. With a magnifying glass they could both clearly see a keel, painted maroon like the hull's bottom, the shape of a dolphin's graceful body: tapered at the trailing end, stubby at the fore, and affixed to the end of a center fin coming off the bottom of the yacht's hull.

Hobson shared what she knew. "The keel on sailing vessels counters the forces that winds create when they hit the boat abeam, that is from the side, that tend to knock her down. The keel opposes these forces and keeps the boat on an "even keel" so to speak." He laughed at the expression; she must have thought he was one stupid landlubber.

"The sailboat didn't lose the keel in the storm," he said. "The photos prove that."

"But," Hobson deduced, "it was unaccounted for after it was taken ashore. In who's custody was it for bringing it ashore and to Scholes Field?"

"Our friends at the U.S. Coast Guard had the entire sailboat freighted by Chinook helicopter after freeing it from the tanker's anchor, directly to the air hangar. After the scanning, while waiting for a pickup crew and their flatbed trailer, local Homeland security staffers couldn't find it in the fenced in *post-security* holding area. Their records show it checked out thoroughly, though, along with all parts of the vessel, for contraband or weaponized materials. All reports, including bacterials, neurologicals, and explosives, negative. What's the keel made of? Does that have any value for thieves?" he asked.

"It's generally pure lead in the better quality boats, and lead is pretty expensive. I'd assume Wet Dream had lead, for she was a custom build, and a pretty pricey one at that."

They mused what they now had. Hobson jumped in. "You said Coast Guard and Homeland presided over a Class A scanning protocol and searched for everything of a threat nature?"

Sweeney nodded and showed her the signatures on the faxed reports.

"What value could lead be to anyone?" Hobson and Sweeney were puzzled. Neither was comfortable without at least a theory. Hobson broke the silence.

"Nothing. Except for one purpose. What if the keel were also custom-built along with the vessel, or even later added on? Keels can be fairly easily exchanged, even in the water, with six or eight bolts. What if the lead itself weren't the contraband of value?"

"Meaning?" Sweeney didn't like where this was going.

"Lead is heavy, yes, and terrific for sailboat keels. But another property makes it far more valuable," Hobson offered. "It's the ultimate insulator."

Sweeney knew he didn't like this scenario, but realized they couldn't ignore it either.

"Radioactivity," the Captain realized. She nodded. Scanners wouldn't pick up isotopes or other spent plutonium rods from an old nuclear power plant if the outer keel contained inches of lead like any normal keel.

The phone rang. "Sweeney here. Great...Fielding, you can keep your pension. Don't do that to my heart again." Sweeney turned to Hobson and said, "You had me going for awhile with this trail, but just got a call from Scholes. They found the keel. It's on a truck back to the field. Must have been a mix-up with so many different departments at the hangar site. Some airfield maintenance folks thought it was part of a cleanup assignment from airport operations and moved it to a dumpsite to be hauled away as scrap." Sweeney knew better than to settle anything with Hobson until her eyes and voice cleared it. She thought a moment. He massaged his hands together, as if readying them for playing a piano concerto and echoed flatly, "they found the keel!" Sweeney seemed to return to his usual state of moderate anger rather than rage. Despite the interruption in the custody of the evidence, whatever secrets the keel hid, it was not a plutonium device or so-called "dirty bomb."

Hobson seemed less relieved about the return of the keel. She'd look further into this irregularity in its transport. She could always find answers to the questions she posed, eventually, with diligent work. What worried her was if she couldn't find the right *questions*. She didn't think she'd yet found the right questions for this case. Too much was mysteriously occurring at sea, in storms, on crewless vessels with keels that disappeared and then returned.

Hobson thought she'd throw in some colorful sea lore for the chief. "Boats generally never change their name."

"And why not?" Sweeney played along.

"Superstition. Seamen have believed for generations that a vessel would be ill fated at sea, unworthy of Poseidon's protection, if the name it was christened with upon its original keel was ever altered," Hobson said. "The Gods will not recognize your craft when the gales blow and woe to the sailor who paints over its God-given name on its transom." Hobson thought this would amuse the chief.

"Seems prophetic in this case, doesn't it?" Sweeney said, more concerned than amused. Hobson thought about what she had just said.

"Maybe not. *Wet Dream*'s keel might *not* be her original christened name."

Hobson considered whether this was good or bad. What were the right questions?

****

On the crew deck of *Hirotu*, now locked down by the FBI with guards in the port of Houston, a Filipino from Luzon, a cabin boy, sometimes an airplane fuel deliverer, was on a VHF radio in a dialect of Spanish informing the receiver that he had a 'wet dream' last night 'at anchor' and the authorities had brought his luggage ashore for later pickup since they lost it. He also got seasick and lost his lunch overboard. He signed off, stowed the radio and hummed another Beatle song, "*All My Lovin' I Will Send to You....*"

CHAPTER 5

Graz 1969

The TV showed the happenings of a three-day weekend rock festival in upstate New York in the town of Woodstock that was all very far away from Graz, Austria. Rock music, the Vietnam War, and hippies were not part of this culture. Graz was Austria's college town situated near the Yugoslavian border, second in size only to Vienna to the north. The Karl-Franz Universitaet of Graz was Austria's largest and second only to Bologna's as Europe's oldest university.

The town had not changed much in the last few centuries. It mistrusted revisionism and modernism. As a keystone location in Europe, it bordered on seven different nations. It found little success historically in grabbing *shoulder room* from its neighbors. In fact, it consistently lost any conflicts it participated in, accounting for its ever-shrinking size.

Austrians were, however, adaptable, if not opportunists, and found the beauty of their female population much to the liking of paunchy royals from neighboring monarchies. This provided a less violent path to expansion, namely one *down the aisle* through marriages of international advantage. It was no surprise that Marie Antoinette was not French, but Austrian, hence adding a good deal of France to the mega empire that was becoming Austria-Hungary. This was Europe's largest, most dominant empire under the patronage and reign of the Habsburg family and their descendants.

Of course, with the rise of nationalism and the *guillotining* of the heads of states throughout Europe, Austria reverted to its pre-marital borders, shrinking in turn, to a less influential posture among its former in-laws who hadn't been beheaded.

The last experiment Graz had with major change involved its shift to fascism leading up to its bloodless annexation by the Third Reich and Hitler's hordes. Graz was the most rabidly fascist of all of

Austria's major cities, due to its proximity to the Communist lands just an hour's drive from its border. They saw the Nazis as the only way to assure Austria would remain non-communist, never considering that Hitler might be worse than Stalin.

Hitler, however, was anti-communist, and he promised a new Empire with the Germans and Austrians at the helm. At least Hitler was born Austrian. Stalin and his Russian thugs had threatened expansion into Austria for decades, so joining the Third Reich seemed the lesser of two evils since Austria's army was like that of a mouse compared to the fierce lion that was the German Wehrmact, Luftwaffe and the largest war machine erected in Europe.

I was studying at Graz University in the spring of 1969 when I met Oskar. He was an Austrian medical student whom I befriended after taking a pathology course together. We became roommates the following semester in a boarding house that catered to students like ourselves.

Oskar was dissecting his cadaver and I was doing the same to my own specimen. We were both quick at our lab work, so we had plenty of time to talk while the rest of the class caught up. We would show each other an organ or a nerve and quiz one another like the professor would do in June during oral examinations.

It was during my oral exam with Dr. Hofstetter, the elderly and erudite Professor Emeritus of the University, that Oskar and I really bonded. These exams were public, so the pressure was on. My German was good, but I worried I wouldn't understand the professor's dialect, him being a Swabian from Stuttgart, this being the hardest dialect of German for a foreigner to understand. It was like a drunken Scotchman's accent to an American.

It was my test day and Oskar was in the audience. The obese, grey-bearded Professor posed the question to me.

"Was haben wir hier, Herr Kollege?" He was asking a question about the intestines and what I noticed about them. In fear, for the life of me, I couldn't think of the word "eingeweide" meaning "intestines" and the only word I could think of would be of little use in answering the professor's inquiry.

"Es tut mir leid aber Ich kann das Wort dafuer mich nicht errinern," I apologized; I couldn't think of the word I needed. The professor looked empathetically at me knowing full well I must have studied one year for this moment and if I failed, would have to wait an entire year to retake the exam.

"What is the word you need? I know some English." He said this in broken, heavily accented English, so I knew he wouldn't know the word I had in mind. I panicked. Now I couldn't even think of the English word *intestine*, which made matters even worse. I had to say something with hundreds of students looking at me in the silence of that great, old, wooden lecture hall with the body before me.

After what had to be a long silence I muttered, "Chitlins."

The professor looked oddly at me and said, "Chitlins. Was heisst diese 'chitlins'?"

Tears of laughter welled up inside Oskar, for he knew exactly what "chitlins" were. He saved the day by translating with a serious face to the professor that "chitlins" was indeed the correct answer and meant "eingeweide" or "intestines".

Oskar and I passed that examination and many more. We couldn't have been closer and were essentially brothers. I had no other siblings, yet couldn't have asked for a better one.

It was on a weekend trip to Vienna that we drove on Oskar's motorbike to a memorial site. Oskar thought I would find it interesting, so without announcing his plans, he pulled up to the memorial. We marveled at the entranceway.

"Matthausen," said Oskar. "This was Austria's largest concentration camp and most of Austria's Jews, communists, homosexuals, gypsies and intellectuals wound up here if they hadn't fled."

A Jew myself, though not a practicing one, I climbed off the back of the motorbike and walked through the front gate. *Arbeit Macht Frei* was the lie above the entrance, as with all concentration camps of the Third Reich. *Work Means Freedom.* It was, in fact, the least accurate statement. Work meant starvation, unmentionable cruelty, and death. I had heard the stories of the horrors of the camps.

The granite quarry at Matthausen where, in lieu of gas chambers, unsuspecting prisoners were ordered to climb the stone steps to the edge of the quarry's steep palisade presumably to carry this or that up there or to fetch something. Once at the top of the cliff, they were met by a group of guards, who barked at the exhausted prisoners to turn around to face the edge of the quarry. The sudden ramming of rifle butts to the back of their skulls sent them headlong over the edge, three or four at a time. The victims' cries, and those of their children and spouses, continued until the final impact with an echo in the ravine.

Death was generally swift by this method, but, dead or alive, the fallen victims were buried in common graves. They were dusted with a caustic lime powder to neutralize the noxious odors.

That day I shared with Oskar was one neither of us ever forgot, and we had grown somehow closer with this experience. We wept together at the photos of the camp operations. Oskar, like his Austrian contemporaries of the new Austria, had tried to fathom why his parents and their generation had propagated the lie that was the Third Reich. How could they reconcile parental love with the monsters that conceived of, or willingly collaborated with, the Nazi death machine?

My father's stories of the war made me aware of the horrors during the Holocaust. Yet, experiencing this actual site, rekindled memories of countless stories and films I'd seen on the tragedy. The images haunted my dreams, turning my youth into a nightmare of terror and fear. I'd learned of typhoid fever and typhus that killed as many as the gas chambers. It was disease, not gas, that ended the teenage life of that famous young Dutch girl who wrote her diary, Anne Frank.

I vowed to use my medical skills to help the children, the innocents of starvation and disease. It was happening in the post-Vietnam era all over again: orphans of war from the Congo, Cambodia, the Idi Amins, Pol Pots and Pinochets.

I learned German quickly, having heard Yiddish spoken in our home. Yiddish, or Jewish, is a language like a Jambalaya or Goulash: every culture has its special dish, which is a mixture of everything left over from yesterday. In the Jewish tradition, due to the far-reaching spread of those of the faith known as the Diaspora, no one dish was carried from land to land, but the language is the delicacy borne of a blend of many languages spoken over thousands of years of wanderings. German, Polish, Hungarian, and Hebrew predominate, but other languages season the recipe as well.

My parents were Holocaust survivors, so the language and horror stories were all too familiar. Both parents were from Odessa, near Kiev, in the Ukraine. They managed to elude the Nazi web casting a far-reaching shadow across Europe ensnaring many, if not most, of its Jewry. That is, until one Sunday, when a detail of a half dozen storm troopers on an occupation mission after the Ukraine fell, were caught in an ambush near our farm. They were cornered by Ukrainian partisans with Mauser machine guns and Luger handguns taken from dead German soldiers whose corpses littered much of the Ukraine that winter.

Two such young Germans managed to survive bleeding to death due to the bitter cold that winter. Superficial bleeding didn't last long; even engine oil froze in the sub zero temperatures day and night. On this Sunday, after a meager farm meal of lentil soup, our family was startled by a knock on the door followed by gunfire. My father hid Mother and me in a shed out back. Then he attended the door. The soldiers, one a badly wounded officer, the other of lower rank, made it clear, in German, they needed medical attention.

It was with great consternation my father, who had extensive medical training in Moscow where he was a Professor of Surgery, consented to help, clearing the dining table of dishes and attended their wounds. Their visit lasted four days. They slept in my parents' bedroom and consumed much of our precious food supply. The only anesthetic available was a bottle of a neighbor's vodka, which doubled as disinfectant. The enlisted soldier eventually suffered hallucinations, which my Mother managed with her nursing skills. The officer emerged remarkably well, considering the multiple machine gun bullets in him. Had sepsis set in, they'd have died for sure. They must have been aware of my father's skill.

Father had not operated in years since he was removed from the Moscow Hospital. Stalin, like Hitler, was no friend of Jews. He purged them from his military and from any position where a trusted Russian might fill the position. Such was the dictator's paranoia and the end of Father's career. Father was despondent; consoled only by my Mother who was grateful they didn't wind up in a gulag prison camp in Siberia. The dairy farm of a distant relative at least allowed Father his freedom and his books.

What happened on that last day upon the departure of the German officer and his enlistee was pivotal for my family. The two German soldiers found a truckload of wounded Germans heading back from the front to Poland to a proper German military hospital. They flagged it down and were being carefully lifted on stretchers in the truck when the officer called to Father, "Thank you, sir, for your expert care. Extend my thanks to your wife's superior nursing skills."

Father bowed courteously, not knowing German, but understood the idea of what they were trying to express. Mother and Father were relieved to have the Germans leave. The German officer smiled and saluted Father. Father turned and was about to walk up the path to our farmhouse. He could exhale now that we weren't harmed, imprisoned, or hung on a nearby tree, like so many other Ukrainians. Just then it happened.

"Achtung, Jude!" This hailing from the truck by the officer was typical Gestapo tactic.

Father knew this word, having heard it in the searches by other German occupation forces they'd encountered. These so-called Einsatzgruppen, or Special Commandos, were nothing more than a mop-up battalion of second-rate soldiers who organized local militias among our neighbors. Their sole purpose was to identify the town's Jews for either immediate execution or for slave labor in a factory or concentration camp back in occupied Poland or Germany.

Father made the fatal flaw of turning around. By acknowledging the appellation "Jude", or Jew, he had condemned himself and us. With that, the officer said that the Reich needed skilled surgeons and nurses. He and Mother could either ply their skills to save lives, be they German or even Jewish, or be hung summarily from our front tree. We were transported by truck, then cattle car, outside Munich to Dachau.

I was an infant at the time. We survived Dachau until its liberation at the War's end. My parents worked in the camp's clinic. Many years after living in a displaced persons camp, we landed at Ellis Island in New York City.

Oskar knew this tale verbatim. He seemed fascinated by its twists and turns, and in many ways, due to the same War, his family story involved many twists and turns and sacrifices, with miracles and survival stories of their own. These, of course, were on the opposite side of the battle line.

After the War, Father was not the same. He was still medically and surgically skillful, but he was preoccupied with his memories of the camp. Mother survived the ordeal and kept her strength only because she knew Father needed her. I'm sure she'd have broken down if he hadn't needed her so or her love for him wasn't so strong. They came from the camp malnourished and in a form of posttraumatic stress disorder from which no one really recovers. They had the prisoners' five digit numbers tattooed on their forearms and hid them under clothing for the remainder of their lives. Me, I was just a baby and don't remember any of it.

There is a kind of guilt that survivors experience, having seen so much suffering and death. They ask daily, "Why me?" My parents did not find any comfort in their faith, or in much of anything except daily survival. They did not appear angry at what had happened, and most did not want to talk about it for many decades.

I made it to Columbia University, then found my way to Austria for medical training. I returned to Columbia for the Ph.D. program in microbiology and pharmaceutical research.

Oskar and I never spoke of the experience or feelings we had at the Matthausen Concentration Camp Memorial.

A year later, when visiting Oskar's family for Christmas, after a bottle of *Schnapps* was emptied, inevitable stories of bygone days revealed what life was like before and during the war years for the Austrians.

It seemed Oskar's father enlisted in the Luftwaffe, the German Air force, the day that Blitzkrieg commenced the war against Poland. His father had been only nineteen years old, and the zeal with which he told the tale was very revealing. He was caught up in the promises of Hitler. He had been well indoctrinated by the Hitler youth camps and was well versed in the rhetoric of the Third Reich. He joined the Party and was in flight school learning dive-bomber tactics in the feared Stukas. He fought over Prague, Warsaw, Budapest and many more of the eastern cities that Hitler wanted under the shadow of his Aryan empire.

Oskar memorized the stories, and judged them and his father a product of the hard times of the German-Austrian post World War One depression. Food and other essentials were scarce, the economy was in a shambles, and social and political unrest of the Weimar Republic under President Hindenburg certainly led to violence in the cities and anarchy. Communism threatened their way of life from the East and the only shining light was a little, mustached Austrian corporal named Adolph Hitler, who promised return to order and the resurrection of a German Empire with pride.

I understood and was careful not to openly judge his parents. Oskar's father conducted a war of aggression on Austria's neighbors.

During these hostilities, Jews from a dozen occupied countries were ferreted out, encamped, and executed. His father was shot down early in the War and suffered for years at the hands of the Russian guards.

Oskar and I remained friends long after graduation separated us. Letters, then email, kept us informed about one another's jobs, homes, and families. But, after years of steady communications, we grew apart with our own separate families, careers and lives. Perhaps we simply ran out of stories to reminisce over. The mail dwindled to birthday and Christmas cards, our relationship to fond memories – perhaps as it should have.

****

Hobson arrived at Scholes Field and recorded the ID numbers on the keel's port side: 070448. It matched the commissioning documentation papers on file with the Coast Guard, which were updated every three years. The hull's ID number, fiberglassed into the port liner under the deck locker just aft of the helm, was also accurately recorded on the original documentation papers.

Her partner, agent Fielding of the Galveston office, was on his laptop researching the owner's name through Interpol for updates since their inquiry six hours earlier. They revealed no more than the same facts about the mysterious Herr Champignon. Whether Herr Champignon had been on board and was now drowned, or at home watching television, they couldn't say.

Hobson thought aloud, "The vessel was not reported stolen or lost by international maritime agencies in Europe or the U.S. Coast Guard. The Swiss couldn't confirm that Herr Champignon was a citizen of Switzerland and he held no degrees, certificates, licenses, credit cards, or diplomas from their country or the EU's. They suggested he might be an alien under another passport, but their Interpol subdirectories didn't list that name. How he obtained legal title to a vessel was a question the Coast Guard documentation officers on site at the hangar could not understand either. He must have produced identification, and then changed his name. This was pre-911 so there was a laxness about who owned what vessel at sea." While that had since changed, it wasn't helping Hobson with this task.

"I'm at a dead end," Fielding reported to Hobson.

"We're dealing with a smart person who doesn't want us to know who he or she is," Hobson summed up. "Let's go fishing. Our fish might be playful, if not overconfident. What's with *Champignon*? Why does he use *Herr* rather than *Monsieur* if he's French Swiss and not German Swiss? It's a conundrum, but let's try bait. Try a search on Interpol for a Monsieur Champignon."

Fielding tried it, and then shook his head. "Zippo."

Hobson pondered other combinations. "What is the good Captain's first name?"

"P. Bello," Fielding said. Hobson took a moment to be creative with her quarry.

"Got it. Now search vessel owners: Swiss, named *Pilzen*.

After a few minutes of furious typing, Hobson sipped her coffee watching Fielding and was gratified when he got a hit.

"Monsieur Porto Bello Pilzen out of Zurich purchased a sailboat of U.S. registry, but terminated the documentation. The reference ends for reasons of owner's name change and vessel's name change, but no further subdirectory is referenced: dead end. But good guess. How did you know that this candidate was our pirate?" Fielding inquired.

"Our pirate is playful and he assumes that we're stupid Americans unschooled in the worldly ways of our European ancestors. He couldn't resist leaving the clue of the false title, which an American might certainly overlook. Europeans are most covetous and careful of their titles. Hence, *Herr* should be a *Monsieur* and *Champignon* is a most unusual name. In French it means *mushroom*; you gave me that clue with his first name: P. Bello, as in *portobello*, a staple for the gourmet mushroom aficionado, as any worthy chef knows."

"Those are the big, old floppy-topped ones, aren't they?" Fielding asked.

Hobson nodded. Her European background, and her French and German home schooling had served her well.

"But what about the *Pilzen*?" asked Fielding trying not to act too impressed with his supervisor.

"The German title was correct, thus *Herr* worked fine, and that was the clue to *pilzen*, the German word for *mushrooms*. Fielding looked dumbfounded and made no effort to hide it.

"Hobs, you deserve a citation of some sort for deciphering all this stuff. I don't think anyone else in the department could have delivered a name from the little we had to go on."

Hobson was lost in other uncomfortable feelings that were beginning to surface from what she'd just learned. She smiled gratefully to Fielding and nodded her thanks.

They alerted all stations in the loop on this case that they were looking for Herr Porto Bello Pilzen, possibly a Swiss citizen, and that Interpol had him listed as the ship's owner and a resident of Zurich. He was, however, Austrian by birth and, coincidentally, held a medical degree. The possible irony of the ship owner's name was not lost on Hobson. She thought this over and what she saw fomenting from this mélange of new revelations scared her. She kept her fears to herself, hoping that they were unfounded. Who would believe her suspicions? It was unlikely to be a real concern; at least not yet. She would need to dig deeper to rule out ancient history taking hold of this case.

Fielding probed Hobson further. "So where are we now? The serial number? Does it match the sailboat factory's number?"

Hobson checked her notes. She nodded. "The keel number matches the one attached to the sailboat when we found her hanging from *Hirotu*. The temporary absence of the keel in the holding area shouldn't be an issue. Only problem is, the ID number is a phony! The factory doesn't use numbers; it uses letters. That's funny." She read her files on the vessel's manufacturing data. "Why use numbers that would red flag our investigators? Unless...."

"These are not ID numbers; this is Herr Mushroom's date of birth." She pointed to the records of their mysterious Austrian Captain from Switzerland. Fielding seemed even more puzzled by this brazen toying with the authorities. This perplexed Fielding. He confirmed that the ID number and their mystery vessel owner's birth date were identical.

He inquired again of Hobson, "Why the mushroom clues? Seems like a clue in itself, doesn't it?" Hobson looked up from the data files, her eyes peering into the airplane hangar's vast space strewn with sailboat parts and equipment labeled and being photographed. He was right. Only one conclusion came to mind.

"Some are delicious and wonderful, some poisonous and dangerous. The trick is, you better know your mushrooms before you acquire a taste for them." They both realized the wisdom of this discovery.

"I think people are like that too, don't you?" Hobson thought aloud.

****

Alexa let the valet take the car at the entrance to the Buccaneer Hotel. The hotel was an old colonial-styled manor, regal and well maintained. She carried her attaché in one hand and the file cabinet in the other. They looked heavier than they were. The doorman offered to help her after letting her in the lobby, but she declined.

She headed straight for the elevator to her room and laid both pieces on the bed. Kicking off her shoes, she resolved to put the file cabinet in the hotel's safe as soon as she showered. It was good to know Alan was still ambulatory. The crash had shaken her and meeting him today left her with a lot of questions about who he really was. There was a dark side to him she'd never seen before.

Of course, she *wanted* to know all about him. She couldn't deny her feelings; she'd known that from their first encounter. What was it he said? People were like certain organisms he'd studied; just when you figure out the right antibiotic to latch on and cling to them long enough to have an effect, the organism recognizes that it's being hugged, possibly to death, and mutates itself. Not recognizing the altered being, they don't die in one another's arms; they co-exist quite well. Was Alan telling her something? Did he think about people when he looked at tiny organisms through his microscopes?

As she stepped from the shower, she noticed that the room smelled different. The jasmine soaps and lotions on the hotel courtesy tray weren't opened. This aroma was more pungent, intoxicating. It reminded her of college. It was marijuana. She'd smelled it at the Wharf when she'd went into her car and said goodbye to Alan. She also noted the Rastafarian smoking in the back doorway of the restaurant's kitchen.

These Rastafarians are a curious sect, she'd learned on the Internet. They believe that they descended from a lost Hebrew tribe of the ancient Israelites. The sect developed under the inspiration of Haile Selassie, the former King of Ethiopia or Lion of Judea, as he fancied himself. Their customs are not widely known outside Ethiopia and some Caribbean Islands like St. Croix, which has a substantial population. The island's rainforest up in the hills is secluded enough for them to squat there in clans and tribes.

Alexa also remembered that some are polygamous, smoke marijuana they call ganga, and ignore civil laws, often stealing to survive, or trading ganga for what they needed. Reggae music was sacred, especially Bob Marley and Peter Toth's. They eat kosher foods and are essentially vegetarian. They don't pay taxes when they can get away with it and if they don't annoy the local populace, are generally ignored. They are African by heritage and wear the Star of David, basing their beliefs on the Old Testament. Israel and its high rabbinical leaders only recently gave them official recognition as a Jewish sect, granting them citizenship on demand, as for all Jews wishing to return to Israel.

Alexa wondered if Alan had put marijuana in that file cabinet and that's why he didn't want to secure it in a safe himself. She couldn't imagine that was the case, but the odor was unmistakable. Drying her hair with a large beach towel, she entered the bedroom. Standing there, his dreadlocks hanging from the fringe of a knitted muffin hat of Jamaican colors, smoking a joint, was the man she'd seen at the kitchen door of the Wharf.

Alexa stopped. She was dripping wet and holding the pink towel on her head. The man only smiled and stared in overt approval, then clapped his hands, the joint in his lips. His eyes were afire and glazed. The smoke hung in the room above the bed between them. She was terrified. She made no effort to cover herself up. She heard a short shriek she hadn't planned on come from her mouth.

"Sweet, sweet, sweet," was all he said. "Like a pink flower. Want some?" he offered the woven cloth sack he carried filled with *ganga*.

Alexa shook her head. She couldn't think of anything to say, so said nothing. She wasn't even sure that she was breathing. There she stood, almost bold in her nakedness, silently facing the intruder without visible embarrassment, just inordinate fear. This intrigued the man. He circled around the foot of the bed, and then approached her.

As he approached, his eyes never strayed below her face. Only three feet from her now, she tried not to show any signs of fear, but the air conditioning on her wet skin was giving her goose bumps. That, she thought, he might interpret as alluring in some insane way. No, she eyeballed him directly, expressionless. He tried to provoke her with one hand elevated from his side, as if to touch her. He had left the joint to fizzle in the ashtray on the nightstand.

With both hands cupped as if collecting water from an open faucet, he gently caressed her face in his large hands. She didn't recoil or rebuff him in any way. Their eyes were fixed and she hoped the drugs would wear off bringing him back to reality, hopefully without a thud or crash.

Now he reached for her purse and opened it. Keeping eye contact with her he grappled with his left hand in the purse among its contents until he found what he was looking for.

"Turn around," he ordered. Alexa didn't move. They continued eye contact, his became fiercer, and she maintained her unwavering stare back at him. Her stubbornness was more out of fear, but no matter, it showed her resolve. He became enraged.

"Turn around." This time the order was issued from deeper in his chest, sounding more like a bark. Alexa reluctantly turned, the towel on her wet head fell to the floor, and she began to shiver. She could see him behind her in the bathroom mirror, just his head over her right shoulder. He was moving his left hand, still in her purse.

"My wallet is over there," she said, indicating the bathroom vanity. His hands were fumbling with something when she felt his hands on the small of her back. She saw something metallic glisten from his hands. Did he have a knife in his other hand? Dear God, let me live another day. Should I scream? Would that scare him or provoke him? What does he want – if not money or me?

She felt a gentle pressure cross her back and when she tried to evade it by inching forward, his other hand gripped her abdomen resisting any movement away from the instrument. It was not painful, but was as if his finger were drawing an imaginary line across her lower back. She dared not move. She froze in place for almost a minute. Then she turned.

He had left, the door ajar, and, after locking the door, she exhaled. She looked around and under the bed. She sat on the edge of the bed and she wept with relief. Her purse lay open, its contents strewn all over the bedspread. Her wallet was on the vanity and her attaché case was unopened on the floor next to the bed where his joint was still in the ashtray.

She would call Alan about this, of course. She would not call the authorities until after speaking with him. What would she say?

Was he there to scare her? Did he have a change of heart and plan a rape he decided against?

She'd dress, compose herself, and then make the call. She grabbed a towel and stopped to catch her breath. No, she'd call Alan right away.

"Alan?" she said into the cell phone.

"Well, this is a nice surprise. I was just having a codeine siesta with the girls on the aft deck hammock en route home. This completes the dream I was having. Paradise is funny like that. Some people think it's about a cocktail, others think music completes the scene. For me it's good conversation with good company."

"My room was invaded by a Rastafarian; the one from the Wharf. Did you see him?" Her voice was rapid and higher pitched than usual. I took a moment to clear the fog.

"I smelled his smoke, but don't remember anything else about him. You okay? He hurt you?" Now I truly regretted involving her in this whole thing. I had no right to, especially when she hadn't a clue about what it was that was happening.

"I'm fine. He didn't hurt me. He caught me coming out of the shower, but didn't touch me. Well, actually, he drew his finger across my back, but that was all. Didn't seem to want money or my attaché case. Left suddenly." Alexa was drying herself when she noticed a blood stain on her towel.

She jumped up from the vanity stool and examined herself in the mirror for injuries. No blood was dripping on the tiled floor and she moved her hands all over herself to see if she was in one piece. Had he injected her without knowing it? Had she been poisoned?

She looked through the doorway to the bed and noticed the bed spread, with all the makeup on it from her purse. She ran her hand over the small of her back and found the blood. It was ruby red and runny because she was still wet.

"Alexa, are you still there?" I asked in a panic, not hearing her for almost half a minute.

"I'm here. I think he drew on my back using lipstick," she said. "He was scary, but really not violent or aggressive. Should I call the police?"

"Did he steal anything?"

"Nope. Wait, the file cabinet. I hadn't put it in the hotel safe yet, but I did hide it in the closet behind my luggage." She paused and went to the mirrored closet door where the luggage was moved to one side.

"It's gone. That's what he was after. I must have interrupted him when I got out of the shower. I'm so sorry, Alan. I should have locked it up immediately, as you asked. Did he get something valuable? Is he Mr. Gasthaus?"

"No and no."

"So, you're saying: no, he didn't get anything valuable and no, he's not Mr. Gasthaus. Right?"

"I'm saying there was nothing in the file cabinet and there is no Mr. Gasthaus."

Alexa was confounded by Alan's obtuse answer. "So I was to lock up a file cabinet belonging to no one that contained nothing in the hotel safe for safe keeping. Do I understand correctly or is there something I'm missing? Because, Alan, this sure sounds like you were using me for bait, and if you're telling me you were chumming the waters for sharks like this Rasti, I'm going to be very angry. Tell me it's not so; I'll know if you're lying."

"Do you think I could use you for bait, really?"

Alexa wasn't sure. "Okay, so I'm not bait. Why the empty file cabinet of the non-existent Mr. Gasthaus?"

"I needed to communicate to people whose names and identities I don't know. I sent them an invitation to communicate and they responded."

"You communicated with Mr. Gasthaus. That's one name you must know. Who is he?"

"There is no Mr. Gasthaus."

"And the name?"

"It's a place, not a person."

"Where is Mr. Gasthaus?"

"It was in Germany."

"Was?"

"Burned down."

"What does the MR stand for?"

"*Medical Records* of the guesthouse in Germany."

"When did it burn down?"

"May 18, 1945."

"Could you be more precise?" She joked to herself for she believed this preposterous story.

"Since you're in a talkative mood, do you know who burned it down?" She asked.

"General Dwight David Eisenhower." Now he really had her attention.

"Yeah, I heard of him. Something about D-Day and running the European Theater of Allied Operations as Supreme Commander of Allied Forces. He won WWII, I heard," she quipped in her satiric manner I loved.

"Okay, so the guesthouse no longer exists, the records of medical care there are gone from the file. What have you communicated exactly and to whom?"

"The records *do* exist and I wanted to let certain parties know I might have possession of them."

She asked, "What do they want with *your* medical records?"

"They're not *my* records."

"They belong to the other parties, don't they? They want their medical records. As an attorney, I have to tell you, patients have rights to their medical records, and not even their physician can stop them. But you know that, of course. What am I missing?"

"The fact that most of these people are either dead or will soon be and have no medical need for these records."

"I figured as much considering they were wartime patients of the doctor or doctors at the guesthouse. There's more I need to know."

"These patients have no rights whatsoever."

"Don't tell me. German military convicted of war crimes. Right?" She knew he was nodding. "These are very bad people, but must be very old or already passed on. You are trying to find out if anyone is still seeking the records by labeling that phony file cabinet with *Medical Records of the Guesthouse*, or is the German a little different?"

"*Medizinishe Rekorden des Gasthauses*" would be the vernacular, but the initials are the same. I couldn't be certain if the ones I was communicating with spoke both languages. In any event, besides you being frightened out of your wits, the communication was delivered and the answer received. I don't know if the police could deal with such an incident. Your *visitor*, being Rastafarian, would wind up in a local jail for some time, but he was only useful for the messaging and is not an active participant I am interested in. Report it if you like, but it won't change the developing events I'm afraid are heading my way. I want you to come to St. Thomas. Take the seaplane and I'll meet you when I dock."

"No, I can't. I've business in Miami. I *am* an attorney. This isn't changing my work routine at all. I understand some of what's happening, but I need more information to put it in context. I'll see you next week as planned. One thing, *Beck*. You said the message was sent and *received*. I don't know how you received any answer."

"Stand up," I said. "Are you in the bathroom?"

"Yes."

"Turn your back to the mirror and look over your shoulder."

Alexa did, and dropped the pink bath towel she'd been using as a cover-up. There it was, as Alan apparently knew it would be. Inscribed on her lower back in her ruby red lipstick, somewhat dripping as if it were blood, a *circle*. But the artist was either sloppy or lazy because the *circle was not complete*; it was more like three quarters of a circle. It certainly did not look like a crescent, but closer to four fifths of a complete circle. I told her, "That's the message:

> *The circle is not complete.*"

CHAPTER 6

On the Hook

Living on a mooring in St. Thomas Harbor forces certain abbreviations to one's lifestyle. Live-aboards call it *living on the hook* or *at anchor*. Closet space is limited, so one cannot accumulate much. Cooking is limited due to the small galley and limited refrigeration space. Energy is limited so luxuries like air conditioning, abundant hot water, big screen televisions, hair dryers, espresso coffee makers, and the like, are not feasible. Island life, in general, requires one to find ways to occupy the abundance of time if one is not gainfully employed: I am underemployed and need to find challenges.

Today, I decided I was to get a newspaper. In my post plane crash condition under the influence of Class "A" narcotics, even this chore seemed daunting. This was especially true from the strain of hoisting sails and dropping anchor on the round trip to Christianstead to see Alexa.

I tied up my dinghy to the dozen other rubber inflatables my neighbor live-aboards used as our main mode of transportation. I found a slightly damp Miami Herald, only a day old. It went with me to Hornblower's Tavern at the end of the docks.

Over an orange juice and English muffin, I sat under the balcony's awning, scanning the paper for news of the day, or at least yesterday. The harbor was already bustling with tourists from the ships jamming the shops. My cell phone rang. It was Alexa.

"I'm back at my place. You made it okay?"

"Slept like a brick. Glad you're home. How are you feeling today?"

Alexa didn't answer right away. I heard her eating breakfast. "Shaken, but not stirred," she joked. Changing her tone, "You're a bit of a mystery man. I thought I knew you. This was probably the greater shock, compared to my *visitor* at the hotel. Please confide in me, Alan. Even if it's not attorney–client privilege, I can keep secrets."

I felt bad. "You can understand that I wasn't sure before yesterday that history, my history, was catching up with me. It's been buried so long.

"We'll need to talk more about this next time. For now, I've got a desk full of forms and questionnaires to respond to – about your last golf junket. There's a meeting in the FAA's downtown offices this afternoon to sum up your statements and sign off on them. Then, I'm meeting tonight with your insurance adjustors and those of Mahogany Run's golf course management."

"I feel guilty about it all, especially not confiding in you. It wasn't out of mistrust, but from fear you'd get *too* involved. In this affair, knowing too much can put you in danger. Your involvement with my past is no longer your concern; I'm officially discharging you from this matter."

"That's like telling the cat in the cage to ignore the canary. But you knew that already, didn't you? In fact, I'll bet you really want me in on whatever you've gotten yourself into and secretly wish I'd get involved. I'm right, aren't I, Beck?" We were back on *Beck* terms. She was right.

"I feel guilty. I would never forgive myself if anything I'm involved in caused you harm. You can understand that."

"And you can understand two things: I'm not a little girl anymore. You know me well enough to know if we're to have a *working* relationship, even across the Caribbean, we're going to have no taboos on what we can or can't discuss. I took you on as a client, professional neighbor, and friend. Now a *mule* for medical records and communications services. If we're to be friends, no holds can be barred."

"You mean like all holds are okay?"

"I'm serious, Alan. A half truth is still a lie," she said. I couldn't disagree.

"I'll tell you what you need to know when we're together, not on the phone."

"All right then. In that case, I'm feeling better."

"Good."

"Good." It was rare when we both couldn't find a word to say.

CHAPTER 7

Dregs

He was sitting on the dock by the fuel pumps on a large, brown piece of luggage. Docks for public and private pleasure craft are frequented by drifters of all kinds. They are usually young, teenagers or college types, a little independent and a little lost. Many have some skill they're willing to parley into a sea berth to sleep in or a ride to another port.

He, in this case, sitting on his brown luggage, looked about twenty-something, very tiny, black, straight shoulder-length hair, almond eyes, and high cheekbones. He was probably from Thailand or Singapore. The standard flip-flops on his feet were rubber, not straw, so he could have been American.

I left a couple of singles for the waitress at Hornblower's Tavern, folded the paper beneath my arm and walked towards *Vanity Fare's* dinghy.

I needed some fuel anyway, so when I limped my aching body down the wooden floating pier, scaling down to the water's level from the dock, I yelled to the young man, "Could you hand me the fuel hose, please?" He looked at the fuel pump next to him, stood up without a word, and handed the pump line to me.

"You'll have to flip up the check switch where it was cradled," I said. He did.
I gave it back to him when the tank was topped off and the harbormaster rode his golf cart by, noted the two and a half gallons of fuel for my account, and saluted me.

"Thanks, Clifford." I acknowledged the dock master, and then thanked the young boy.

"What happened to your head?" he asked.

I'd forgotten why my head hurt so. "I found out why they call the horizontal spar for the main and mizzen sails the *boom*."

He didn't get the joke, so I knew he was a landlubber and of little use to sailors.

"Know how to cook or sew?" I asked.

He shook his head.

"Can you fix a diesel engine?"

He certainly knew how to shake his head.

"My suggestion is to find a skill you can trade for transport, so you'll be of some use around here to somebody. Waiting for someone?" He nodded yes.

"They're late, huh?" He looked at me and nodded again. At least the headshakes had turned to nods.

"I have a phone if you need it. And I know almost everyone around these docks and nearby islands. Your host have a name?" I waited for a response. He ignored me.

"I could leave you my number if they don't show. Most of the hotels are pretty busy and certainly overpriced with all these liners in town. Would that help a little? Without a hat, you're gonna get pretty hot by noon today." Now he looked as if he were trying to size me up. I didn't much care for the attitude, but chalked it up to youthful caution rather than rudeness.

"Need a roof? I'm anchored over there on my ketch. If you need a place or some food, just hitch a dinghy ride from the harbormaster, Clifford. Mention my vessel, *Vanity Fare*, and he'll ferry you over. Knock on the hull. I'll put you up if your friends don't show." With that I proceeded to start my Yamaha. Before it kicked over he said, "I can cook."

"And apparently, can speak as well. Have some biscuits and soup on board for a snack, if you like. Eleanor and Rita don't cook much, and I could use a home-cooked meal." He thought it over and I'm certain the mention of other females onboard compelled him or reassured him in some way. He nodded and almost fell trying to board the dinghy after lowering his brown luggage piece and bag.

"Got a name?" I said.

"Dregs," he said.

"Pardon me, but you don't look that bad." I joked as I started the outboard.

"It's really Phuong Hyundh Drg, but everyone at school calls me *Dregs*. It's Vietnamese and very common back home. I never adopted an American name."

His accent was almost non-existent, so I assumed he came over here at a fairly young age. I smiled and engaged the gear on the outboard. I wondered where he would have wound up, or his body washed up, in these tough dockside areas, if I hadn't found him. I thought his parents' prayers were probably answered today. I'd advise him to contact them right away.

We neared *Vanity Fare* and my furry white burglar alarms went off.

"Why *Vanity Fare*?" he asked.

"I know a plastic surgeon who gave me the down payment on her. It's the *price of beauty*." Meet Eleanor and Rita." He smiled and I knew he was expecting a pair of bikinis with Pina Coladas. The girls licked my hand to identify me and to see if I'd brought them any snacks. I tied the dinghy's line to a deck cleat.

He lifted his luggage aboard. The girls licked his ankle for future identification purposes and to check for treats.

Once below, Dregs seemed mesmerized by the teak-paneled main cabin with its brass light fittings and bronze portholes and hatches. He smelled the beef stew simmering for a late lunch.

"The woodwork. It's amazing." He ran his hand over every surface to feel the varnish. He removed his shoes. "Even the floor is so smooth and shiny."

"The *sole*," I corrected him. "Boats don't have floors, this one being made in the traditional manner of alternating strips of teak and holly. It's called a *sole*."

His face grew more serious now as his thoughts strayed.

"My father worked with teak back in Saigon. He made statues of dancing girls for the G.I.s to support our family." He was clearly going down memory lane with the teak and mahogany paneling in *Vanity Fare*. I also noted he was carefully inspecting the galley. I hoped that his parents had taught him the superb cooking skills at which many Vietnamese are so adept. It was like Chinese food, but with the French colonial influence with more creative sauces and seasonings.

"You can put your things in the V-berth forward." He didn't seem to know what I meant, so I lifted his luggage towards the guest cabin in the forepeak, and pointed to the head. He went in immediately with a "thank you," almost bowing subserviently, though I knew he was only being polite for the hospitality I was extending him. I waved off any further thanks.

I fed Eleanor and Rita their biscuits after toting them down below. Eleanor was a middle-aged West Highland White Terrier of independent disposition and good sea legs. She was a good friend who'd sailed more than a few seas with me over the past eight years. Besides a little seasickness in storms, she'd kept me awake and alert on more than one night watch at sea, maybe saving both of our lives. She would snuggle next to my hip when I sat at the helm. We spent many a midnight passage seeking shelter in this or that island's safest harbor when the seas turned hostile.

Which hip she'd snuggle on depended on the attitude of the boat's angle of heel with the prevailing winds. She'd always sleep secure on the high-sided hip to windward, and if I stopped moving for some time, she managed to sense the lack of wheel motion or body movement and would try a shove with her nose in my ribs. As a last resort, a couple of sharp barks would usually rouse me into a frightening start. Beaching *Vanity Fare* in heavy seas on the rocks, leaving no trace of any of us or the ship, was the worst of my nightmares: a mid-sea collision with a tanker or cruise ship ran a close second.

The codeine depressed me. It also prevented me from taking my regular medications due to interaction warnings. I'd have to stop it soon or lose my DEA narcotics license to an addiction problem.

Dregs ate every bit of food I offered. "If you're still hungry, there's ready-made biscuit mix in the freezer and some eggs," I pointed out. "I don't bother cooking much, just for myself, and you're welcome to it." He nodded in gratitude.

"I'm from Miami Beach. That's where my family settled eleven years ago. My father works in a beachfront sundries shop my uncle owns and my mother cleans hotels. Both of my sisters, one younger and the other older, are in school at the University of Miami. I quit there this semester to travel before I settled down. I met a girl, Yao Yo, and we were serious about each other. I love her and she and her family want me to settle down with her, so I quit college and, you know, get married. My family got furious. They threw me out of the house. Having children is very important to my family, but only *after* I finish my education. I want to be a physical therapist and that's three years of graduate studies after college. Our families fought about my future with Yao Yo, and I couldn't take it any more.

"They want me to finish college, my girlfriend's parents want me to marry their daughter and work for her father in a restaurant they own in Ft. Lauderdale. It would be a good living for both of us, but I'm really interested in the medical field first. If I fail, I'll work in their restaurant.

"I got so confused; I didn't know what to do. Two weeks ago, I got a ticket on a steamer leaving Ft. Lauderdale for the Bahamas. I got this far today after traveling all night." He was starting to tire. His eyes were closing between breaths. His hand slipped off the counter table.

"You need some rest. Is there anyone you want to call?" I offered him the cell phone.

"Thank you. No, I don't want to call anyone right now. Not yet, anyway. Thank you. You've been so nice and I'm very tired of traveling." He was petting Eleanor who was used to having the occasional guest aboard. She was resting her own head on Dregs' right thigh. The bench in the main cabin where Dregs was sitting was about six feet long and he began to lean over a bit as sleep overcame him.

"You can rest right where you are." Rita was immobile on the rug beside us spread-eagled on her back with all four legs up in the air with total abandon, if not immodesty. It was her dead dog impression.

In the cockpit, I opened the now-damp issue of the Miami Herald. My plane crash was no longer newsworthy, but there was a last page about the NTSB's ongoing investigation. My name no longer appeared in the copy and, thankfully, neither did Alexa's.

I was about to turn to the crossword puzzle when a very odd photo on the front page caught my attention.

The color photo showed a huge oil tanker with a sailing ketch hanging by its rigging from the tanker's anchor. The article on the next page didn't give much information, only to say that a mid-sea collision had ensnared the two and that the tanker's crew was unaware of it since it probably happened in the storm that had just passed in the Gulf of Mexico. No crew were found aboard the sailboat. The sailboat's port of origin and destination were still unknown. The sailboat was being held in Galveston at the nearby airfield while the tanker and its crew were being detained indefinitely in Houston. Investigations by the Coast Guard and FBI were underway. Homeland Security assured the reporters that this did not appear to be related to a terrorist threat on Houston or its coastline of flammable refineries.

This was truly an astonishing affair. It would appear an entire crew of indeterminate number, perhaps a family, was missing at sea in the middle of the night in a ferocious Gulf storm without so much as a trace. Every sailor fears sudden squalls at sea during the night when you could scream, sound bull horns and set off fireworks and no one could hear or see you.

I was about to tackle the crossword when I spotted another item on the front-page photo: the name on the ketch's transom: *Wet Dream*. I turned my full attention to this article, less for its obvious amusing double entendre, than for something about it that jostled my memory. It had to do with a name from long ago and far away. My limbs turned cold despite the rising morning sun. I remembered a traumatic experience in my youth. But this couldn't be related.

I tried to work the crossword, but one name kept surfacing.

Wet Dream sparked the memory. I prayed *he* wasn't aboard.

CHAPTER 8

The Fencing Club

There is an old restaurant near the University in Graz, Austria where they serve the finest shish kabob of paprika-ed pork. I often ate there back in the sixties while in graduate studies for human anatomy. Oskar and I frequented the Wartburg Restaurant two to three times a week for lunch, after morning dissection sessions in the cadaver lab. Oddly enough, human body dissection never seemed to interfere with our appetites.

The inexpensive pork paprika was a good value, so was a favorite of most of the poor graduate students. One day we were seated in a back corner of the restaurant. I'd never noticed it before: there appeared to be *another* corner room, a private room, with two closed doors, even further in the back. A young student opened the unmarked doors, and then closed them behind him.

A seemingly endless parade of students, interspersed with some older gentlemen, professors perhaps, quietly entered this unmarked, double-doored chamber. Curiously, most of the students wore a silly looking hat of drab olive green with a black band about its crown, which was flat on top. The green material I knew was loden wool, a traditional material Austrians used in their local anoraks and traditional suits for special occasions.

"What's with the back room there?" I asked Oskar in German. He turned around, shook his head, and continued picking his shish kabob. We always spoke German since my studies needed to be conducted in German and I spoke it better than he spoke English. "And what are those silly hats? I've never noticed them on campus." He looked at his cabbage soup, put down the spit of pork, and wiped his face and hands.

"They're idiots," he said, sounding somewhat annoyed. "It's a *fencing club*, of sorts. These fanatics fancy themselves as athletes. It's a secret society and illegal. Forbidden on campus. That's why you won't see those hats there. In the middle of the night, they organize *duels* for new inductees, the ones with the traditional military hats."

"Are they fighting about something to settle a score or an insult?" I asked.

"The score they are settling is not with one another, but that's another story."

My interest was definitely aroused. He continued.

"No, the duels are a demonstration of their bravery and commitment. It's a little like your hazing and blackballing rituals in America."

"I don't think swords and duels are a part of that, but I see the connection."

"They don't really fight at all. The Master of the *inductee*, as they call the pair, raises his sword and proceeds to take threatening swipes at various parts of the candidate's anatomy, including the face."

"The face?"

Oskar nodded. "The face is the most important. The candidate must demonstrate his bravery by not flinching or reacting at all. The sword is wielded on his body, inflicting deep lacerations. If he flinches, he will be blackballed."

"Why is the face so important? It could ruin his complexion and chances of finding a suitable girlfriend or wife."

"The facial scars are the most visible and, therefore, the most important. This ritual of scar bearing is like the stripes on a soldier's uniform. It's a rank of sorts and, as such, these ugly scars are to be admired. There are plenty of women, certain ones to be sure, who consider those scars worthy of dating and marrying above all others."

Oskar appeared to lose his appetite, even though I knew he loved the pork paprika.

But he added, "Of course, I've seen their scars and hats, but the meaning goes far deeper than a sports club; *they're political.*"

"Why don't they solicit new members with at least a sign on their club room door? Could I join if I ever decided to take up the sword?" I joked.

Oskar ignored my ridiculous question. I must have sounded naive.

"We Austrians know what they really are. Back in America, you call them skinheads or neo-Nazis, or *right-wing radicals.* It's really more than that. These are the children of former SS guards, Gestapo Polizei thugs, and all sorts of violent criminals who are remnants of the old Reich. They are not sanctioned by the University, but as they are a *sports club*, they use that cover to mask their subversive activities. They are arsonists, muggers, rapists and...." He stopped, almost spitting up the fine meal. He took a swig from his beer. He looked me square in the eyes for the first time since this conversation started.

Ever since our trip to Matthausen, there wasn't much between us we couldn't share; our cultural differences seemed to evaporate. We were brothers, with no secrets from one another. Only our backgrounds separated us. Language differences we overcame by first semester. Oskar had presided over my first years in Austria, teaching me Austrian customs, ways of thinking, rules of politeness, methods of dating, how to respect professors, Austrian history and geography and, of course, Alpine skiing.

I had developed a love of this tiny nation and even considered relocating there permanently. It was an idyllic country with wonderful manners and a culture at the forefront of European taste, as Vienna had historically always epitomized. Its music and art were the most admired for centuries and it maintained its castles, museums, concert halls, and opera houses at the pinnacle of world class. I loved Oskar after living with him for four years in Graz. We double-dated together, studied together, and our classmates knew us as the academically top students and, essentially, brothers. He shared his family at Christmastime with me and he came to Florida during our summers to enjoy my family.

This day proved difficult for him. He had to tell me about this fencing club and I could see his pain. Are these fascists? "*Verdammte Idioten,*" he'd called them. I knew he was angry when his German penetrated with its rolling R's and inflamed his eyes. His fist slammed our table. I feared it would attract attention among the other diners; and it did.

He paused a moment. "They are proud of their anti-Semitism, proud of the camps and Himmler's *final solution*. They are proud of their scars and even prouder of their parents' roles in the Third Reich. Proud of the Holocaust! This is *Sheissdreck!*" The German for *crap* expressed his sentiments.

They'd hurt his pride. His father had fought in the Luftwaffe as a pilot with honor and was military, not political. I knew and liked him. Oskar's family had suffered through the pre-War depression, suffered in its aftermath of starvation and decades of allied occupation. His mother told him that she had been attacked by a drunken British soldier one night. It took many years for her to admit the details about this assault, and Oskar wondered if she'd been raped.

During the years of Allied Occupation of the remains of the Third Reich, crimes like these were rarely reported among the vanquished to their occupiers for a multitude of fears and mistrust. Better to be silent.

"So what you're saying is, this club is a political anachronism. They still hate Jews, homosexuals, gypsies, and Communists. This, despite the fact that almost all the Jews of Austria had escaped to the West, been gassed, or worked to death in the camps. Few have returned since the War; am I correct?" Oskar acknowledged this.

"Some have come back unnoticed. Some change their name and return. Some have intermarried and returned. Some even converted during the war to avoid Nazi extermination."

"What more can they want? Virtually all Jews would not *want* to come back for any reason I can think of. The vast majority of the multitude of Jews who called Austria home, they had everything taken from them; land, factories, loved ones, educational opportunities, civil and professional jobs. Only very bad memories of a nation gone mad, of suffering at the hands of neighbors, only dead friends and family, most without so much as a memorial headstone or a grave. *Who would want to come back if they were Jewish?*" I looked at Oskar. I thought I detected a Mona Lisa smile hidden in his expression. He looked up from the pork paprika and stared right back into my eyes. I understood.

CHAPTER 9

The Seventh Hole

Hobson gazed at the lead keel, alone with it at the hangar at Scholes Field in Galveston. It was late, long after her dinner with Special Agent Jameson at the local tavern on the Strand. Jameson, a partner during her first months with the Bureau in Houston, was now in his last year before retiring.

"What did the scanners find?" he queried, bringing a couple of beers to their corner table at the Strand Tavern.

"No toxins, no biologicals. The sniffers were calibrated for anthrax, Seran, Ricin. All the usual substances. No narcotics, crystal meth, cocaine derivatives, formalin compounds, Cannabis. Negative, too, for the whole panel of explosives." He hadn't read her daily report so she reiterated the things they *hadn't* found.

"That leaves us with..." his voice dropped off. He looked at her and saw her flipping back over her memo pad, then looking again up at him.

"I'm going back to the hangar. You don't need to come if you're going off shift. I can handle it tonight. Chief's going to want more than this." She scanned his face for a decision.

"You got it. Thanks. There's a bed and a chocolate Lab waiting for me at home. Molly gets hungry for dinner about now. Wife's taking her art class tonight at the adult center, so Molly has me and *Columbo* tonight. Any new ideas about what was with that keel that went missing for an hour? You know, this isn't adding up." He finished his pie and beer, wiped his face, and almost hid a burp. Hobson was lost in her thoughts.

Then she looked at him, or through him, as if staring into space. She was one bright field agent with a terrific career ahead of her. She'd only been in Houston one year, her first in the field, but

Jameson never felt he had to pull her along. More often than not, it was Hobson driving him to dig deeper to get the facts right; "roll them around" she would say and, if you don't come up with the right answers, at least get the questions right. That was it! She needed the right questions on this case. This silence from her was beginning to *creep him out*, like his son used to say.

"All right then, you poke further into finding the right questions, and I'll feed Molly." He rose and she smiled and nodded, then returned to her notes.

****

Scholes Airfield was deserted, except for the night guard who checked her ID. Wisps of clouds floated across the moon. Standing before the massive, lead keel in the dark hangar, Hobson ran her hand over its cold surface with her tiny fingertips. She marveled at its smoothness for a very heavy, forged, lead piece of metallurgy. The six threaded bolts lying on the ground that formerly anchored it to the bottom of the fiberglass hull of Wet Dream were each over sixty pounds. She had difficulty trying to push any one of them with her foot to even roll an inch. They were mighty, but she would get one to the lab, somehow.

She walked around the keel. It was painted maroon, and leaned on its starboard side. It was eighteen feet long from its blunt end to the finer, tapered trailing point. She walked around it several times. She pushed her fingers through the bored out holes for the keel bolts to fasten it to the fiberglass hull. At the other end of the hangar lay the sailboat's bare hull. Like a beached whale, it looked unnatural on land, despite its beauty and grace in the sea. Masts and rigging spars lay next to it.

While running her hands near the keel bolt holes, Hobson noted something odd. There it was. She hadn't noticed it before, even in daylight. She took her pocket flashlight from her key chain and with her fingers, detected a seam along the top-most portion of the keel.

The keel bolt holes went through the plate and then into the body of the lead keel. *Why was there a top plate?*

She wondered if this was a fastening plate that might be typical of keel construction. Or, maybe, *something else?*

With a screwdriver she found at a nearby workbench, she tried to pry the plate loose from the keel. Many nautical miles submerged in the salty sea had caused this plate to become part of the keel. She'd need help. A crowbar, she thought, and retrieved one from the trunk to her car. She used a hammer found on the workbench to pound the crowbar's flat tip driving a wedge between the cover plate and keel.

Repeating this operation a dozen times around the perimeter of the keel caused the two to suddenly separate. Out of breath and exhausted, she collapsed to the floor. The echo of each pounding of the hammer on the wedged crowbar rattled the old windows above the hangar's door. It was deafening in the middle of the night. No one heard all the noise she had made. She wondered why the security guard had not checked in about the noise. Sweat pored through her silk blouse and her hair was matted like she'd just come out of a shower.

She resolved to give one more final thrust to drive the iron deep into the crevice she'd started. It drove in firmly. Putting the hammer down on the counter, with two hands and using her weight, she tried to lower the lever she'd created to free the cover plate from the keel. It suddenly gave way and she fell again to the floor. The plate fell to the floor as well, to her left, narrowly missing her left foot. Where was that guard? She could use some help about now.

After a few minutes she regained her normal rate of respiration. She'd torn the right sleeve of her shirt and there was blood on her right knuckles, probably from falling to the floor and sliding. She ached, but was glad her curiosity had found *something* she could report to Sweeney in the morning. *That was only a couple of hours away.*

She stood and peered at the exposed keel. What she'd seen before her made the last hour's work worthwhile. She found her flashlight and confirmed what she thought she had seen. *It was hollow*!

She looked around to see if anyone else was here to help her. She was alone. She found a plastic crate and brought it to the edge of the keel. She kicked her shoes off and stepped up on the crate. Even with the keel on its side, she would need a little more height to peer further into its abyss. She lifted herself higher, as if doing a chin-up, and peered over the edge.

It looked empty, as far as she could see. Her flashlight went out. It was dark in the inner chamber. She decided to climb in. The lead was cold in the night air and more than a little damp from the onshore breeze from the Gulf.

As she lifted her weight over the brim of the chamber, her hands slipped, and she slid all the way down inside the keel. The inner surface was not as smooth as the outside and the slide abraded her buttocks and palms. Her butt was protected by her pants, but her palms, acting as brakes, must have been bleeding for the moisture did not account for the warm liquid accumulating in her palms. Salt stung her palms. What had she fallen into? Could she get out? She was shivering, her injuries hurt, and she was alone.

She remembered a time when she was in middle school and two young boys locked her in a school janitorial closet back in Sweetwater, Texas. There was some chemical used for cleaning materials in there and the lid on the metal cleaner's container was not sealed. The darkness and the awful smell of the ammonia or acetone were overwhelming. Hobson was found twenty minutes later by a janitor, passed out on the closet floor.

Hobson didn't like this situation at all. She had to focus if she was to avoid passing out. She could scream, but who'd hear her? The flashlight wasn't working; she cursed it aloud. There was a slight echo in the keel's inner chamber. She felt around the chamber; it was large enough to take perhaps half a step in any direction.

Still, she knew that she'd found something worthwhile. She didn't know much about keel construction, but what purpose could hollowing it out serve except...?

She was getting the *right question* and it excited, no, it *disturbed* her. What a convenient method of transporting contraband beneath the radar of U.S. Homeland Security: create a transport space impervious to radar scanners *with lead*! Lead being the natural material of choice for a sailboat's keel would innocently also prevent any scanner, even X-radiation, from penetrating its secret contents. That is why the sniffers and scanners failed to detect any threats. Nothing could sense or detect this secret compartment. It was hermetically sealed. Clever.

What had been in the keel? Now she realized that the disappearance of this keel for even a short time had potentially sinister significance.

It was only logical that something was concealed beneath Wet Dream by Herr Pilzen, the mysterious mushroom man. The serial number on the keel was clearly not a proper serial number. Herr Pilzen, or someone, had replaced this vessel's keel with another to transport items he didn't want the authorities to discover. No, Herr Pilzen was so confident in his ingenuity that he'd created an obviously humorous ID number for his custom keel: his birth date. Hobson took a moment to consider this.

Was he being brazen and bold? To go to all of this expense and risk to transport something so vital to his interests, so cleverly, why even tease the authorities with such a clue? The keel was the key; she just didn't know the right question about it yet except that it must have carried something of value or of danger. He was a smart smuggler and if it wasn't for the collision at sea with *Hirotu*, the plan would certainly have evaded detection.

Why the keel was empty now meant either something was picked up during its absence or was removed in the storm at sea. The cover plate she'd just managed to jimmy off could have been replaced after opening by someone on the docks using a common adhesive caulking material. Thus far, no suspicious activities about this keel, like a covert team opening and removing something, had been reported. She would get the surveillance camera videos from around the hangar and holding areas to confirm this.

She took out her cell phone and prayed it would work. If not, no one would find her until the first shift arrived at sunrise.

The phone showed reception. She dialed the chief. He wanted to know everything on this mystery ship as soon as she found it. She'd have to wake him. Knowing him to be an insomniac she'd either find him happy to talk or angry with her for waking him from the little sleep he had. "Sir, have some info on our sailboat."

"That's good news. I'm paid to hear the bad news though." His sense of humor at this hour told Hobson that Sweeney hadn't been sleeping.

"I found a hidden inner chamber in the sailboat's keel. This is not usual; it was probably fashioned as a custom replacement keel for an otherwise stock sailboat."

"What did you find inside?"

"Empty space."

"It was missing for an hour due to Fielding's carelessness. What do you think it was holding?"

"First, let me tell you one more item of concern. There were six holes drilled in the hull and keel perfectly matching the six bolts. But I found *one more hole*, a smaller one I could only feel with my fingers, drilled among the others. It went from the sailboat's hull and bilges, entirely through a cover plate topping this inner chamber in the keel's hollow. This concerns me most of all." Hobson didn't know how far her suspicions should be revealed to the Chief at this time.

"Okay, you got my interest," He was in a relatively good mood for this hour of the morning. "What do you think might have been hidden in that chamber, Hobson?"

"Chief, it's not *what*. I'm thinking it might be *who*."

There was a silence neither of them liked. She could visualize Sweeney's face going from curious to grim.

"You're thinking we have had someone smuggled into this country by a closed lead keel affixed to a sailboat found hanging from a supertanker that snarled it at sea? A little farfetched, Hobson, don't you think? I know I've pushed you hard at this case, but it is top priority from Washington. We don't want to be the butt of a joke inside the loop."

"Two other facts suggest *living* cargo, not contraband. The keel's ID is our mysterious yacht owner's birth date. Cargo has no birth date, only people. But this alone didn't make me think a person might have been smuggled into the country. It was this other small hole. It could be for an air-line for someone hiding in the keel. There is no reason to have a seventh hole between the keel's inner chamber and the inside of the cabin."

Hobson felt better about what she'd been thinking from inside the keel for the last half hour. Solitude promoted her thinking and the hole she'd spotted in the deck plate as it lay on the ground after coming within inches of crushing her left ankle, inspired her. This had to be a living crypt for someone who was so obviously wanted by U.S. authorities that the only way to transport them into the country was with a very extreme, highly risky method, forged out of desperation. Her breathing became heavy.

"Chief, this person, I suspect, is already in the country and is very desperate. I think he is a known criminal, internationally probably, who was willing to go to great expense, is well funded, is fearless, and has something to do which is worth risking his life over." Hobson felt justified in what she'd just revealed by the facts and the cleverness of Herr Pilzen or Monsieur Champignon, or whoever he or she was. There was one more thing she almost forgot to tell Sweeney.

"I'll need someone to fish me out of this inner chamber from the keel at the hangar."

"I'll call security at Scholes. You okay? Sounds like good work, Hobson. Get back here for a debriefing with the team at 0800."

"Roger that, Chief." He hung up. Her phone battery was dying. She was getting giddy from the pain she'd endured in her body from her bleeding palms and aching buttocks. Being isolated too long in a dark, closed space, like a coffin, was beginning to make her lightheaded as well. She'd come a long way from a school closet fainting to sailboat keels, and possible terrorists. She tore the remainder of her right sleeve off and made a bandage for one palm. She sat at the bottom of the keel's damp chamber and tried to stop thinking, if just for a while.

One thing was for sure: she'd found the right questions.

CHAPTER 10

Ghosts

Dregs slept all afternoon. At sunset I took my decaf on deck to the cockpit. The air in the harbor smelled smoky from a barbeque pit on shore where a party was given with the Caribbean flair of steel drums playing *Island in the Sun*. I liked the islands in spite of the tourists. I was healing from my wounds and grateful to be alive.

"Evening, Alan," spoken with a familiar soft voice. The codeine hadn't quite worn off. I looked at the foredeck, which was pitch black since I hadn't lit any bow or anchor lights as yet. From the cockpit I reached in the companionway below finding the breaker panel and turned on the anchor light. It was enough to illuminate his form even though I couldn't really see his face.

He leaned casually against the stainless bow pulpit rail.

"You startled me! Even Eleanor and Rita didn't hear you slip aboard. I wish you'd knock on the hull when you dropped by."

He had always been a little shy around other people and remained a loner over the last fifteen years. He avoided most human contact and no one, except his patients, visited him much up the hill anymore. I worried about him at his age living up the hill, but that's the way he liked it.

He said, "You need some feminine company, don't you think? I watch from the hill and you're alone a lot on *Vanity*. Since Mom's been gone, we both could use a little conversation. Have you been all right? Look a little thin, even for you, son. I hadn't seen you since the ER."

"I've been fine. What's doing at the clinic? Amy doing well?"

He looked at the moon. His face was gaunt and withered, but his mind, as traumatized as it had been from war, torture, enslavement, disease, rejection, isolation and surviving the loss of my mother, seemed remarkably lucid.

In the loom of the anchor light, we could see many similarities in our faces. Our dark complexions, long frames, and similar facial features would make us look more like brothers twenty years ago before I lost my hair. I was always proud of my Dad. He was a well-regarded physician and surgeon, just like his father. He was an even better scientist. The potions he'd concocted by trial and error, from fungi and algae, were astonishing.

He nodded to the question about Amy, his companion and head nurse at the Bougainvillea Clinic up the hill in Morningside Heights. It was a beautiful estate donated by a Danish colonial family who, lacking heirs, ceded it to the island for the purpose of providing needed healthcare. Dad, Georg Becker, M.D., accepted the post after retiring from the U.S. Navy Medical Corp where his last tour was at Bethesda Naval Hospital in Maryland. He'd spent the last five years of his hitch in the military as a general surgeon. During the war, he had pioneered far more advanced surgical techniques he'd performed routinely for very high-profile patients back in the old country. At the clinic, he handled minor and preventative care, even an occasional appendectomy or delivery of a baby.

"I think a lot about grandfather, don't you?" I asked.

"He'd have been proud of your lab. You do a lot of good for a lot of needy people." We buried Dr. Samuel Becker with his brother in our village outside Odessa in the Ukraine, before the War.

"I sometimes think he's still doing surgery somewhere, maybe even teaching it like he used to at the University in Vienna before...." Our eyes met, our faces grim.

"Guess I'll be going. Amy will be wondering where I'm at." We hugged each other, not knowing if this would be our last visit.

"Night Ellie," he said to Eleanor, his favorite, who'd wait for him to leave because he always had a biscuit in his pocket. He gave it to her and she chomped it in two bites. Rita was standing by and when she didn't get hers, murmured pathetically; of course, he had one for her as well. A pat on each of their heads, then he turned to me as he untied the line holding his dinghy in the blackness below.

"You be nice to those little girls and stay away from anything that flies. No bedtime stories tonight."

He was the kindest man I'd ever known. If his eyes continued to cloud, his days as a surgeon would be numbered. I worried about him finding his way back to the tiny pier he built in an isolated section near Frenchman's Reef, where his comings and goings were not noticed by anyone. He always managed to get home all right though. Amy would call me if any emergency developed. She was good for him.

Just as he was about to climb down, he turned and said. "I've got a busy morning, but I can meet you for lunch if you like, after patient hours. Like to hear about your lawyer friend. Ring me if you can make it. By the way, it is Mom's birthday next week, so I thought you and I would sail to Virgin Gorda for a visit. It's been a year."

I nodded and said I'd call. He climbed over the rail and with his long, still lithe frame, stepped on the wooden seat of his inflatable. I handed him the bowline and he used the oars to put distance between him and my boat's forecabin. As he faded in the darkness of the harbor, the Calypso music veiled the sound of his outboard starting. He was gone.

CHAPTER 11

Mosad

Alexa's office, like mine, was located just off Brickell Avenue in an efficient, two-story office building of tinted glass with a parking lot underneath. She had her own condominium on Brickell, so with Miami's fair weather, walking to work wasn't an issue unless her briefcase was too heavy. Today it was moderately heavy with FAA and NTSB documents. While the morning rush hour traffic clogged the avenues, she was walking to her office when she spotted another pedestrian who seemed to mirror her pace and direction. He was tall and stocky, and wore a tie and sunglasses. She sensed he was averting his eyes so as not to seem to be watching her, but a wave of fear overcame her; *she was being stalked.* Her breaths quickened, as did her pace. She made no secret that she knew he was there. She turned her head in his direction. She didn't want to panic. This side street was not busy, just one elderly woman walking a white poodle. She lifted her cell phone as if to dial. She turned and her stalker was gone.

She was almost at her office and had to make a decision. Was this a random street criminal or was it the *Federales*? She looked over her shoulder and stopped in front of her office. She faked talking on the cell phone and looked around. No stalker, in fact, no one was on the street.

Then she heard a voice close behind her. "You'd probably have to turn that phone on in order to make a call." She dropped the phone and grabbed her attaché with both hands and raised it high in the air to defend herself. The voice belonged to a large, square-built, dark-complexioned man in a dark blue suit. She was about to lower the attaché on him when he grasped her wrists with one hand and produced a leather-cased ID with the other.

"You don't want to do that," he suggested. "While *I'm* immune from prosecution here, *you* could be charged with assault." She realized that he wasn't the shadow she'd been running from. This man was fiftyish, his hair black with a grey shock, tightly kinked.

She lowered her attaché. She noticed her shadow across the street was joining them, though not in a hurry, just a walking pace with both hands in his pants pockets. He didn't look to either side of the street for traffic. Was there a third person in their group watching out for them, possibly communicating with them?

She focused her vision on the ID. As best as she could make out, it was diplomatic and issued with a U.S. seal. The name was Middle Eastern, Ben something or other.

"Ari Ben Yorel; my associate is Yitzach Sanger. We're attached to the Israeli consulate here in Miami and would like a few words with you, if that would be all right." He lowered the ID. Judging by the way his eyes moved, perhaps one was artificial. Alexa accepted the cell phone, which he had picked up. She confronted his face and suggested they go into her office. They nodded and followed.

She unlocked the door, her secretary was not in yet, so she turned on the lights and they joined her in the two client chairs in her office in front of her glass topped desk while she sat at her oxblood leather chair behind it.

"So, what's this about? I've never been to Israel and you're not here to issue a visa, I suspect." They seemed glad that she'd relaxed enough to trust them in her office and to make a modest joke.

"No, you've never been to Israel. Wichita Falls and New Haven Connecticut where you were educated."

She could see they'd done their homework, but why was she a *person of interest* to these Middle Easterners? "If this involves a client, and it must since I've no connection to your country or any other international connections, I must tell you, as in your country, I can't discuss a client's affairs." She was becoming a lawyer again, and had regained most of her composure. She reminded herself to buy some Mace or pepper spray.

"The barristers in our country have the same privilege yours do, of course. We do not need to violate any such privacy. However, Ms. Grey, there are some matters a client has probably not informed you of that may be of concern to *you*. These matters may be construed as criminal or espionage." Alexa had a bad feeling about what was coming next.

"You know a Dr. A. Becker, do you not?" He issued a photo of Alan and laid it on the desk. It was black and white and looked recent, taken candidly from the dock where Alan was on *Vanity Fare* drinking a cup of coffee. She nodded. "Yes, he's a client. I can only confirm he is a client and I represent him. But you already know that, as does most of Miami, if you read the papers."

The older man, Mr. Sanger, smiled warmly acknowledging that he did, indeed, read the newspapers.

"Do you know what kind of product his lab manufactures by any chance?" the older man inquired. She noted he was far more serious in his expression after asking this question. In fact, if eyes could pierce one's soul to act as a lie detector, this man had, with probably many decades of experience under very violent conditions, had to make life and death decisions based on a subject's response to his interrogations. Of this Alexa was certain; he was no amateur.

Alexa thought that, to learn more, she'd have to give something to her *guests*. She was very curious about Alan for two reasons. He opened some new windows into himself and his background she hadn't known before which has surprised her. This wouldn't have tempted her to play *let's see what you know* unless she was falling in love with him and had to know *who* he was. She gave them only his business' public documents: annual stockholder's reports and pro forma outlines, the business plan, and SEC filings.

"He had briefed me on his remedy for a type of fish poisoning. I hadn't heard of it before, but he manufactures and distributes a tree-sap extract that he's discovered is a remedy for a toxic fish poisoning. He holds the patents for the treatment. While it is profitable to many nations who need it, he applies much of these profits to providing the remedy to nations less able to afford them.

While he doesn't lose money, apparently there are many who applaud his noble work and are satisfied to own stock in such a company with a good heart. It's not a charity, but it's not the usual way most firms do business either."

Alexa let all this settle and was looking for a sign that they'd felt she'd given them something. She wondered if she was volunteering *too* much information. She was an attorney and knew better. She was so relieved not to be in immediate danger that she was letting her guard down too far. She didn't want to get Alan into any trouble that would also possibly violate her client's privacy and privilege. Ari Ben Yorel could see she that was starting to think and become curious about the interrogation. He volunteered a little.

"May I suggest, you visited him this past week in St. Croix, and you did some legal work for his business matters. We are interested in his business because he distributes his products in Israel and we are always interested in Americans bringing Israel trade. We have been asked by our health department to commission his lab to expand its production for Israel. This fish poisoning you mentioned recently developed in our southern port city of Eilat. We are concerned about fish because Israel depends on good fishing for our diet. Just across the Red Sea and Jordan River from Israel, we have seven hostile *neighbors* who would prefer we don't eat *their* fish. In fact, they prefer we don't eat at all. In fact, they prefer we move elsewhere. You understand, Ms. Grey, our government's concern about which fish poisoning's we can't treat." Mr. Yorel studied her eyes to see if she was getting this, or perhaps, believing it. She wasn't certain which.

Alexa mulled this over and determined it sounded like a fish story of the first order. The truth must be more than they are willing to divulge. She assured them she understood their need for Dr. Becker's antitoxin.

Both agents looked at each other. Ari Ben Yorel said, trying to appear congenial and affable, "I knew his father. Did you?"

Alexa seemed surprised now that a personal connection had emerged with Alan that she did not know about. She shook her head and admitted she did not and had only heard mention of him in occasional discussions with Alan. She volunteered, so as not to sound too ignorant of Alan's family, that she knew Dr. Becker had participated in some of the original research that helped in the subsequent development of the treatment of Ciguatera.

"I only know he is a physician and surgeon. He had been a well-respected surgeon back in Stalinist Russia in his younger days. Now he works at a free clinic with his companion and enjoyed his semi-retirement. Alan speaks of him fondly and talks to him weekly. I've never personally met him." She looked at the two of them looking at each other. With some trepidation, Ari Ben Yorel volunteered.

"It might surprise you to know, Dr. Georg Becker, Alan's father, is indeed well known throughout Austria and Germany, especially since the War. There obviously is much about the elder doctor you are not aware of. Shall I go on?"

Alexa braced herself; in fact, she knew little about Alan and his family.

Yorel continued. "He was truly a gifted doctor and surgeon and saved many lives. Years after World War Two ended, he became more notorious than famous; he was sought by many nations as a Nazi war criminal for decades." The two men saw the shock in Alexa's face, too real to be anything but genuine. She sat back in her leather chair and tried to recall what Alan had ever said about his father. It was all very positive. He worshiped his father. They were Jews, non-observant ones, but still Jewish and they had a close father-son relationship.

Yorel continued, "Did you know Dr. Alan Becker has been institutionalized for mental disorders? He was diagnosed with schizophrenia, and was treated with electroconvulsive shock therapy. He was last in Texas, Austin State Hospital, and released with medication to control his psychotic delusions."

Alexa must have turned pale. "You wouldn't have access to those records."

Sanger pulled papers from his coat pocket and showed them to Alexa. "As you see, Ms. Grey, these are Alan Becker's hospital records. There's more, I'm afraid," Sanger added. "Based on his pharmacy records, Dr. Alan Becker has not been taking his full complement of prescribed medications for the past six months. This would suggest his psychotic delusions might be re-surfacing. His medical records at Austin State Hospital indicate that he might be a danger to himself and others."

Alexa couldn't hide her devastation. "I'll need to verify all you are alleging." They nodded. Alexa could understand their concern about Alan's patents on this fish poison remedy being unavailable to Israel should its enemies use Ciguatera as a weapon and the Manchineel extract becoming unavailable. This could incapacitate the Israeli Defense Forces in a crisis and render the nation vulnerable. Alleged enemies could have the convenience of *deniability*, since the poisoning is known to occur naturally. These diplomats could be on the level, simply seeking nothing more than to be proactive in defending their homeland.

"Ms. Grey, I assure you, my associates have the ability to obtain the intelligence I've shared with you including those of an historical nature and the younger Dr. Becker's medical and pharmaceutical records, despite your elaborate privacy laws here." He stared at her with a cautious and knowing smile to reassure her of the veracity of his assertions. Alexa, for her part, was certain Sanger was the superior and Yorel, the subordinate.

Alexa sensed a specter of truth in what he said and was sinking into despondency, one shocking revelation at a time. She had not decided how to confront Alan with her new information. As for Alan's father, he was a fugitive from justice. Alexa could not imagine any Jew, especially Alan's father, committing atrocities of any kind against his own people. She needed to know about the status of the elder's warrants from law enforcement or war crimes tribunals. She couldn't harbor fugitives she was aware of and still practice law, not even for Alan. Could she still love Alan? Both situations required resolution.

"You said 'the elder Dr. Becker *was* sought'. Does that mean he is no longer being pursued for the alleged crimes?" The agents looked at one another surprised by her question. Sanger spoke first.

"That would be most correct. You see, Ms. Grey, Dr. Georg Becker has been dead for over twenty years."

CHAPTER 12

Crisis

Dregs awoke and climbed the companionway steps to the deck where I was coiling some lines. He was carrying the girls up the teak steps. The boat rocked a bit more than yesterday and we saw a police launch motor by. It created a mild wake that rocked the sailboats in the harbor making them look like toys bobbing in a bathtub.

"Morning," I said. "Have to straighten up the deck lines so the girls can do their business." He put the girls down gently.

They licked his feet; he didn't seem to mind.

"Morning," he said.

"You've had dogs before, I see," I suggested, since he didn't seem to mind the licking as so many other folks did.

I noticed his eyes were dry and red. Salt air and sunlight were probably affecting them. I suggested he shower, and borrow a hat and sunglasses I had below. He thanked me, this time without a bow.

Just then the phone rang. It was Alexa, who sounded cool. I couldn't be sure if it was the result of her ordeal only a few days ago at the Buccaneer Hotel, or something else. Her next statements clarified this.

"Two men came visiting me from the Israeli consulate asking about you and your father. We need to talk," she said, again with that icy tone I had never heard from her before.

We both silently acknowledged that the future conversation on this matter would need to be face to face and not on cell phones.

"I'll come up there tomorrow morning. Are you available in the morning?"

"I'll make it. Let's meet where our first lunch together was." She didn't want to announce the location in case others were eavesdropping. "My visitors really creeped me out, even more than my visitor at the hotel."

I knew she was under stress and I wanted to get to her sooner than later.

"Alan," she said. "They seemed to know more about you and your father than I knew. Frankly, that disconcerted me quite a bit. I mean, if I didn't care about you, if you were only a client...." her voice trailed off as I interrupted.

I couldn't find any way to allay her concerns just now, but had one card to play. "Trust me," was all I could muster to deal with the matter over a public phone.

Alexa hung up. Emotionally, she knew she had to end this mix of business and pleasure. Alan's mental state crossed her mind as well. What was her legal obligation if her client was a madman? A CEO who was nutty as a fruitcake would cause an ethical dilemma she hadn't confronted before. Was he a danger to her or himself? Why didn't he take his medications? What would she testify to when the FAA and NTSB asked her about his health and condition while being the pilot in control of a private aircraft? How could he have a pilot's license if he was mad and medicated?

Back on deck, I hung up the phone and looked at the young fellow from Miami. I offered to take him to breakfast. He gratefully accepted. He must have noticed that my phone conversation had upset me.

"I have a favor to ask of you, Dregs."

"Sure."

"I need to take a day-trip to Miami tomorrow. Could you boat-sit for me? The girls just need to be fed around noon and six, and put on deck for a bit."

He agreed, but seemed concerned and asked, "The trip to Miami is not to notify my folks or anything, is it?"

"You're old enough to make your own mistakes."

We motored away, me at the throttle of the dinghy, Dregs holding onto the bow line, in the direction of the dock. Neither of us noticed the two clusters of air bubbles on the other side of *Vanity Fare's* hull.

The divers waited for the dinghy's engine to fade and gradually came within two feet of the surface. One had a waterproof white marking board attached by a loop to his wrist and was writing down the serial numbers of the vessel's keel. The other pointed a flashlight at the ID characters. In their wetsuits, neighbors would assume they were the owners or guests. Nothing to be alarmed about. They grabbed the rope ladder on the port side and climbed aboard. The girls continued their naps, thinking it was just me and Dregs re-boarding from a short hop ashore.

****

Fifteen workstations were arranged in two rows in Department Helix at the National Security Agency located at Fort Meade, Maryland. This department was charged with only one mission: listening to phone traffic. The Helix software program, which gave the department its name, was specifically designed to alert monitors of certain *key words* or *suspicious phrases* in conversations. It was then fed into the Cray supercomputer. Key dialogue from cellular phone traffic was extracted.

It was a program and process that generated many leads and, even though most were dead ends, this method of technical surveillance was clean, low risk, involved minimal manpower and payroll, and could reveal plots to harm American assets.

Hector LeBron's workstation was particularly fruitful today; he had no problem with the invasion of privacy issues. Controversial hearings on Capitol Hill were being conducted this month on this subject. Being a Puerto Rican by birth, he could easily compare his life with those in Communist Cuba. He knew the alternative to democracy. He'd willingly listen to private conversations post-911; it was a small price for his freedom. Most of his co-workers agreed, but there were dissenters at department meetings who wanted the software *softened*.

Today's scans revealed one particularly worrisome word. That's what the program was configured to detect: a word or expression from voice conversations was transposed to written, voice recognition format and digitized to a list. Hector's job was to classify the level of risk or *peril level* associated with the program's curiosity about a certain phrase or expression. He classed today's word as *orange*, which meant *warrants further inquiry* by active investigation on the ground.

From this point, the data on this dubious expression and word was channeled real-time down to both Langley and Quantico, Virginia. These addresses, said in the same sentence, represented a new level of cooperation under the guise of Homeland Security with the CIA and FBI, respectively, residing at them.

Kelly Hobson, in Houston, noticed a text message from Quantico flashing on her PDA:

> Alert: source Helix NSA, threat level orange coded text to follow, pursue. Sender's phone source: A. Becker, Charlotte Amalie, U.S.V.I., receiver no. 23745544 GSM Europe based, no name assoc with phone no. Interpol no ident. Proceed priority A/B, HELIX WORD ALERT.... "CRISIS." 16 repeats, sender last 48 hours ending 18:56 Greenwich time.

Hobson wondered why Dr. Alan Becker, the newest lead in her maritime accident investigation, had spoken the word *CRISIS* sixteen times in forty-eight hours. Was he, or someone else, in trouble?

CHAPTER 13

Mushroom Cloud

Hobson, Sweeny, and Fielding sat casually in their high-backed chairs nibbling kolaches from a tray on the conference table. Hobson took the lead at this morning's skull session. The Chief sat at the opposite end of the long, walnut conference table in the poorly lit room. The smell of coffee filled the air, and it was hot this morning. Everyone noticed Hobson's bandage on her palm; they'd already heard about her call for help to lift her out of the keel.

The Chief stayed out of the dialogue, letting Hobson brief them straight away.

"We have a possible collision of two vessels, but the actual site of impact on the chart and when it occurred is unknown. Debriefing Captain Sorensen of the tanker, *Hirotu*, and the crew members who were on station the night of the storm, revealed nothing remarkable. The logs noted that an early morning potential target was sighted on the radar, which likely was a *false echo*. No confirmation of impact could be determined from data tapes of telemetry of the ship's monitors or written ship's logs." She eyed the others, waiting for questions. It was too early for questions; they needed coffee.

"It seems that the collision of such a large tanker with a small private craft as this ketch, would probably go unnoticed in such rough sea conditions. The differences in the vessels' sizes would make this collision possible even in smooth seas in daylight. Radar was all but useless for anything but another supertanker of comparable size."

"Don't radar reflectors on the sailboat's mast make the vessel much more visible?" Sweeny offered.

"True, but with the size of the waves reported that night, a sixty-seven foot mast, even with radar reflectors as Wet Dream had, would simply appear as another wave among the artifact and sea chatter the radar recorded. I think the questions we should be more concerned about are the following: Why was a private vessel like this sailing in well-charted international shipping lanes in the first place? The safe thing any oceangoing captain would do would be to *avoid* these lanes in this kind of weather. Unless," she paused for effect, scanning the team's faces. "Unless, the crossing of courses was not accidental, but *planned*." Sweeny wiped his mouth with a napkin having finished the kolaches from his plate. The acid reflux in his stomach would start soon, but he already medicated himself, as he did every morning. Sweeney seemed a little uncomfortable with the direction this debriefing was going. Fielding jumped on the bandwagon after seeing Sweeney's expression.

"You think they planned to meet up? Sounds a little far-fetched." The others seemed to agree. "I don't know a lot about ships in heavy seas, but from the movies I've seen, there's no way two ships could park themselves next to each other and arrange the entanglement of the sailboat's rigging onto the tanker's anchor. No way. It's impossible." Fielding seemed pleased, as if he'd redeemed himself in Sweeney's good graces. Sweeney saw the merit in Fielding's statement; he turned to Hobson.

"I agree, but because we can't explain it right now, doesn't mean it didn't somehow happen." She continued. "Besides, until late last night, I hadn't realized just how clever our subject perpetrator is. In light of this, the meeting of two ships of dissimilar size in a Gulf storm seems plausible." Sweeney felt she had recovered herself nicely despite the fact she didn't have *all* the answers. She went on.

"The sniffers and scanners picked up nothing, because the *cargo* was embedded within a hollow space in the keel. There's no nautical reason to hollow a keel. Normally, it's simply deadweight to offset wind forces hitting a sailboat on its beam. Hollowing a keel is counterproductive. Homeland scanned and sniffed the keel *prior* to discovering the void inside. It was negative for everything on our Homeland Security panel for Gulf Coast international borders and seaports."

"There must be more," Fielding said trying to anticipate what was about to be discussed; he wanted to seem alert and involved.

Hobson had countered his last criticism and he couldn't deny she was on to something.

Hobson continued cautiously, in deference to Fielding's screw-up in losing the keel for almost an hour. "The keel was *mislaid* for half an hour, and possibly as long as one hour *after* scanning. It seems the that in the lot where Homeland guards keep an eye on the fenced, quarantine zone, the keel could not be accounted for. The station was immediately notified of its absence and, ultimately, it was found a mile away. No one spotted its transport or can account for this lapse in security. Since it was found on its original flatbed truck near the airport parking lot, we cannot rule out the possibility something was inside the keel, and accomplices were parked nearby awaiting its *arrival*." Her bandaged hand was starting to throb; she hoped her face didn't reflect it.

"I think another question we want to pursue is not *what* was in the keel, but the possibility of *who*." This word perked up their ears better than the coffee.

"C'mon, Hobson, there's no proof that anyone was smuggled in there," Fielding countered again.

"I climbed in there myself last night and it seemed custom-made for one person to hide inside for a brief, if cold and damp, trip. A strong, healthy person who was highly motivated, who was very high profile on our most-wanted lists might risk this method of transit. It's scanner- and question-proof. The absence of the mislaid keel for almost an hour would make exiting the keel possible. That's not all."

The Chief jumped in. "Listen up, gang. She's onto something here."

Gratefully, Hobson went on. "The serial numbers on the keel didn't match the records of the original yacht built back in Clearwater, Florida ten years ago. It was titled and documented in Grand Cayman by an owner, Herr Champignon of Zurich, Switzerland. The original papers filed in Brussels for a vessel with *her* hull identification number says it was named *Mushroom*. Swiss authorities have no ID for this phantom owner, according to them or Interpol or our databases. Now for the suspicious parts."

"You mean there's more than a crewless ghost ship with a phantom captain and owner of unknown nationality, identity, and whereabouts, found hooked by its rigging to the anchor of a giant oiler mid-ocean during a storm?" Fielding was in fine form, trying to compensate for his lost-keel screw-up. Hobson's hand throbbed with perspiration that penetrated her makeshift bandage. It kept her alert.

The sarcasm was not lost on Hobson, but she let it roll off. "Actually, I think we can infer a lot about the mind or minds behind all of this. The theme is *mushrooms*, and they made no secret of it: the alias *Champignon* is French for mushroom; the recurrent mentioning of *pilzen*, German for mushroom; and *portobello* being a species of mushroom."

"Our subject does not fear us. He, she, or they wave clues in front of our eyes recklessly. Perhaps our profilers can determine if they feel he, she, or they want to either *be caught* or to *rub our noses in it*. I think this is encouraging, and my hope is that they didn't expect us to catch the clues so quickly into their operation."

They mulled over what she had just said. They were writing the essential details in their memo pads and PDA's.

"The key now is to determine not *what*, but *who* we are looking for."

Fielding had his doubts. He finally put his finger on what was bothering him. "Kelly," his tone softened. "How did our *invader* breathe?"

"Right. Of course. I found a seventh hole drilled from the vessel's cabin bilge, directly through the hull, and further into the concealed crypt within the keel. It had to be for a ventilation tube of some kind." She was sweating from the heat of the room, the stress of the debriefing, and the exhaustion of not having slept.

Fielding asked, "Why didn't the sniffers pick up anything like human scent through that hole?"

"Good question. I found a sticky substance plugging it up, which would account for that. I've sent a sample of the substance to the lab for analysis."

The Chief rang in with, "This type of transport of a person across our border had to be risky, so there's certainly some desperation involved. It must have been nauseating, freezing, and could have killed them in the collision."

Hobson agreed. "It's possible our subject was even on board *Hirotu* and climbed down when the vessel was snagged. What we can't figure is how the sailboat was actually snagged on the anchor."

They all looked dumbfounded by this whole case. Some suggested it be shelved until there was more evidence for what they were actually looking for and if a crime definitely *had* taken place. Washington and Homeland had their antennae up on this one, though, and Houston didn't know why. Sweeney wondered if they had more information about why this was so suspicious, beyond the obvious publicity in the media.

The Chief put any thoughts to the contrary to rest. "This is priority-one, all of you. I want leads developed and followed through, and a progress update, let's say," he checked his watch, "at 0700, in forty-eight hours." Hobson was satisfied she made her logical case that a crime was committed and an operation underway. The consequences of one man, a criminal at that, loose within our borders, frightened her. If she was reading his calling cards correctly, he was highly intelligent, knowledgeable of U.S. security methods, and brazenly confident.

She almost forgot to look at her PDA text message that she'd received during her briefing. It beeped a reminder to respond and act immediately. She acknowledged the message with her sore hand, *received*. Why would someone under a security watch from NSA repeatedly use the word *crisis* sixteen times in forty-eight hours? It would appear Dr. A. Becker was in a good deal of trouble with someone listening on the other end somewhere in Europe?

She was asking the wrong question again. She thought a moment, then it surfaced: Why did this piece of intel wind up on *her* PDA from NSA while she was working on a maritime collision, border security case? *This* was the question. Someone, somewhere knew more about her case than she did.

****

Two days later, after getting some medical care for her palm, Hobson read the Houston Chronicle's national news section. Over orange juice at her desk, a story with a photo caught her interest. A light aircraft had a forced landing and caught fire out on the ninth fairway of the golf course at Mahogany Run on St. Thomas. Although the pilot had not been able to be reached for an interview since he was at the hospital as of the writing, his attorney, Alexa Grey, commented at her office in Miami that she knew nothing yet of the accident, but that Dr. Alan Becker, the pilot in command, was experienced. She had only just heard of the accident prior to being contacted by the reporter, but had spoken by phone with him in the ambulance and he was conscious. He had reported that he'd suffered only minor injuries and that his two dogs that were flying with him were okay. The attorney also reported that NTSB and FAA had already initiated their inquiries, and that Dr. Becker would, of course, cooperate fully. The article further mentioned that Alan Becker was CEO of a pharmaceutical firm that marketed unique medications derived from plant sources. Hobson couldn't remember, but she thought that *mushrooms* were plants, of a sort.

Hobson re-read the article. The name A. Becker was already on her PDA from a text message.

She resolved to run *search protocols* on A. Becker and his attorney, Ms. Grey, and get to know them better. Furthermore, she'd track down, with Sweeney's authorization, the source of her mysterious text message.

It was a long shot at best, but the coincidences were too great to ignore. It took both she and Sweeney a few phone calls, but she was right. Someone at NSA in the Helix department had already named A. Becker as being connected to her only active case. The maritime accident predated Dr. Becker's airplane accident. The plane wreck sounded more like sabotage. Dr. Becker had more of a *crisis* or two on his hands and Hobson would find out exactly what they were.

CHAPTER 14

Bedtime Story

In the Land of Oz, there dwelt a Wizard known to all. He resided in a walled kingdom and served those within and without its walls. The Wizard's skills were sought by many, for those he served were ever at peril.

Inside and outside the kingdom's wall, a multitude of ogres roamed. They knew of the Wizard and his magic. The Wizard had succeeded in conducting miraculous transformations like never before. The Wizard, himself at peril within the walls of the kingdom, was forbidden to ply his craft and would be put to death should his powers be known to the ogres.

The years passed and the Wizard was aging. He feared his skills would soon leave him and the secrets of his magic that had eased the suffering of so many would vanish with him. He also feared that, in his absence, his family would be in danger from the ogres. Hence, the Wizard had vision to see to it that the secrets of his potions and incantations, and the art of his transformation magic, were passed on in secret to his scion, his only son. It took many years and much patience for the skills to be passed on to the son.

Too soon, the elder Wizard weakened from poor health. He could not perform his magic much longer. His wondrous transformations had suddenly become very much in demand, for the reign of the ogres over the kingdom was soon to end. It was the ogres themselves who sought his magical transformations. They no longer wished to be recognized as ogres once the kingdom's reign ended.

Thus it came to be that, towards the end of Oz, many sought the Wizard's transformation magic in desperation. They would pay him with a guarantee for the safety and transport of his family from Oz.

Secretly, the Wizard kept records of all he had done to the ogres. They wanted no record of their transformations. To assure this, they planned to eliminate the Wizard and his family once their transformations were completed. But the Wizard was wise and planned well.

He knew that, if the ogres could not destroy them, the records could serve to keep him and his family alive. Furthermore, the world outside the kingdom could identify the ogres who'd wronged so many of the kingdom's inhabitants. In the hope that one day the ogres would be punished, he'd hide the records in a deep, dark place. Knowing torture and threat could pry the secret of the records free from him, the Wizard himself knew not where they lie.

The plan needed a method to have the records discovered by someone who could be trusted to reveal them when it was safe to do so.

Finally, the last days of Oz were imminent and the ogres were busy destroying the last traces of their former identities and deeds. They traded all appearances of what they had done for alibis and lies that they would tell after Oz fell.

Thus did the Wizard, his wife, and his son manage to survive. When they passed from Oz into the forest, they wandered through many kingdoms until they found a new land across the sea. Much had changed in the years following the world of Oz, much many wanted to forget. The Wizard's craft was put to good use. The potions were sought by innocents afflicted with curses no others could heal.

The evil done by the ogres of Oz could not be forgotten. They turned the Wizard's dreams into nightmares for many years beyond those days. The son grew up on the Wizard's skills, but also on his bedtime stories of Oz.

The son always remembered the motto at the entrance to the mythical Land of Oz: ARBEIT MACHT FREI.

Oz was a fairytale of dreams, but those who survived its horrors, called its nightmare Dachau. Its ogres were easy to recognize for they always wore a symbol of their evil: the swastika. The Wizard was born Georg, and he would have a son named Alan. For Alan, the nightmare never ended, torturing his soul, some said his mind. The Wizard would recite the story of Oz over and over for *it should never be forgotten. Ogres would deny their deeds, but this family had proof. The Wizard's family lived because of what they knew and would live to retell it again.*

Being too young to fully understand the purpose of the story, Alan learned the tale as a children's story. A popular book, *The Wizard of Oz*, was a format suitable for such a young child to swallow such a repugnant piece of history.

Dr. Georg Becker gambled that Alan would feel the passion his mother and father did about rectifying acts they alone could. Only they had the information to right so many wrongs. Never before had such an opportunity existed. This would be their family's justification for survival, and for the spiritual survival of so many millions who didn't leave Oz.

It was only later in life that Alan made the connections necessary to understand the drama his family had endured, what had been done to survive, and the moral rectitude of their deeds.

His family's good name, their reason for surviving, was the legacy his father had instilled in him. It was both his passion and his obsession.

****

Dregs closed Dr. Becker's diary that he found in the cabinet next to the master berth. He was more than a little confused by the fable. He'd seen the movie *The Wizard of Oz* on TV at holiday time, but he wasn't familiar with *Dachau* or *swastika*. He was too young to remember. He didn't have a clue as to what the records were about. The girls were on the bed watching Dregs read this with curious looks on their faces. The final page of the diary was dated November 4, 1972. There was identification at the very bottom beneath the date:

Austin State Hospital, Assignment #7, group session, Dr. Delaney.

CHAPTER 15

Dorothy

Alexa sat at the same table where we shared our first lunch in Coconut Grove. Her dress was businesslike: dark blue, three-piece, with a tailored blouse, pump heels, a silk scarf, and a pearl necklace. I didn't like the tone of the outfit.

"I got here a little early and was sitting at another table," I said.

There was no handshake or kiss on the cheek.

"Okay, no secrets. Shoot away." I'd said this as an opener to help thaw the iceberg sitting before me. The waiter brought my fruit punch over from the bar and she ordered lemonade.

"The two agents you met, Sanger and Yorel..." I said.

"You know their names?" she said, amazed.

"Why yes. So do you. You've written to their institute in Haifa where they are employed."

"I have," looking more amazed than from the first revelation.

"The Chaim Weizmann Institute for medical research. They're actually clients of mine that you have drawn contracts for to secure Triton Pharmaceuticals' Manchineel extract formulation for Ciguatera toxicity."

Alexa took her lemonade and threw about half of it back in her throat, probably wishing it *had* been stronger. "They are our Israeli clients?" Then why didn't she recognize their names?

"They're not in direct contact with you because they work in a different department than you're used to dealing with," he explained, anticipating her next question. "They're security to make sure they get our product *undisturbed*."

She admitted, "I assumed they were with Mosad, not really concerned about their country's fish safety issues, like they told me. Apparently, they *were* telling the truth."

I nodded. "However, recently their concerns have less to do with the Israeli Medical Institute's concerns with fish safety. Their medical concerns go back to the perpetrators of medical experiments in the concentration camps during the Nazi Era of World War Two. That is the extent of their *medical* angle with you, me, and missing medical records."

"So I was right. They are tracking war criminals who might happen to be doctors." I nodded.

"What you need to know is there were experiments. In retrospect, they weren't experiments so much as cruel methods of torture using medical science as an excuse to ultimately dehumanize and then murder their patient-victims. A camp called Dachau, outside Munich, had such a clinic. The clinic had two sections; one was *within* the walls of the camp and the other was something special *outside* the camp's walls."

Alexa didn't ask questions since I was freely speaking.

"The clinic within the camp was farcical; there weren't any instruments, medicines, nothing to aid those suffering. But, of course, that was precisely the idea. The prisoners were there to die, be it by working and starving them to death or by gassing in the *shower* chambers.

"There were no Nazi doctors at the camp since they were ordered to treat wounded German soldiers in hospitals. There was no medical care for the internees, mostly Jews, but also homosexuals, dissidents, gypsies, and some mentally ill and handicapped. They were labeled on their drab uniforms by a system of colored stars of David, stripes, or symbols for their *crimes of birth*. All were deprived of medical care."

"You're talking about the Holocaust. What does this have to do with you?" she asked.

"I'm getting to that. Late in the War, one doctor who arrived at the camp was taken from the ranks of the prisoners. He was ordered to treat the military staff and their families, and even the Commandant. An inn outside the walls was converted and equipped to perform surgery for German personnel. His training prior to the War was superior so the Nazi staff were pleased, thus he was able to keep his family alive."

"I assume the doctor was Georg Becker, your father." I nodded. Alexa continued, "But, I don't understand what that has to do with what's going on now."

"He bartered his talents after helping some particular officers. You might think it was immoral to treat those who had so oppressed one's peers, but survival was the only thing that was on any prisoner's mind. If Father could ease the plight of his fellow prisoners through some minor care or advice, or even some secreted food that he could secure, he was their only hope of some civility, some kindness in this wasteland of burning flesh.

"Father had no medicines for prisoners, so he learned to apply some of the old world lore associated with Russian farmers' folk medicine. Herbs didn't grow in Dachau, *but fungus did*. This was the source of his medical improvisation, his genius. He could treat the main diseases that threatened the prisoners and Germans alike, typhoid fever and typhus. All his medicines were derived from fungi and other forms of primitive plant life that he could find in Dachau.

"Certain plants grow quite well under severe extremes, even if they lack nutrients, irrigation, freedom from pests, and temperature extremes."

"You mean fungi and molds, don't you?" Alexa now understood.

"Also yeasts and algae. They're all primitive species of plant life; been around for millions of years and survived ice ages and volcanoes. They predated dinosaurs as well as man and the advent of water or sun. Dachau was a breeding ground for these primitive plant life forms."

"They're still around today, so who am I to argue?" Alexa relaxed more.

"Don't forget all the good things they make for us." I added. "Yogurt, cheese, wine, beer. But one product caught Father's attention. He'd heard of an English scientist who'd discovered the wondrous ability of a little green bread mold to inhibit the growth of staphylococcus and streptococcus bacteria. The Englishman called it *penicillin*, and his name was Dr. Alexander Fleming.

"While the penicillin production towards the end of the war was nowhere near what the soldiers needed, rumors of this wonder drug hit local news and radio, for it provided hope of saving wounded soldiers' lives from infections associated with bullet and shrapnel wounds and burns."

"I'm going to guess your father became adept at treating some diseases without real medicines, by culturing whatever disgusting fungus, mold, yeast, or algae that contaminated the rotting food scraps he could find in garbage cans or the dark corners of a closet." Alexa was right again.

"Some of the strains were cultured from other protein sources around the camps," I said.

"You're talking about the stacks of corpses, before they were cremated. The smell must have been awful."

"That's exactly what he did. By night, he would take culture samples from those already dead and use the products as various medicines. It was the only protein source available. In a way, they saved the lives of their prison mates *even in death*. This was one of the horrible choices my father had to make; to save the living despite the fact he used the *corpses* of the victims as his medium. He didn't have the luxury of a slice of bread like Fleming. In wartime, hard choices had to be made."

"Thus, your father was construed as a *war criminal* himself for complicity with the Nazis. He and his family were alive and the envy of those less fortunate."

I nodded. There was a tear in my eye. I didn't care if Alexa saw how painful this was.

"I'm going to take a wild guess that some of your lab's work was the result of your father's pioneering use of molds, fungi, and especially, algae. Ciguatera is the toxin of gastrointestinal algae which laid the foundation for you putting two and two together using Manchineel sap to counter its toxicity." I nodded again.

"According to Sanger and Yorel, your father died over twenty years ago. They didn't say how. They also said you were under the care of a mental facility in Texas for schizophrenia. They said you had shock therapy and need to stay on medication. Alan, are you really delusional?" Alexa sounded more concerned than angry.

Where would I begin? "Imagine how important it was to my father to keep his medical files secret. His mold and algae studies paved the way for many medications to come to fruition decades later. Moreover, *it was proof of his innocence from war crimes*. There were also some accusations by his former patients who were not successfully treated by my father, who lost many family members to the Holocaust. You can imagine why these survivors were bitter, but much of the bitterness was misdirected at Father's work, even though he tried to cure some of their diseases.

"In order to keep the medical records available, they had to be hidden very deeply indeed, for they would be sought by many parties for many reasons." I let this sink in before coming to the current menace awaiting me. Alexa followed the saga.

"There's more I need to tell, but first, you need to understand this is not ancient history. This story is current, and the key players *very much alive*, obsessively pursuing their goals. Towards War's end, officers at the camp could see their situation, and that of the Reich. They knew they'd be castigated and hunted down for their crimes against humanity. The Allies would see to it that they'd face a firing squad or hanging to humiliate the Nazi command structure.

"To survive, the officers needed new identities. Papers and passports were of little concern; they had access to the presses and even help from foreign sympathetic sources, like a certain cardinal in the Vatican. Vatican documents wouldn't be questioned and the Nazis could pay for them with gold pilfered from the Jews. No, what they needed was something far more dramatic to camouflage their past. They needed new faces! Plastic surgery had not yet been completely successful and under war conditions was of little interest. This changed towards the War's end for two reasons: Soldiers were disfigured by burns and battle-related deformities. My father was a gifted surgeon. Many Jewish prisoners had been beaten or tortured, causing facial and other body deformities. When Father needed to reset a facial bone, nose, ear, or jaw, he had an artist's hands. He could reform or redesign, so to speak, many a patient's end results to be more cosmetically acceptable."

Alexa thought it ironic that frivolous vanity surgery could be a stepchild of the death camps of central Europe, but she could understand the rich learning resource laboratory it must have been for a doctor as talented as Georg Becker. "He must have been quite a man to have developed revolutionary medicines from molds and such, and cosmetic techniques for surgery on patients who'd likely be gassed, never to even see themselves in a mirror."

I said, "He provided a little hope for a future, even if there wasn't one." The Nazi officers within and those unrelated to the camp SS squads, sought Father to alter their appearance so, in fact, they could evade the Nuremburg War Crime Tribunals. They could affix a new photo to their new passports and, after proper demotion in rank to a corporal in the supply corps, they could return to the remains of their homes and rebuild upon the remnants of what had been Germany.

"Father complied with their wishes only to keep Mother and me alive, not to facilitate the escape of these criminals. I am certain my father wasn't anything less than pragmatic. I'm also certain any court that performed a perfunctory investigation would exonerate him. His hundreds of patients kept alive to tell the tale of Dachau owe every breath of freedom they have to Father. Those tortured and maimed can look in a mirror today as a result of his handiwork. That officers of the Reich escaped detection with the benefit of his work, meant survival for our family. Those same skills repaired tortured prisoners and cured many with disease.

"Our family had lived through so much that to refuse the Nazis demand for new faces, while no guarantee of living another day past the fall of the Reich, did allow us to live *that* day and to hope for the day to follow. My father's sole aim thereafter, was to preserve the medical records of what he'd performed and on whom. This was his legacy, his hope for justice not just for his name and family, but also for the souls of those who were executed in the camps. For *their* memory, he insisted on keeping the records and their meaning alive."

Alexa's heart raced with the fear of where the story was going. She nodded for me to continue, and held my hand in support. I was in tears from exorcizing all these long-hidden ghosts. I felt purged – for the moment.

"Mother agreed she would be custodian of the records. In our family, she was the administrator, the planner, the one who thought out details far better than Father. He was the mechanic and theoretician, she the pragmatist. He didn't want to know the details about hiding the records. He insisted the plan be durable for the years to come, portable should they relocate, and contorted to foil the enemies he was certain would pick up the trail. Finally, it had to be foolproof, so only I would be able to decipher the plan when it was necessary to reveal their identities and deeds."

Alexa jumped in. "But the written records your father kept would not necessarily show the transformations he had performed, would they? I mean, a written document with references to former names and possible current ones would have limited value, wouldn't it?"

"Do you know what a Leica is?" She shook her head. "It's a very fine camera. My father had the foresight to trade for one with an officer, for a facial alteration. It was of little use to the officer, but of immeasurable value to my father's documentation of changes he'd made to their identities. These are the photos that several parties seek."

"Sanger and Yorel, for example."

"Yes, but their interest has less to do with finding very old Nazis for the purposes of justice, than for more current concerns. Their fear has more to do with Father's fungal research. There might be groups seeking Israel's destruction that would apply some of Father's work to developing strains of fungi-based toxins to attack Israel with. Yes, the two do indeed work at the medical research arm of the Weizmann Institute, but they are also involved with the Israeli Defense Forces for military operations involving biological warfare."

"You mean the records are photos taken before and after your father's Nazi criminals had cosmetic surgery? Why did they allow it?"

"They didn't know. He only photographed them while they were under anesthesia. *After* photos do not exist, but my mother had some artistic ability, so she could draw how they'd look based on the work Dad performed. She would trace the original photos, years later in safety, and render what they probably *would* look like today.

"Father's zeal to keep the past alive, his daily tales of the events at the camps, the need to get justice for those who never survived, the details of tortures, defacements, brutalization, firing squads, and the hangings of women and children tormented my youthful soul. I ultimately went mad with anger, guilt, insomnia, drugs, shock therapy, and even attempted suicide to free my soul. I understood Father's activities had saved us, but his guilt must have blinded his paternal instincts to preserve my sanity. I don't blame him." I needed a pill.

Alexa was becoming uncomfortable, because the man seated at the table to her right, although reading a newspaper and sipping tea, was eavesdropping on every word I was saying to her. Perhaps it was just an interesting story, perhaps it was just a boring day for news in the paper, but her paranoia when I mentioned *certain parties* on my trail and *now in communication* with me, had her worried.

"I was treated on and off again with electroshock. It would only help a month at a time. The voices of dead souls floating above Dachau's *showers* haunted my dreams every night. I was exhausted. I couldn't talk to anyone about this, except Father. Mother was buried on Virgin Gorda. She left me a cryptic key to the hidden site of the medical records."

Alexa stopped me. The man seated beside us took a sip of his tea and started doing the crossword puzzle. If she could see his eyes, she'd know how innocent he was. "I'll assume that explains the *Gasthaus*, or guesthouse, on the file cabinet." She was piecing the whole story together.

"Dachau Gasthaus was booked for the final months of the war with as many dignitaries and semi-dignitaries as the schedule would allow. Father's facelifts and chin implants using newer plastics the Nazis had developed for war purposes, and nose jobs and even some eye and ear alternations, were not yet in the textbooks, but he had willing Nazi guinea pigs to experiment on, who were motivated by fear for their own lives without it."

"Hence, your father became a pioneering plastic surgeon. I assume he practiced for many years with your mother at his side." I nodded. "What was the key to the trail your mother gave you to find the records?"

"Twenty-five years ago, when we vacationed in St. Thomas, Mother brought me to a specific site on the docks. Then she turned me to face two markers set upon the hill. Today, I know these two markers, one halfway up the hill, and the other almost all the way to the top. The top one is an orange triangle and the other is a square. Both are four or five meters in diameter. They are navigational markers known as *range markers* used to guide sea captains coming into Charlotte Amalie's harbor, right down the middle of the channel. If the captain sees the triangle on top of the square, his vessel is properly aligned in the channel.

"Mother stood me directly below them and then turned me to face beyond the harbor's entrance, out to sea. She said, "One day, forces will compel you to return to this spot and find what you were destined to discover." All I knew was that she loved me very deeply, and was very worried about my mental health after years of Father's daily war tales. I was thirty-three years old. She was aging and, with Alzheimer's setting in, she knew her lucid years were numbered. She also knew that her mission would be in jeopardy if she couldn't pass on the *key*. Father had become an emotional recluse, waiting for the future to turn its attention to him.

"I begged Mother to tell me *why* and *where* I was to discover *what*. She put her hand on my heart, looked in my eyes, and said,

> *When the past finds you, then you*
> *will crack its cloak. Beneath its*
> *mantle, you will find the depths of*

*its true secrets and your soul. I
know you are not only your father's
son – but your mother's, as well."*

I wrote down her exact words; she repeated them often, without
alteration or modification, in the same level voice, with the certainty
I admired in her."

"So that was literally what she said?" Alexa asked. "I don't
know much about ciphers or code keys. Are you translating her
words to me from German?" I nodded.

"When Mother spoke in earnest, she always addressed me in
German."

"Word for word. Write it down for me in German, and write it
in English."

I did, having learned it by heart, and I handed it to Alexa.

"It is the key?" she asked. I nodded.

"Whew, that's quite a story. I do believe it, and you, Alan. You
probably need to do some treasure hunting. Your father was truly a
remarkable man. The world should have known him and his work.
His contributions must have been enormous to the world of
medicine, plastic surgery and...."

"Mycology, the study of fungi, molds, spores and algae."

"Mycology. Indeed, he was a genius."

"A Wizard," I said.

"I guess you could characterize him that way, but genius would
certainly suffice," she said.

"He became known at Dachau, in fact throughout the Reich,
among those who mattered most, as the *Wizard of Dachau*."

"But you never mentioned how he died after your mother was
gone. It must have been about five years later, based on Sanger and
Yorel's Israeli Military Intelligence."

"No, my father's death was a necessary convenience, the result
of being pursued by so many rabid factions. His death was an
apparent suicide." Alexa's paled; she was shocked at my callous

remarks about my father's death. With that, I smiled a little, stood up, moved to the table beside us, and took the newspaper from the man who sat patiently through the entire tale. The stranger suddenly stood.

"Alexa, I'd like to present my father, Dr. Georg Becker. The Wizard of Dachau."

****

Alexa's face paled and tears welled up in her eyes. She needed to be prepared for this meeting and I'd done the best I could. My father, the old world gentlemen he was, took Alexa's hand from the table, bowed, and kissed it gently, then smiled with his gaunt, graying countenance. She, for once, had no words, and flushed pink, an improvement over her pallor. I didn't know she could blush, but her intensity showed on her face. She cried and smiled, and then looked at him, then at me. She stood and embraced him. Father was caught off guard by all this fuss, but he didn't mind it.

"Never knew an attorney who could cry," he said, trying to lighten the mood.

She gazed at me. I noticed that the ice was gone. She felt our suffering. She understood our isolation. And, I think she treasured our confidence and trust in her.

"I, well, I don't know what to say. Now *that's* really rare for me." She took a tissue out of her purse and wiped her eyes. My connection with Alexa had changed from deceit to honesty, tentativeness to trust, hollowness to wholeness.

"I'm afraid you know all about me and I know very little of you. We must rectify this." His faltering English was a sure sign he was either tiring or was filled with emotions too great for him to handle; in all likelihood, it was probably a little of both.

Alexa smiled at him. She turned to me and held my hand firmly. "There's much to do and we must plan our course of action. As your mother predicted, the past is coming to call and it is time to follow her trail."

Leave it to an organizer to see to the details. Alexa's thinking was so much like Mother's. "We have a key which neither of you understand. I want to go to the spot where you and your mother stood when she gave you the key. I need to feel her presence. I want to see the clinic on the hill where you work, and, of course, I want to meet Amy." Then she moved closer to me. "Most of all, I want to be with you as often as possible."

Who could refuse such a wonderful woman?

CHAPTER 16

Wannsee

"Doctor Becker?" The voice was deep, the tone firm, almost ghoulish. The accent was German.

"Keep talking," I said.

"We have much to discuss. Are you available today?"

"Keep talking," I said again.

"There is so much benefit one can derive from history, don't you agree? I refer, of course, to recent history. It influences our current lives so much. I have been aware of your firm's numerous patents and licenses in the field of Ciguatera toxicity. My firm's interests are also in the area of Gambierdiscus toxicus." It was clear he knew the exact genus and species of the algae causing Ciguatera.

He continued, and I listened. We might, however, be able to benefit mutually, financially, from *interfacing*, as you Americans like to call meetings. You are American, are you not? No matter, my background is more European, Prussian in fact. I'm sure if I were speaking my native tongue, you would have guessed that by now, Berlin being familiar to you."

I switched to German. "A place called Wannsee is the only area of Berlin I'm familiar with." I was probing, and the voice at the other end could see where I was going. I continued in German, which Alexa had never heard me speak. Her face revealed how different I must have sounded in this guttural tongue.

The stranger's voice reverberated, "I would have guessed your accent would be more Bavarian than Prussian, but it has been many years since Munich. I believe your Russian and Yiddish would be equally good." I continued in German, "My firm has no interest in mycology, only viral and bacterial disorders. A meeting would, therefore, be of little interest."

"*Aber, Herr Doktor*," his tone somewhat elevated and the pace of the intonation of every syllable he could squeeze from his German made his tone as emphatic as a military order. The conversation convinced me I wished no meeting with this former officer.

"You must consider, Herr Doktor, that I have gone to a good deal of trouble to locate you and to determine your identity and profession. It would be more useful information to other parties, due to a recent sea disaster you've certainly read about, would it not?"

Now my expression must have puzzled Alexa, for she made a funny face that must have mirrored my own. There was no humor in my mind about this, but what did that sea wreck have to do with me?

The stranger let this information set in before he proceeded. "In fact, certain inquiries from people in Virginia have come across my own desk that would startle you as they surprised me. Since they have reached me in Berlin on Kurfurstendamm Strasse, how long will it take them to locate Doktor Becker on their, how do you say '*auf* English,' *Ach, ja*, on their radar screens?"

The genus and species of Ciguatera's algae Gambierdiscus toxicus was public knowledge, but his use of the ambiguous "Doctor Becker" concerned me. Did he mean it as a threat against Father perhaps? Now his voice softened. "Lieber Kollege Becker, I have even understood that Mosad has you under scrutiny, perhaps even now as we speak. Better you speak to me sooner than later, *nicht wahr?*" His addressing me as a colleague suggested his medical degree. I knew Sanger and Yorel could be listening to our conversation.

I stared at Alexa the whole time, and she could see my concern. I agreed to meet my unnamed host at noon at Blackbeard's Castle lounge on top of the hill. At least it was a public place, and daylight.

Alexa and I were having coffee in *Vanity Fare's* cockpit when the phone rang. She had just arrived on the early flight from Miami.

"Do you want me to leave?" she inquired, referring to the meeting I had just agreed to.

"A man who I don't think I know just spoke words I hadn't heard in a long time, from a nightmare I lived a millennium ago." Alexa said nothing. "He said he had a firm interested in my work and that his field was mycology. He spoke Prussian German like a native, was probably a military officer at one time, and knew of the significance of Wannsee. He might know that my father is alive." I let Alexa participate in decisions. "Oh, did I mention that the CIA, FBI or other authorities might have contacted him? I'm both worried and a little intrigued about meeting this person."

"What is Wannsee? That's the only part I didn't understand."

"It was, is a very old, very grand castle, a mansion, on a lake just outside Berlin."

"Sounds like nice real estate."

"It's where a dozen of Hitler's finest military and political planners calculated how to exterminate every last Jew in the eleven countries the Nazis had conquered during the War, efficiently and inexpensively as possible, without wasting a single bullet."

Alexa said, "The *final solution*." I nodded.

"The concept of the death camp was invented at Wannsee. The Germans, in their obsessive need for efficiency and supremacy to do things better than anyone had ever done, made an assembly line of murder that the world had not seen before or since. They could transport entire villages by rail. The Nazis could remove eyeglasses and gold teeth, confiscate belongings, conduct them to the fifteen-minute *showers*, which were gas chambers, and thereby dispose of 1200 frightened transferees within one hour of their arrival. The limited space for incinerating their remains in ovens created the backlog in the process necessitating the multitudes of stacked corpses rotting in camp. This went on day and night for many years."

I feared spooking her and maybe even making her gun-shy. Judging by her expression, I had nothing of this to fear. She seemed, as always, rock steady. I wanted to make it clear that the people I was dealing with were ruthless, smart, cruel, desperate, violent, and, above all else, efficient.

She smiled. "So, when do we go?" We held hands, and she was serious again.

"Alan." I liked *Beck* better. "Do you think this has anything to do with the plane accident?"

"Maybe, I don't know. There was another accident, and the voice on the other end confirmed my fears."

"What accident?"

"The papers a few days ago mentioned a wreck at sea with a supertanker and a sailboat. It wasn't exactly a crash as much as an *entanglement* they said. The ketch was hanging by the tanker's anchor. No crew or passengers, dead or alive, were found."

"Sounds like a ghost ship from a Stephen King novel. What concerned you about it?"

"The sailboat had been christened Wet Dream," Alexa smiled a little.

"When I was very young, prepubescent even, my father had already taught me about our family's history. His tales were frightening, but he had resolved to keep their secrets alive in me. I memorized every horrible day he was at the camps. Who'd have known this would land me in the depths of depression, escape via schizophrenia, and return to sanity in electroconvulsive shock therapy and on medications for life?"

"What did Wet Dream mean to you?"

"There was never a night from the age of eight that I didn't awaken from a troubled sleep, swimming in a pool of my own sweat. My parents were tormented by the idea that I was suffering with the Oz fairytales, but Father felt the truth would keep the Becker name free of aspersions. Mother's documents backed it up. Privately we called them my wet dreams and simply changed my linens every day. I never knew a sleep of peace and rest after the age of eight having heard of the gas chambers."

"So your nickname became Wet Dream or Wet Dreamer among your friends when you overnighted with them."

"For a woman without children, you are sure insightful."

"I like the name Beck better." she said.

"My mother loved double entendres, but she was sensitive enough to me not to ever use that epithet, Wet Dream." I saw Alexa cataloging my mother's love of puns.

"So, you suspect someone may have known you by that name and is, therefore, intimately aware of your sensitivity about it and possibly taunting you to *come out and play* so to speak. Sounds like the schoolyard bully to me."

"Unfortunately, the sailboat that was snared on this supertanker, was suggestive of a connection to me in more than just a name. It was a ketch of identical manufacture as *Vanity Fare*." Alexa was processing this information, deciding if there was more here to be concerned about.

"This would alert NTSB and we're already in the hot seat with them since you used your plane instead of a golf cart at Mahogany Run. That could certainly do it. However, your name specifically is not known to be involved in this maritime affair. I wonder if our other smart party is communicating that it wouldn't take much for him to drop your name, cross-reference the air crash here on their databases, and Dr. Alan Becker becomes a person of interest. Voila!"

I had to agree. This was no coincidence. It was a blatant, well-conceived, expensive, risky, highly coordinated plot that likely involved more than one smart person. Alan couldn't be certain who'd qualify as suspect in this plan or exactly what they wanted. He had some ideas he wasn't ready to share with Alexa.

The girls lay beside us for their first nap of the morning, and I told Alexa the fairytale I'd known since I was eight years old, not knowing if it was truth or fantasy back then. I told her about the land called Oz and a wizard unlike any other, who prepared magical potions of great power and the promise of life to the walking dead. It told of his deeds and misdeeds in Oz, and how his legend lived on long beyond the time of most mortals. Alexa listened to the fable attempting to decipher its metaphors with her legal mind and historical recollections of darker times.

I cautioned her. "So you fully understand the implications of the meeting I just set up. You don't have to go, probably shouldn't. You understand?"

"I understand, but do you?" Now I was puzzled. She'd put so much together. "You've heard about the Land of Oz your whole life. Dachau was a dreamland of horrors from long ago; one too terrible to have been real, but it was. Your father knew you'd have to cope with understanding it, even in children's terms, and to prepare to resolve the threats to the Becker family. The camps were the *motivation* that you'd need to pursue revealing his secrets from his work and medical files. He must have hated himself for burdening your dreams at such a young age, but he also knew his life was at risk, as was yours, simply because others suspected that he, you, and your mother knew the contents of the files.

"Your father was, is a wondrous Wizard. He has delivered many to find their *yellow brick roads* to the shores of freedom and survival. Your father wants you to become the successor to the Wizard's talents, and with your lab's successes predicated upon his fundamental discoveries, your future looks bright."

"Sounds rosy, so far."

"A gauntlet has just been thrown down in the guise of a threat on your life by sabotaging your airplane, by threatening your father, and now a reference to your nickname, Wet Dream. How this sailboat could be connected to *Vanity Fare* and to you, I don't understand, but I'm sure this *master planner* has demonstrated his resolve and skill thus far. You have a worthy opponent, Beck. Now let's eat lunch. I want to see where your mother positioned you on the docks with the cipher code on the way."

"Why is he doing this? What does he want?" I asked her.

"I think he's applying for your job of Wizard: just needs something from you for the promotion. I have a feeling he'd be a malevolent Wizard. I also think you know him. He's too familiar and knows too much to be just a good detective. He's doing this with passion and that concerns me. You will need equal passion to discourage him, for I fear he's afraid of very little. Now, we're off to interview a Wizard from Oz."

"How do I introduce you?" I asked.

"Well, I'm from Kansas, so, just call me *Dorothy*."

The sweats were starting again.

CHAPTER 17

The Minister

He was a general surgeon, who rose to Department Chairman of Surgery at Graz's General Hospital. This position put him in the parlors and smoke-filled anterooms of important leaders on the rise in the Viennese Volkshaus, Austria's Parliament. He married a beautiful German girl, an attorney, whom he had met at the Opera Ball in Berlin. A year later, a shift to the Right in Austria's national elections made him Austria's youngest Minister of Health

The *Minister*, as he was known, with his medical degree and political position in the State Hospital, was himself poised for higher office, when the political winds of the post-War era changed in Austria. In dark corners of smoke-filled rooms, old men told younger ones that the time for apologizing for the Jews and the camps was over. Was Hitler himself not an Austrian from Linz? Were not a disproportionate number of the SS troops who ran the camps Austrian volunteers?

The Minister hated the political correctness sought by the whimpering cowards of the current party of Socialists in the Viennese Parliament. That the head of the Socialist Party, Josef Friede, was a Jew added further insult to their Austrian sensibilities.

The room was dark for a meeting room. A horseshoe-shaped table sat at one end, with three rows of seats for the general membership. Plaques, awards, and photographs of members decorated the walls, and highly polished fencing swords of honor were displayed in walnut and glass cabinets behind the table.

The Minister stood and three-dozen fencing club members rose with him. They sang the club's somber, patriotic anthem that clearly voiced their goal: re-uniting with their true Fatherland, Germany, which had united its eastern and western halves with the world's blessing, why shouldn't Austria be able to take its rightful place as its Eastern Empire? Had not the Austro-Hungarian Empire started the same way, by a happy marriage?

That the German economy was the driving power behind Western Europe's economy was obvious. The Frogs and Limeys couldn't but sit back and envy the German Economic Wunder that had long out-produced them each year. Austria needed to latch on now, since so many Slavs, Serbs, Croats and other *mixed* races were cropping up in Vienna's urban ghettos. Now that Serbia and Bosnia were separated by war, under the watchful eyes of the eunuchs at the U.N., Bosnian Muslims were immigrating into Austria. How dare Austria's leadership shelter these Muslims who accused the Orthodox Christians of Serbia and the Catholics of Croatia of *ethnic cleansing*. Austria could not tolerate the Muslim refugees filtering into their homeland and competing for jobs with real Austrians who had rebuilt these factories from the post-War rubble.

These non-Christians were *demonizing* Austria, making it a Muslim satellite. The Fencing Club, as the Minister defined them, were crusaders, who would reverse this tide, making life for émigrés uncomfortable, to say the least. Couldn't the NATO nations see what they had created in Austria and Germany? Even the French, drowning in their own liberal-socialism, believing they were the only *enlightened* people on the Continent, were infested in every city with Algerians, Tunisians, and Moroccans, their former colonial subjects. The Mosque burnings had already made headlines in Lyons, Marseille, even as far as free-thinking Paris' northwestern suburbs. Paris would soon be ablaze, the Minister thought, but the French didn't realize that in the backroom of the Café Balzac on the Champs Elysées there was an affiliate chapter of the Graz *Fencing* Club. The French club members wore the same flat-topped hats, but recited their own patriotic agenda made from ideologies of the former pro-German Vichy government of World War Two.

The Minister's portrait hung behind the officer's table. He was in his sixties, narrow-waisted, and his head was shaved clean. They, twenty-two men and four women, seated themselves and ceased their private discussions. He remained standing and addressed them from behind the lectern. The *Minister's* charisma permeated the room.

"We have a problem," he stated flatly. "We have lost something important to the club's *master agenda*." They looked at one another. "Certain papers that we thought were buried are at risk of exposure. We do not wish this data to become public, for this would make us public. Our connection with the master agenda is deniable, but it would be preferable to re-bury or destroy these documents. I seek recommendations to retrieve and destroy the information."

There was discussion around the room about the papers. Many had been told about them by their senior members.

An elderly Professor Emeritus from the chemistry department stood. Dr. Grabel was the Old Guard; the Minister was of the brave, new Order.

"I believe I speak as one more closely tied to the data than you younger pioneers of our cause. Speaking as Professor at the University, it could damage our Party, our plans and, most of all, our agenda, if this data surfaces." The elderly chemist with the straight waves of thick, full hair yellowing like his fingertips, from years of nicotine, paused for effect. His broad smile revealed too-white, porcelain-smooth teeth. To thousands, that smile was the last image they'd see before going to the *showers*.

Grabel had slept well all these years since the War's end, undisturbed by his conscience. Indeed, Dr. Christopher Grabel had long since made his peace with his wartime. He was a war hero; he was even awarded Hitler's Golden Palm honor. Mores and laws had wavered with the times and the War's outcome. The fencing club's agenda was to finish the good work their Party started in 1933.

The Minister spoke. "With the Board's approval, we have put certain operations into effect that the task force had in the planning stages for several years. These involved *unfortunate accidents* that would agitate certain desirable activities abroad to further our agenda."

The others listened intently. They understood the Minister's meanings in his indirect discourse. He sipped some water and continued. "The accidents provoked the authorities to help us on both sides of the Atlantic. We could not count on them after all these years, due to post-911 pre-occupations dominating their operations, to pursue certain records we now seek. The current custodians of the records have been slow to uncover their location. My concern is that, after all these years, even *they* are no longer interested in opening the files."

The Minister paused, pretending he was sipping espresso, which he'd already finished. The Minister's real concern was that Alan Becker could not determine where his parents had hidden the records and that they might no longer be salvageable. This would be catastrophic. Decades of preparations by the Club would be vulnerable. The Minister didn't want to discuss this possibility to the group until he could communicate directly with the records' custodian. They had Alan Becker under surveillance for so many years. The Minister could not communicate with Alan directly lest his own name and identity appear on the *watch list* of organizations he couldn't afford to be on at this stage of his career.

The Minister said, "For decades, the medical records were of little concern to us. Then we learned that they contained pictures of interest to the Club. The Board has already discussed the repercussions should these certain pictures reach the authorities: we fear that our political efforts might be severely jeopardized. We must determine whether the records still exist and, if so, can Alan Becker locate them. To accelerate his acting on our behalf, we enacted our task force's use of a seagoing vessel with certain documents, identification numbers and names to be reported in the headlines."

The seated members whispered to one another, then nodded. Dr. Grabel seemed less satisfied, but knew that his one vote carried little influence with the youth. Grabel thought back to the time he wore the swastika with pride, along with a silver Medal of Freedom personally pinned upon him in Berchtesgaden, Hitler's *Eagle's Nest*. A visit there was reserved only for Hitler's pet commanders who excelled at fulfilling his wishes. Fraulein Eva Braun, *der Fuehrer's* girlfriend, stood next to him during the ceremony. Grabel had performed a service for the Party on the *Jewish problem* that made mass eradication of European Jews a reality. Zyklon B was a hydrogen cyanide gas that left many gas chambers filled with over a thousand naked bodies of men, women and children who were told they were to get a shower. Only minutes later, the guards could open the chamber doors to reveal victims heaped in a pile, one on top of the another, a pyramid of corpses reddened by the poison, unsuccessful in their attempt to find oxygen at the roof of the chamber. Grabel had had a little *work* performed by the so-called *Wizard* at a so-called *guesthouse* outside Dachau. Pictures would be disastrous. What idiot would trade a Leica to a Jew? *Do not keep records of camp activities*. That was Himmler's directive at Wannsee, in the planning of the camps.

The Minister knew very well what kind of work the Wizard of Dachau had performed inside the camp and at the inn. It had been frequented by VIPs of the Reich who frequented Dachau to see the accomplishments of Hitler's policies. There were too few ovens to keep up with the efficiencies of the Grabel's showers.

Many of these VIPs spent a night or two at the guesthouse Inn to rest or, towards War's end, to have some *alterations* performed by the Jew. Most signed the guest book kept by the doctor's wife; what harm could come from a visit to this innocent Inn? There was no shame in signing. Soon they'd be somebody else with a new name and appearance.

The doctor and his wife could not be allowed to survive the end of the War. The camp commanders would see to that. These records, along with medical charts the doctor and nurse meticulously kept elsewhere, along with photo documentation of *before* shots of sleeping Nazis, would have been useful to the Nuremburg War Crime Tribunals immediately after the War. But the guest book never did surface, nor did the medical records, or the photos. At the War's end, the foremost objective of the Becker family was to resettle, survive, and forget the nightmare.

Survivors told of their inability to discuss the Holocaust years. Some said it had been too great a trauma; some said it was better to ignore since humanity had turned its back on them. Why trust anyone again? Retribution and punishment were far from their thoughts immediately after being freed from the Nazis. They had years of mourning for their family members who'd not been so fortunate. They had the guilt of surviving. They had to live when those they'd loved could not.

****

The meeting at the back room of the Wartburg Restaurant was over. The three dozen members exited with little discussion. Other patrons eating dinner in the restaurant tried not to stare at the members filing from the meeting room. Many of the older patrons knew of the Club's official fencing purpose; several of the members did have scars from duels. Two members in fencing uniforms stood at attention at either side of the double doors with arms crossed. Tonight, the Minister was the last to leave. He acknowledged the guards, and then lit his cigar.

One elderly couple had lost their appetite at the sight of the exiting members. They put their napkins down, beside their apple strudels, cold and unfinished.

"These verdammten idiots of the New Order. Have they learned nothing?" the old man asked. He was a teen when he served in the final defense of Berlin in the last days of the War. His wife, her fox fur about her neck, was sickened by the sight of them. She'd lost two brothers in the siege of Stalingrad because of that idiot Fuehrer, from Austria of all places.

"What do they call these *clubs* these days?" she asked.

"Der Kreis," he said.

"And they have always met in that back corner, have they not?"

"Jawohl," he said. "And it's always been called *Die Ecke des Kreises.*"

The Circle's Corner

CHAPTER 18

The Wizard's Apprentice

I looked at my watch and realized that Alexa and I would be late for our noon luncheon meeting at Blackbeard's Castle restaurant. Taking one of the waiting taxis from the Yacht Haven Marina Hotel, we sped up the mountain to Blackbeard's.

Alexa wore shorts and a white blouse. She looked like every other tourist in her sunglasses and wide-brimmed straw hat with the pink scarf.

As we walked in, the receptionist directed us to a table overlooking the harbor. The breeze was wonderful. I needed to take one of my pills. Sitting with his back to us, inspecting the cruise ships below, was an elderly silver-haired gentleman.

He raised his head as if he knew we'd arrived, but didn't get up or turn around. I assumed he'd learned to sit with his back to the entrance to rooms to hide his identity. He must have become skilled at seeing people coming up behind him after all these years of looking over his shoulder.

"Herr Doktor. I did not know you were bringing such charming company. Please, please, setzen sie sich." He gestured to Alexa and gently held her hand. "Dr. Felix Sobotta."

"Miss Alexa Grey. My legal associate." His eyes were cool, blue, and more alert than I would have expected from a man his age. He moved like an athlete: energetic, quick. The eyes were cold, calculating, and condemning. They gave him away if you ignored the toothy smile. This man had seen a good deal of death. It occurred to me whom he might be. His age, his manner, and the description Father had given me of him back at the University. He fit the description even more as our meeting proceeded.

"You must truly enjoy your work together," he said, as I was trying to place the face.

I ordered iced tea for myself and Alexa. I noticed another gentleman of similar vintage, dressed in old world clothing so out of place on the island. Like my host, he wore black leather shoes. The suit my host wore was dark grey wool. He must have been perspiring all over the double knit shirt he sported. Thank God he skipped the tie.

I wondered about the relationship between these two gentlemen. The coincidence of them both being at Blackbeard's at noon so inappropriately attired, led me to believe they had just arrived from Europe on the same plane and probably worked together. Both were elderly, but the one at our table was more forceful in his manner while the other pretended not to be snooping on our conversation, seemed more mild-mannered, gentler, almost effeminate. I thought about being smart and asking our host if his associate at the next table, the one nursing a Pina Colada, would care to join us, so he wouldn't have to eavesdrop. Then I figured that these men knew far more about me than I knew about them. The less I let out of the bag, the better the odds of this meeting being productive.

Alexa made conversation. "So, you're from Europe. Do you have business there, or are you retired?"

The host smiled at her American audacity to pry. "I am in business for myself. I produce medical products, not unlike Dr. Becker does, but in a very different manner. I have a factory in a place familiar to the doctor."

"Graz, I'll guess," I said. Alexa liked the fact that I was on top of the talk.

"Jawohl, meine colleague."

"The name of my firm is *Oesterrisches Zeugnisse*, or Austrian Enterprises in English. It's just a small factory and laboratory. You would call me a CEO, I believe."

Now it was becoming clearer. "Yes, I know the firm. We have been doing business together, have we not?" The old man with the steel eyes nodded, seeing I'd made the connection.

I didn't look at Alexa, who just had a refill on her iced tea. But it was for her benefit I didn't go ahead too fast. She was entitled to know what I did. And, I had promised: no secrets, not even half-truths.

"You produce the growth mediums used by Triton and many other labs worldwide. You are far too modest, sir. Your company is likely the largest producer of growth media for medical purposes world wide." The man relaxed his stare at me and smiled, then nodded, as if tipping his head to thank me for the compliment.

I needed to fill Alexa in. "To grow the algae for toxin production to be neutralized by Manchineel sap, we need a very special medium for the Petri dishes we use to isolate the strains of algae. The particular medium I needed is called Sabourad's. It's only used for fungi, which is my field of interest. Austrian Enterprises produces the finest purity Sabourads that can be found."

"Your discovery of a viable antitoxin for Ciguatera poisoning was predicated upon my making Sabourads available in large quantities, just for you." He looked more sternly at me. I wondered if he expected something in return, thinking he was owed a favor for selling me medium. He went on. "Ms. Alexa, may I call you that?" She nodded, but I could tell that she didn't like this man and his duplicity. She smelled slime, and it wasn't from the kitchen.

"Sabourad's medium comes in many varieties. We label them types 1-1V. Letters are subclasses that are essentially the same as the group, but specialized in their nutrient content. Dr. Becker has been ordering types 1-III for years. He is to be commended for continuing his noble research in the name of science. Who knows what wonder drug he'll develop next, and to combat what disease?"

This man was keeping records of my research orders from him. I couldn't explain why, but was certain he'd tell me.

Alexa said, "I assume Dr. Becker's paid all his invoices to you and that you're not here to collect a past-due account." The old man smiled and patted her hand that rested on the table. I could tell Alexa didn't like this man's brazen manner. He acted like he held all the cards. The man at the next table stood up. He asked a waiter for the men's room. I mused that his prostate just couldn't hold out any longer with the two drinks he'd finished.

Our host continued. "Dr. Becker's research has progressed to the point where he has entered new areas beyond the usual frontiers of mycology research. In the last three months, he has ordered a new type of Sabourad's medium, the experimental type IVb." He looked to me for validation. I nodded half-heartedly.

"The only problem with this is, that while this variety of medium is extremely rare, difficult to produce and very expensive, no one is quite sure what its validity is. What struck me even odder was that this medium is now on a *watch list* for Homeland Security. Certainly you knew this, Herr Doktor, did you not? This put me and my laboratory under scrutiny. An extensive audit by Austrian authorities of my own work in perfecting pure media for fungal growth came under suspicion, which you can imagine caused me more than a little consternation and considerable expense." His face reddened. Alexa's pulse was racing, and she needed something stronger to drink. She ordered a scotch for herself.

I said, "I apologize. If my orders have caused you any distress, please send me a bill for your legal expenses and emotional suffering, and I will be delighted to remunerate you." Alexa didn't like my offer to compensate him, but assumed this old man was telling the truth.

He said, "That is most kind, but that is not the subject of today's meeting. I cleared my lab of possible violations. I explained to the inspectors that we were trying to make the more customary IV type, but an amino acid was added in error, hence, our invoices to our customers, or customer, were erroneous, but harmless."

"I am grateful for your assistance and clarification to the authorities on this order. I frankly did not make it myself. It must have been a form incorrectly filled out by an associate. I will look into it immediately and correct it. Please send my apologies to your staff and firm."

The old man knew I was telling the truth. *I had not made the order.* I would never order such risky media, especially since 911. "The authorities were certainly only doing their job. With so many scares these days about *weaponizing* strains of this or that, like anthrax a few years ago and the Ebola virus before that, it was to be expected. It would be a little scary for my lab to be a breeding ground for something in the fungal family that no one would have the antidote or antiserum for." I knew who'd ordered it, and I would have to reprimand him immediately. I wondered if my host also knew who ordered the medium and was simply probing.

The man at the next table returned from wherever and sat back down. Our host rubbed his hands together like he was washing them, but he might have only been stretching his fingers to ease arthritis stiffness.

"I am confident that the authorities were convinced of my candid explanations, as you now confirm, and that there should be no further inquiry on either side of the Atlantic. However, there is a far more important favor I would like from you: I need certain documents of an historical nature." There it was, his ace-in-the-hole. "I believe you know exactly which ones I refer to. While they have little meaning to you or your deceased family members, I have associates who would be most generous in their appreciation to you for their return to their rightful owners."

How he could rationalize that Father's medical records and photos of his work were *his peoples'* property after all these years was a tact I couldn't fathom. Alexa saw the conversation sour and wanted to intervene, but couldn't think of what to say. A moment later, she spoke.

"The documents to which you refer are gone. As recently as last month, Dr. Becker has tried to understand where his deceased parents would hide such material only to learn that they were destroyed."

I'd wished Alexa had not insinuated herself into clarifying to this man, what she knew and didn't know. She was making it clear, as well, that I cared about her enough to trust her with some very sensitive information and family history. I feared this could jeopardize her safety.

"What my attorney has said is accurate. My mother, the custodian of the documents you allude to, destroyed them. If their contents concern you, I submit that they are gone and never to be found." The man at the next table paid his tab and slowly left.

I could see our host was quietly fuming at our lack of cooperation. He said, "Well then, this is most unfortunate." I thought that he meant *unfortunate for us*, but couldn't be certain.

"I believe we, therefore, have concluded our business. I'm sorry, you have wasted a trip all this way only to fish in an empty pond," I said.

Alexa stood as I pulled her chair away. We didn't shake hands, but he tipped an imaginary hat on his head. His forced smile made me think of Alice's Cheshire cat in another Wonderland.

****

The two elderly men met in the hotel's lobby after Alexa and I had left in a taxi.

"He may or may not be telling everything," our host said. "I have already anticipated that by sending a *calling card* from him about the missing files to the FBI. They are already on the island as a result of my clue." The other man nodded. He seemed to have other issues on his mind besides medical and photographic records, but he couldn't discuss these with the host. They told the desk clerk that they would stay another week.

****

In the cab, Alexa said, "Well, that was uncomfortable. It seems you were right about being traced. Certain parties sought both you and your records. You don't have them, do you?"

I didn't like her questioning me, but could understand her doubts after my lack of candor over the last few weeks.

"Did you know this man you were dealing with in Austria for your media?"

"Now it makes sense. I didn't know he was CEO of the Austrian Enterprises Company. My father used to tell me about him. He was a professor at my university in Graz, although I'd never taken a course from him. His name is Christopher Grabel. He's actually quite famous. He received Hitler's personal scientific honor for achievement, received it from the Fuehrer himself. Invented an insecticide based on hydocyanide."

"Zyklon B. Don't tell me that. He's a cold-blooded murderer." She thought it was good they hadn't actually eaten lunch, for she had become nauseated. "How do you break bread with a mass murderer? And do you think he'll drop his pursuit of the records and leave you alone?"

"No, not at all. He is determined not to fail in his mission. But why now, after all these years? There must be something major planned back in his club, der Kreis."

"Oh, the restaurant and fencing club you'd talked to me about last week?" I nodded.

"Who was the other visitor at the table next to us?"

"I can't be sure, but I think he is also famous. If I'm right, and remember that I have to add a half a century to a face from an old documentary I'd seen; I believe he is Werner Lobel."

"Another mass murderer I suppose."

"No. He worked through the War in non-military capacities. He was a chauffeur and valet at one time. I imagine he's never killed anyone. No, his manner gave him away. Very neat and a good servant to the wealthy."

"What could he possibly want with those records if he isn't a war criminal?" she asked as she rolled down the taxi window to get more air.

"I don't think he's here for medical records. His face has not been altered, like our host's, which was clearly Father's work. I think he must be a member of the club in Graz, maybe works for Grabel, but he must be here as an assistant to his boss or, perhaps..."

"What?" she said. "Maybe he worked during the War for a client who'd become a war criminal and he's here at their behest?"

"Yes, but not at *his* behest. He had only one client I know of. A man named Herr Schickelgrueber."

"Maybe he's a war criminal?" she asked.

I nodded. "You know him better by his adopted name, Adolph Hitler."

Now Alexa really was nauseous. Thank goodness the window was open.

****

Sweeney, back at the Houston FBI office, received the lab report Hobson requested. She stated that she'd taken some sticky trace material off the vent hole of *Wet Dream's* keel. He opened the report: Growth medium for culture, fungal uses, name Sabourad's type IVb. Exotic and rare, sole lab supplier, Austrian Enterprises, Graz, Austria, director and owner. Dr. Felix Sobotta. No known criminal history. Austrian national, no war records found, ALERT RED: this medium on terrorist watch list for possible weaponizing of fungi strains related to Ciguatera fish poisoning. NO KNOWN TREATMENT. Sole purchaser following Austrian Polizei lab audit: Triton Pharmaceuticals, Inc., CEO, Dr. Alan Becker, M.D., Ph.D., Miami, FL. Current residence, Yacht Haven Marina, St. Thomas, U.S.V.I.

Sweeney shipped Hobson and Fielding to St. Thomas for surveillance of Dr. Alan Becker. Grabel's calling card for Alan had worked. Hobson didn't know she was doing pro bono work for Dr. Grabel, now known as Dr. Sobotta.

****

"All things considered, our situation looks lousy until we find those records." Alexa grasped the situation.

"What are their motives, besides the obvious ones? Grabel wants to preserve or erase his criminal history, but at his age, it can't be just a matter of pride, can it?" I thought this over. "No, I think something more sinister is motivating him. In the absence of those records, his current identity, whatever it is, has afforded him a certain success. He is a doctor, after all, and a member of *The Circle*. They have an agenda that's more political, even malicious."

"What do you think is the agenda, Alan?"

"It's in the name *The Circle*. It means something, I can't be sure, but imagine how a bunch of aging Nazis feel about being free to be successful businessmen and judges, leaders possibly, since the old records attached to old names no longer exist. If I were aging and had achieved economic success, before I died, I'd turn my interests to reaffirming the principles and lore that had created the *Reich*, or Empire, that I'd devoted my early years to. I'd want to show my grandchildren *what could have been*. No, I think these records mean something much more to *The Circle*."

"A circle represents payback, or a return to where you started, doesn't it?" She was good, and was getting ahead of me again. "

After the Treaty of Versailles that ended World War One, the terms were very humiliating to the Germans. They weren't permitted to rebuild their military and were required to pay harsh reparations in Deutsch Marks to the nations that had defeated the Kaiser. Germany was weakened, as the result, and a severe depression ensued. Political unrest resulted in over 150 political parties that created turmoil making Germany a hopeless, bankrupt nation. Communists threatened from the East, unions ran the factories. The weakened Weimar Republic could not suppress Herr Hitler. I think *The Circle* is about payback, about restoring German glory. Perhaps they want to show the current German generation that what they tried to do back in 1939 would have been best for them all. *The Circle* members are the old guard. There may be one last demonstration of what a world with a united Germany at its helm can and should be." Alexa took this in, and mused. What could it be they were doing?

"You think Grabel and *The Circle* have grandiose plans along those lines." I nodded. Their determination after half a century convinced me I was right.

"I specifically think Herr Grabel is experimenting with the weaponized fungi. I think the type IVb medium was for his personal use. I also think he suspects I was not the one who ordered the IVb medium, because my reaction was too surprised. Furthermore, I'm thinking that he's questioning my father's death. My father might have made a major error ordering this medium through my firm. How could he have suspected that Grabel was on the other end of his order?"

Alexa said, "So, your father is still trying to be the *Wizard*? He still does research?"

"Always has. These last few years, his work has been on lung disease treatments using fungal extracts." My thoughts returned to Grabel's plans.

"I think Dr. Grabel wants to become Dad's replacement, to serve his own purposes through *The Circle*." That was it: Grabel seeks to humiliate and replace the Jew Wizard of Dachau by mastering weaponized fungi. "He's here to get his old medical records to either conceal his criminal past should he become high profile or to use them to extort, from those identified in the records, access to European and American sites where his formula could potentially do the most damage. Many of his old cronies, former Nazi commandants, are well placed ranking politicos, like governors and judges.

"He could cause upheaval in the German government by threatening to release the true identities of their current parliamentary leadership. Ultimately, he could so weaken the current German government that whatever he planned would be easier with a strong threat over key leaders who don't want to reveal their past. NATO itself couldn't be trusted to stop him since Germans are in its leadership as well. He was ambitious, even brilliant. A new Reich could reemerge unnoticed. Imagine *The Circle* running the world's military?" It scared the hell out me and Alexa. Grabel sought the power of toxins and blackmail to re-align the political landscape as a new Reich.

"So you think Grabel aspires to Wizardom? I don't see him in that role," Alexa said.

"My father told and re-told this awful history, in the guise of the *Wizard of Oz* so I could understand it." Alexa acknowledged this and felt sorry for me having to suffer so by my father's tales. The records needed to be resurrected; this they both knew.

"Remember the name of his company?" I asked. "His motives are in the name."

Alexa thought about it. "Yes, it's Austrian Enterprises."

"No, in German it's *Oesterreichisches Zeugnisse*. OZ. He wants to be the Wizard of Oz." Now she knew Grabel and the Elder Dr. Becker read the same children's books. I secretly hoped that our aspiring Wizard didn't think he could use Alexa as his Dorothy to squeeze me for the ruby slippers. Father and Amy were also in danger if Grabel discovered their clinic on the mountain. I needed to warn them.

CHAPTER 19

Hannah

"Dad, it's time for a trip to visit Mom," I said on the cell phone. "Take the car and I'll pick you up at the dock. Bring Amy, too."

"I have one more patient to see, and then we can leave."

Alexa and I had come from meeting Dr. Sobotta, née Grabel, and his friend Lobel more than a little scared for Dad, Amy, and us. It was time to make a plan. The sail over to Virgin Gorda would be a good opportunity. Dregs had become a good hand on the boat and cooked well enough. He agreed to crew for the day trip.

Amy and Dad came aboard. Dad has his spear gun; he loved fishing with it. Even at his age, snorkeling was a favorite hobby.

With me at the helm, Dregs dropped the mooring line and we motored out through the channel past the Frenchman's Reef Hotel. I put *Vanity Fare* into the wind so Dregs could raise the main sail and jib. The sound of wind filling the sails replaced the noise of the diesel auxiliary engine. There was a gentle heel to leeward and we were all, including the girls, comfortable in the cockpit. Dregs and Amy brought out some breakfast rolls, as we made way for the British Virgin Islands.

From the balcony of the Frenchman's Reef Hotel, Special Agent Fielding photographed *Vanity Fare's* departure using a long, telephoto lens. He'd report this to Sweeney and Hobson. He wondered where the sailboat was headed, but the transmitter beacon he and Hobson had placed on the hull while scuba diving to record the vessel's keel ID numbers, would certainly answer that question. He called Sweeney.

"Fielding here, Sir. The vessel's leaving St. Thomas with the clinic's doctor and nurse, and his attorney. They're sailing west, but I'll know more when the GPS gets a fix on them."

"Notify Hobson and have her call me right away. The lab analyzed that trace material she found on the keel at Galveston from *Wet Dream*. It's an experimental culture material for what could be a very dangerous fungus that could be used as a weapon. CDC says they don't have a remedy for it."

Fielding realized this case just became more important than he'd originally thought. "I'll call Hobson immediately." He noted the GPS located *Vanity Fare* passing Red Hook, heading to St. John. Fielding couldn't be sure if they were planning to stay in the U.S. or to head further towards Tortola and the other British Virgin Isles. He wondered if he should alert British authorities that Dr. Becker was a fugitive.

****

We'd made a glorious day sail past St. John and its beautiful green hills and gorgeous beaches, one after another: Cinnamon Bay, Trunk's Bay, and Hawk's Nest. The waters here were what attracted the tourists most to these islands. Three quarters of this island was a U.S. National Park, which assured a pristine appearance, free from hotels except for the harbor area. We decided not to stop at this point, but to continue closer to our destination in the Sir Francis Drake Channel, to Virgin Gorda in the British Virgin Islands.

"Are we going to check in?" Amy said.

"Not today. We're only staying one night, and it'll take too long. Better we move on and visit Mom," I said.

"Not checking in where?" Alexa asked.

"With customs," Amy said.

"Wait a minute, Alan. Are you sure you want to do this?"

"I'm not supposed to be leaving the U.S. waters. If the Brits know I'm a fugitive, they could arrest me. Remember that story you told me about the jail Houdini couldn't get out of?" She nodded. "It's right up there on the hill, to your left on Tortola in Roadtown. There, you can see it now."

"But if they discover we haven't registered at customs, we'll all be illegal aliens, won't we?"

"Let's take a vote. Who wants to check in?" Dad and Amy nodded and Dregs didn't seem to have an opinion either way. The girls just looked at me, wondering why they hadn't been fed.

We sailed on past Peter Island and Dead Man's Island of *Yo ho ho, and a bottle of rum* fame. A pirate had left three insubordinate men to die on this rock where he buried some treasure. They couldn't spend the gold, and they died rich, with only a bottle of rum. We saw the hills of Virgin Gorda, the contours of which looked like a woman on her back with a large belly. Virgin Gorda was "the fat Virgin", or, as some said, "The pregnant Virgin". We anchored at the Bitter End Hotel for the day. Dad and Amy took the snorkel gear out. I gave Alexa hers and some flippers.

"You know how to snorkel?" I asked, realizing that I'd assumed she did. She nodded.

"I learned in the Caymans after doing some banking arrangements for a client last year."

We all climbed into the dinghy. Dregs turned the outboard on. The girls woofed and wagged on *Vanity Fare's* deck, as they always did when they were excited, continuing even as we motored out of sight.

Alexa asked, "Where are we going to snorkel?"

I said, "to Mother's grave."

The Bitter End Hotel was the last point on the end of the Virgin Island chain before a very long sail – several days – to reach the next group of islands, starting with St. Martin in the Lesser Antilles. A Bitter End also refers to the end of an anchor's rope or *line* that attaches it to the boat it's supposed to be tethering. If you needed more line than you had, the end is truly *bitter*, for you'd soon be adrift.

The sandy white beaches around the resort were served by the hotel's bar that ran along its length with beautiful views of the aquamarine ocean. Only one island could be seen now, Necker Island, owned by Sir Richard Branson of Virgin Island Records and Virgin Airlines fame and fortune. It rents for ten thousand dollars a day. But you can bring a dozen or so friends to enjoy the privacy and accommodations and the full staff. There were only a few names on the guest book that weren't immediately recognizable as celebrities who sought privacy.

Our dinghy rounded the point of the Bitter End, and we were in more open water. It was less than fifteen feet deep. I cut the engine and dropped our Danforth anchor in the sand. Alexa noticed the reef nearby. We all put our gear on, and I was the first in. Then Alexa, followed by Amy and Dad, dropped into the warm, clear waters.

Dregs stayed on board. He said snorkeling wasn't for him, but he'd dip a little to cool off. I swam on the surface, leading the group to the spot. About fifteen yards towards the rocks of the beach was a cove of still water, protected from the waves by a spit of land. I indicated to Alexa, who was swimming fine on the surface, where the spot was. She didn't see anything special about it. Dad and Amy were already submerging about eight feet to reach the spot.

I dove the few feet to the rocks where I helped Dad and Amy rotate the stone. It moved with both Amy and me standing on the rock floor just under the water's surface. Alexa could not stand; the water was too deep. With a snorkel, I stood on the cluster of rocks below and used the firm leverage to pull one rock free. The rock moved a couple of feet. I used my hand to wipe away a year's accumulation of plant life and sea scum. The lettering read, *Hannah Becker, devoted Wife and Mother. Unsere Ewige Geist des Herzliches Seeles.*

Father stood on a nearby rock and contemplated the underwater tomb. Amy, Father told me, had known Mother, having worked in his hospital in Miami for a brief period. She loved Mother very much and wound up caring for her in her last years on St. Thomas. Thereafter, she became Dad's caretaker, companion, and nurse. She was totally devoted to the widower, especially after Mother's death. I found a small stone to place near the headstone. Dad did the same, then Amy. Alexa looked at me. When I nodded, she added a stone to the small pile near the headstone. I then rolled the large stone back to cover the crypt. After a last look, we surfaced and swam towards the dinghy.

"I had no idea your mother was buried like this," Alexa said.

"Dad and I decided it would be safer for her. If the medical records were interpreted unfavorably for my father's name and his family, there is a risk her grave might be vandalized or searched for more information. He wishes to be buried, when he really passes, next to her."

"And the stones?"

"In the Jewish tradition, we mark our sorrow, upon the anniversary of a loved one's passing, with a stone. Under the circumstances, flowers would be futile. A stone is practical. A stone is permanent."

The motor revved as we departed. Dad was quiet as he always was when we visited Mother. Amy held him to keep his trembling body warm in the wind created by the boat's speed.

"What did it say on her tomb?" Alexa asked.

"Roughly, she is our eternal spirit and soul of warmth and kindness."

"And there was no date." I nodded.

The dinghy arrived at *Vanity Fare*. A boat from the BVI Water Patrol was tied to her.

Alexa saw it and paled. She knew we were caught. She must have been thinking she'd get to see that prison that Houdini couldn't get out of. The two men stood aboard *Vanity Fare* with their hands on their hips, looking grim. Dregs must have been trembling; his family would certainly be notified of his incarceration. Amy and Dad held each other from the cool breeze. The girls stood on deck, barking at the visitors.

The officers watched as we climbed aboard.

"Nothing like fierce guard dogs to protect one's property," I said.

They didn't smile, nor were they afraid of my silly looking dogs. They wore police caps and automatic pistols. They were both about forty-something, very black-skinned with huge shoulders exaggerated by the tightness of their fitted police shirts. Their chrome badges glistened in the bright sunlight.

"It seems you neglected to stop by customs at Soper's Hole on Tortola when you entered Her Majesty's waters. You must know the law. Your papers please."

"The newspapers, Officer?" I asked.

Alexa sat in the cockpit aghast at my awful answer. How stupid, acting cocky with two armed police officers.

"No, your toilet paper, you jackass." They laughed hysterically, knowing full well they'd put on a great show for my guests. They especially liked Alexa's face that was reddening as she realized the charade that had just been performed.

I sat down and embraced her. Her face was already changing from angry red to embarrassed red. I knew the difference and she started to laugh along with us in relief of her tension.

Dad stepped up, "Alexa, these are our good friends, Officers Vernon and Roger Callaway of Her Majesty's Marine Patrol. They are our family on the island and they see to it we don't clutter up their jail."

They all shook hands and I asked Dregs to get some refreshments. Amy got the lemonade that had been chilling in the fridge. In the cockpit, the girls licked Vernon and Roger, as they had been doing for years.

It was Roger who asked, "Been to Mom's grave?"

Dad and I nodded. Dad explained to Alexa that Mom had delivered two of Vernon's and one of Roger's children. She was a good midwife and would stand by at island homes for days waiting for the new arrivals. Without a midwife, the lack of medical care on Virgin Gorda would require expectant parents to stay at the hospital on Tortola in Roadtown until they delivered. This was expensive, inconvenient at the least, and took them away from their jobs and their families.

Mom was available for any Virgin Gorda islander to assist them in their homes when the time came. Her kindness was never forgotten and many islanders, like Roger and Vernon, knew where she was buried and visited her on occasion. Her location was known only to those who knew and loved her.

As we sat in the cockpit sipping lemonade, I asked them if they'd heard anything that might concern me.

"We received a report about your plane crash; Dr. Becker, I assume the living one," smiling at Dad, "was restricted to U.S. territory. Customs is to arrest the doctor if he tried to enter our territory. Guess I'll just have to arrest you. Look pretty dangerous to me, especially with those vicious guard dogs."

"They'll lick you to death, so be forewarned." I cautioned them.

"There's more. Day before yesterday, got a call at the base from an FBI Agent Hobson. Said she was investigating a lead here about a lab in St. Thomas that may have been developing some dangerous poisons. Mentioned your name. Asked if we knew where you had your boat serviced. Said there was a problem with your keel. Might be smuggling something. I gave him nothing; played stupid island cop." Vernon said.

Now it was beginning to make sense. Alexa was connecting the dots as well.

Dregs didn't know what we were talking about.

I started with, "So, the sailboat I'd read about in the papers, the one that was hooked onto some tanker's anchor, had a keel very similar to mine."

Alexa looked at me. "No wait," I said. "Is it possible it actually was mine?" I thought about this possibility. "I get the bottom work done on *Vanity Fare* at a yard in Roadtown, Tortola, just over there." I pointed to the horizon where we could see Tortola in the distance. It only takes a few minutes to remove a keel if you have the right equipment. I left the boat there for a week when I stayed with Amy and Dad at the clinic.

"Why would someone do this?" Alexa asked.

"I guess to get my ID numbers in front of authorities, if that accident at sea was not an accident after all. Was there something else? You said two other things, Vern. Something about smuggling, and that they also knew about a lab down here making experimental poison."

Vernon said, "Yes, they indicated that the keel gave them both pieces of information. They could have been lying."

"A keel could be a neat little smuggling method, when you think about it," I realized aloud. "Would have to be hollowed out though. It would take special work and welding tools, but it's not impossible. Clever. X-rays can't penetrate lead." I nodded, and Alexa had another question.

"Would it be possible Grabel had stirred up this affair by sending American authorities enough data to make them think you're a smuggler and a terrorist with toxic fungi? It would motivate you to find the documents they want. It would alert the authorities who had been ignoring the Holocaust and old war crimes." Alexa was certain she had the answers.

The plan was brilliant. Alexa's respect grew for Dr. Sobotta or Grabel, and for *The Circle*, and for the criminal minds that were sick enough to contrive this. They made yesterday's news of old Nazis today's headlines of a terrorist plot with poisons. The only problem was that Dr. Becker and son were on their terrorist list of suspects.

"But how do they know about the weaponizing of fungi they think is being done?" I asked.

Alexa thought about this. "It would have to be a clue they would follow that would lead to Dr. Alan Becker, or even his father. I'd take a sample of IVb and leave it for the authorities to analyze, and then to trace back to Triton Pharmaceuticals." Alexa was confident about her theory, and I had to agree that it made sense.

"We know the source of the referral to us. The sole client for IVb might be my father, which would be an added benefit, if he should still be alive." I said.

Dad and Amy listened to the whole story about our meeting with Dr. Grabel and Herr Lobel. Dad had been waiting years for this. I saw no fear in his face, but rather resolve. He would have a chance to set things right with his former masters. I resolved to protect him. I knew he would fight me on this.

Dregs was in the galley making lunch, so he missed most of this conversation. Vernon and Roger knew most of the story, but for the recent meetings and new players.

Just then, Roger pulled something from his boat: a huge conch shell. He handed it to Alexa who admired its size and beautiful shades of coral pink.

"*Conch* is its name in the islands. Technically it's a Triton. It is named for a mythical Greek God," I said.

Alexa, Greek by culture, added. " Let's see, Triton was the son of Poseidon, ruler of the Seven Seas. Triton was half man, half fish. Your typical *merman*, I guess. When Triton blew his horn, the conch shell, he heralded his father's coming and presiding over all sea life."

We didn't have to *act* impressed with Alexa's knowledge because we really were.

I added, "The occupant of this shell is a gastropod and a delicacy in the islands. Looks like a giant oyster. It's eaten raw, chopped with onions, tomatoes, celery and cucumbers, and soaked with lime juice. Vern and Roger have already removed the occupant, see the hole here?" Alexa noted the two-inch diameter hole where a hammer had punctured the shell. "Here, the attaching muscle of the tenant is cut loose using a knife, freeing him from the protection of the shell."

I pointed to the spot from which they'd evicted the gastropod. Then, Vernon produced it from his ice chest. It was obviously naked without its shell.

"That's really awful looking. What is that long, spiny projection from that thing?" she asked, wincing at the slimy, squirming creature with a hooked spine hanging from it about 6 inches long.

"You eat it. Around the islands, we swallow it whole," Roger volunteered with a smile.

"Islanders believe it fortifies them in many ways, not the least of which would be sexually," I said.

Amy blushed. Dad just smiled.

"Caribbean Viagra." Vernon added with a smirk. "Puts starch in one's bamboo."

Now Alexa was either blushing or very sunburned. With that, Vernon handed the entire live creature to Alexa. She winced through her first bite, but then appeared to enjoy it.

"Dad has a particularly large specimen of a Triton on the shelf in his office. Mom gave it to him when we came to the islands. She inscribed it to use it as a greeting card. She was both artistic and resourceful," I said.

It was a great reunion with old friends: the Callaways, Alexa, Dad, Amy, and, of course, Mother beneath us, but forever with us. As we drank rum punch, I toasted Mother; "May Triton and Poseidon, watch over and protect her soul."

CHAPTER 20

The Valet

Vanity Fare sailed into St. Thomas Harbor. I spotted the two range markers ahead, using them to confirm that I was centered in the channel. Alexa noticed them, too, and they reminded her of Hannah Becker's cipher.

We had said our goodbyes to Vernon and Roger Callaway back at the Bitter End Hotel. They promised to update us on anything new they'd come across from FBI bulletins. They mentioned that the agent in charge was a K. Hobson out of Houston. I had suggested that Dad and Amy remain in the British Virgins, perhaps with the Callaways, who agreed it would be a good idea. But they refused to be intimidated, and felt responsible to their patients back at the clinic.

Dregs picked up the mooring line for us to tie up to after I'd dropped and pleated the sails. Alexa straightened up the galley and cockpit. The girls were already napping on the aft deck in the shade of the mizzen mast. It was late afternoon. After taking Dad and Amy back to the docks, Alexa and I shared a rum punch in the shade of the bimini in the cockpit.

"I'm glad you took me to see your mother's grave. I feel closer to you and your family. I think your Dad is a wonderful man, and maybe I understand his dedication a little better and can appreciate what he had to do as a doctor during those awful times. If he exposes the identities of these criminals, this would be justice. It would certainly invite investigations into their past and present activities. Their names would be infamous in recorded history. Maybe these names and photos in the files are the rank and file of *The Circle* internationally. Now, that would be a frightening possibility." Alexa had changed since she'd become involved in my family history.

Just then, I noticed a dinghy approaching. I took the binoculars out, seeing him chilled me.

"We have a guest," I said. The girls started to bark.

"Should we be concerned? Do we have a weapon?" she asked.

"We should be concerned about him, but I always have a weapon handy. The universal sailor's weapon," I said holding up one of several winch handles located on both sides of the cockpit. She looked at me with that *get real* look, but I reassured her that they were very effective.

I gave a good hard stare at the elderly, thin but not yet frail man with the light skin of a tourist about to suffer his first sunburn tonight. He was dressed in Bermuda shorts, long black socks, black slip-on loafers and a cap that said *St. Thomas.*

"Remove your shoes. Bad for the fiberglass decks," I said to our visitor. Alexa went below to change from her bathing suit. The guest needed a little help to steady himself on the now rocking boat. The girls barked and did their usual threatening wag dance.

"Thank you for allowing to see me. We must talk, Herr Becker." He didn't offer his hand and I didn't extend mine. I gestured to the seat. Alexa brought up some lemonade and offered him a glass. He drank the entire glass and took a pill. This was a sick man. He looked awful and that pill suggested he had serious heart maladies.

He caught his breath and looked around to see if anyone on a neighboring boat was looking at us. I assumed he was concerned about Professor Sobotta, née Grabel.

"Are you feeling better, Herr Lobel?" I asked. He did not seem surprised that I knew his name. Alexa was. "Hitler had only one valet, or manservant, during his entire tenure as Fuehrer," I said. Alexa was impressed. "Lobel was in the Bunker in Berlin until the last days of the Reich and at Berchtesgaden, the mountain retreat, with Hitler."

He seemed to be used to this recognition and was proud of the distinction, at least in certain *circles.*

"You look same like your father. I knew him, also your mother. They were good people. I am sad they are not with us."

I didn't react. I was trying to picture this man fifty years younger.

"What brings you to St. Thomas, especially with Grabel?" He noticed the disrespectful lack of any of the Professor's titles.

"There is a concern to me and others," he said.

"Missing medical files of my father's, yes, I know that already. Since I recognized you from your many photos, I can assume your name is not in the files, and I see no sign of you having used my late father's services," I said.

"This is true, but your father *did* treat my friend at his clinic at the camp. Herr Gustav Levitsky. It was of my special request; my authority help Gustav to have medical care *outside* the camp walls." Lobel looked at me for judgment. Alexa and I understood the relationship was more than a friendship.

"I suspect your employer would have frowned upon you having a Jewish friend at all, a violation of the Nuremburg laws, and that your friendship was far ahead of its time. In fact, when you served der Fuehrer at Berchtesgaden, you must have spent your days off visiting your friend Gustav outside Dachau."

He nodded, "Jawohl. Gustav be my partner, more than brother. Whatever you think, we care for each other. I risk my position, nein, my life for Gustav. Gustav become sick at camp. 'Typhus,' doctor before your father say. Verboten to treat Jews. Later, when your father arrive at camp, I visit the Gasthaus asking about Levitsky. Your father treat him inside Dachau with his, how you say, Pilzenmitteln?" Lobel was having trouble speaking English; spittle appeared at the corners of his mouth. Alexa turned a fan on in the cockpit to cool him down. He took a breath.

"Mushroom-derived herb treatments," I translated. "So my father, as a favor to you, got Levitsky some special treatment, meaning he could come to the Gasthaus and get some real medicines which he couldn't give him on the inside. Are you here to acknowledge that and to thank me in his stead?"

"Nein, nein, but I wish I have thank him before." I thought to myself, if you'd been here an hour earlier, you could have. He continued, "Nein, I wish to discuss other matter. Do you make interest in the Nazi history period?" He took a moment to catch his breath. This was a sick man with obstructive pulmonary disease. His emphysema had caught up with him. "Of course you do, you were born to it. I accompany Herr Hitler in the Bunker, the Berlin Bunker, so Allied bombs not interfere with der Fuehrer's War. He could radio from there with his generals. It was only for the highest in the command staff and we live there. It is comfortable, like the Eagle's Nest at Berchtesgaden, but not sunshine and beautiful scenery."

Alexa listened intently. The girls sat besides her sniffing the scent of the fish the seagulls had caught in their beaks just off the stern.

"Please continue," I prodded. He looked tired, and I didn't want a long, drawn out affair going down memory lane with a nostalgic old Nazi. I was sure he was a nice man, but politeness and gentility in manner compensates little for Nazi brutality. In his case, he had someone who he cared about inside the death camp, telling him about the cruelty and horrors his employer had concocted that was the Holocaust. That left him with no excuse. He was well informed.

"You know of last days of War, naturlich. Field Marshall Zukov and Russian tanks are on the East outsides of Berlin, your General Patton and Englishman, Montgomery, coming from West, so I have work to do in the end. Herr Hitler and Fraulein Braun are to marry in little ceremony in the Bunker, and then they to right away kill themselves. No music, no flowers. I see it and bring dry Edelweiss leaves I find so she have small bouquet. I love Fraulein Eva. She is beautiful and make all men around her feel young. She childlike, not grown up. She have the trust for me. She know about my friend, Gustav, at camp and help me make to visit him at your father's clinic at Gasthaus. Guards see my special ID papers as *personliche staff to der Fuehrer* give me *carte blanche*, as French people say. Eva know

Gustav must to be Jew. She not believe of Herr Hitler's philosophy. We go visit him together with her help, I trust her with my life."

I tried to look bored, but was actually engrossed in these revelations. Alexa knew she was hearing part of history from a key character in a unique position to tell it.

"Eva and der Fuehrer to kill themselves right after wedding. Hitler have black cyanide capsule for her, and pistol for him. They kiss. It very sad. We hear tank shells from outside come very close. Militia reports say they two blocks away from us. Shells echo loud in Bunker. Dust from ceiling make everyone uniform white.

"Eva and der Fuehrer go to private room and close door. Two guards stand by. We hear shot and wait few minutes. We find them on floor. She have red face from cyanide. He lay in blood on floor. The guards help me. I am to cremate both bodies with petrol, outside Bunker in *strasse*. The guards they bring petrol tanks and we wet bodies. I light match to burn bodies. Russians come around corner and see flames and troops chase us back to Bunker. We surrender with other staff. We be arrested and go for questions. I live in jail six months with the torture over and over."

Alexa brought another round of lemonade and she put a bottle of rum on the table in case we needed something more bracing. She poured a swig of rum into her own lemonade.

Lobel continued. "I cry when I see Fraulein Eva's body on floor. This girl be my friend, is only family. To destroy her with flames be too much." He was crying as if this had happened yesterday, not sixty years ago. "The Russians being cruel. I swear Hitler and Fraulein Eva dead. They do post-mortem, how do you say, oh, autopsy, on bodies. Russians try to stopping fires. I live in gulag in Siberia for three years." He showed us both where two fingers were missing, presumably from either torture or frostbite.

There were tears in his eyes. He was a pitiful sight. In another age, I might have admired this gentle man. He'd suffered a bit, but at least was alive.

"Why are you here with Grabel?" I said.

"Dr. Grabel think me asset for I know your mother and father. I am here for very different purpose. Russian autopsy prove Eva and Hitler dead. This be true."

"I've read the reports for the autopsy documents. They were only recently made available from the Russian Archives in Moscow for inspection confirming the bodies to be Eva's and der Fuehrer's. And you're here to tell me they actually *are* alive," I joked a little.

"Nein, nay. Hitler and Eva dead. Eva's body was much better condition. Her organs autopsied for identification."

"And was that Eva Braun you cremated?" I asked.

"Yes, Fraulein Eva. But," he swallowed another capsule and wiped his brow with a handkerchief. "Report not see everything."

Alexa couldn't stand it. She said, "What did they miss, Herr Lobel?"

"Fraulein Eva be pregnant."

****

"What could this matter, since Eva and her fetus would have been cremated?" Alexa asked.

Lobel looked at me and I made a facial expression giving him full authorization to continue.

"I visit Gustav at Gasthaus and your father. Gustav's health improve. Your father risk his life and your mother's with treating Jew. Eva want to go with me. I not imagine why, but think she want to meet Gustav. I introduce her to your father. Eva meet him, and also meet Gustav. Then, Eva ask to speak to your father alone. After they talk, I take her back to Berchtesgaden before our *trip* become, you know, suspicious." Lobel was exhausted. I thought about bringing my oxygen tank from below just to keep in the cockpit along with my emergency medicines.

He rearranged his position. He was probably getting stiff from the dampness and from sitting so long. "On drive back up to mountain, Eva ask I must find camera for next trip. I not imagine what for. She say it be a gift for doctor. I think to pay for care of Gustav. She go with me on next trip. I see Gustav, but this time Eva go into clinic room for long time. When she come out, she look very white like she sick, weak, like she have surgery. Your mother say she be fine. Eva later tell me she be pregnant. I assume she had an *abtreibung*, how do you say?" He looked at me for translation.

"Abortion," I suggested.

"Ach, jawohl. However, she be good Catholic girl from farm family. She could not do such thing. I ask what she did at clinic. She heard Nazi doctors experiment with egg transplantation. Hitler order research, for it good for Reich. You see, Army need more soldiers, but only those of *pure race*, his *uebermenschen*, how you say."

"Master Race," I offered.

"Aryan women Germany have many, but many man killed in war. Nazi doctors say if they can transplant cow embryos in cows, why not in people? They want to produce blond, blue-eyed babies Hitler need in new Germany."

I could see that Alexa didn't like where the story was going. Dregs was below listening to his CD player. The sun was beginning to set and the cockpit was cooling off a bit.

Lobel continued. "Eva ask your father to take her baby and find new mother for it. She hear secret reports at home. She fear for her baby with bad news from Eastern front, how D-Day landing succeed, how Battle of the Bulge fail, and that Fatherland fighting its own borders, her baby never come to be born, not in *her* body with the relationship with der Fuehrer. This is her baby's death sentence. Your father tell her this not kill baby, the fetus to survive, but it is experiment and have risk. She good Catholic girl."

"Herr Lobel, this is where I must disagree with your tale. My father would never attempt such a procedure if he knew the truth about the father of the fetus." Lobel stared right at me, waiting for me to take in what I'd just said. Then I understood.

"You are suggesting that Fraulein Braun was less than candid about the father's identity. She could have even suggested that her life was on the line for a possible fling she'd had one weekend away from Adolph. The threat to her life was obvious, Hitler being the paranoiac maniac he was. He'd be intolerant of her infidelity, for sure, anger best expressed by snuffing out the focus of his affections. The betrayal would cost both her and the baby their lives. It wouldn't surprise me if he'd simply send her and her love child directly to Dachau for processing like the Jewish prisoners."

"Would it surprise you she make threat to name *me* father? Dear God, she become protective mother even risk *my* life to save baby. She be fine mother, this I know, so I forgive her. She not believe Hitler's genes to be crazy or disease." He seemed to be apologizing for her.

"Since she was virgin, she not have experience. Der Fuehrer her one, how you say, intimate companion. If he discover her baby, he be humiliated. Nein, this child have no chance of life. The reports she hear and moods of der Fuehrer make clear experimental transplant was not so risky as baby in her womb with name of Hitler."

Alexa and I were stunned by this revelation. What relevance did this have to the present? Did the procedure succeed? *What happened to the child?*

I posed the question directly to Lobel, who had taken advantage of the pause to drink his lemonade, this time with a nip of rum. He swallowed another capsule. He knew what we anxiously wanted answered.

He said, after swallowing the whole drink, "This why bring me to you, after half century, to get answer to question."

****

None of us noted that, even as the sun was setting, there were eyes on us. On the Frenchman's Reef Hotel balcony, Hobson and Fielding viewed us through their long-range cameras. With their acoustic directional dish, they heard a good deal of the conversation. On the patio of Blackbeard's Castle Restaurant, Grabel could see Lobel with us. In a nearby boat, Sanger and Yorel recorded our conversation, transmitted by a tiny transmitter attached, unnoticed, under the cockpit table. We had no idea our conversation was so public. It was already being discussed on three continents in English, German, and Hebrew.

CHAPTER 21

The Opening Gambit

Lobel stretched as he climbed aboard the dinghy, and his shirt rode-up to expose his lower back. There it was, an incomplete circular scar. That he was a *member* of the fencing club of the Wartburg Restaurant was of little surprise to me.

"Alan, did you see it yet on CNN?" Alexa sounded terrified on the other end of the phone. I'd sent her to Miami after Lobel left.

****

At many of our post-cadaver-dissection lunches, Oskar trusted me with more information about the fencing club. He described the initiation ceremony as *duel-like*. They took place in a densely wooded, pine forest outside Graz that was isolated from prying eyes and from law enforcement authorities. The land was part of a compound owned by a member. The clearing was known to the locals as *Sonnenfeld* or *Field of Sun*.

"The candidate removes his, or her, shirt while a dozen hooded Board of Directors in black robes, holding torches, preside. One of them reveals a polished, steel sword with the swastika engraved on a scarlet red background in its grip. The ritual sword is heated in a bonfire. The candidate's sponsor approaches the aspiring member, who now faces away from the other robed observers. With a nod from the leader, the sponsor removes his cowl, thereby identifying himself. Using the glowing ritual sword's tip, he embosses a circle into the trainee's lumbar region. But the circle is not complete; the upper right corner is open to symbolize what is left undone; repaying the Allies for defeating them, for suffering the humiliation of the terms of the armistice, their unfulfilled dream of reestablishing the Reich, and of finding their future Fuehrer empowered with dominion over the inferior races, not yet realized."

Their mission of resurrecting the Reich in today's Europe had not yet been fulfilled. How could Oskar know so much of this secretive group of fanatics? I never saw Oskar cry, but I think he was ready to. He was so sensitive and I loved him as only an adopted brother could. Although our bond was strong, our futures, based on culture and geography, would probably draw us apart. We always feared this. Then I understood.

"It's your father, isn't it? It is through him that you've learned of these secret rituals. He was bitter from his years in a Russian prisoner-of-war camp where he was starved and tortured after his plane was shot down. This must be very hard on you." I empathized. Oskar loved his father. We were closer than ever, and I was certain Oskar's association with me, an American Jew, was a source of argument between him and his father. My weekends at his family's home would have been far more political if his father had revealed his association with *The Circle*. This also must have been a source of strife between Oskar and his father.

****

"What are you talking about?" I said. "What's on CNN?" Alexa's panicky voice ended my reminiscences of after-school lunches with Oskar.

"There was a terrorist attack in Haifa, Israel. Several hundred people were affected. They don't know anything except a gas exploded in a B'hai Temple. The emergency rooms are reporting bizarre symptoms of nausea, headaches, double vision, muscle and joint aches, and something bizarre."

"Which is?"

"The victims report feeling cold when something hot is applied to their limbs, and hot when something cold is applied. These symptoms seem to be unique to this inhaled substance. The victims are starting to have respiratory arrest. They said a dozen or more who were closest to the temple site have gone comatose from hypoxia and some have died. The death rate is climbing and little else is known. The hospitals are overloaded and exact information is unavailable. The military made a radio announcement that they will institute martial law immediately. Alan, are you there? The Israeli Defense Forces are activated for more attacks."

I understood so much more. This was an opening salvo, a warning shot, the opening gambit of a chess game. In chess, the opponent tries a move even if it involves sacrifice to ascertain his opponent's strengths. This gambit had been played.

"This symptom of sensation reversal is a hallmark of Ciguatera toxicity. The location being Haifa is obvious, as it would be a Jewish State target and politically desirable," I said.

"For *The Circle's* aim, you mean?"

"Yes, and the delivery system was a powdered form of the toxin I've never worked with. This never came from my lab."

"You're thinking it came from a lab in the Land of Oz, aren't you?"

I had to suspect that. "Very likely, wouldn't you agree? The fact that Grabel is away from the lab and here *vacationing* in sunny St. Thomas would absolve him of any direct involvement. Clever, isn't he? He told us his lab in Austria was given a clean bill of health by Austrian inspectors. He also could be counted on to come and visit us. This attack only makes him more imposing, more credible in our eyes, and we should take him seriously."

"Why the B'hai Temple? Isn't that a Muslim faith? Wouldn't that make it look like a non-Muslim cell was involved? I assume there's a message in targeting a B'hai Temple."

I saw the message immediately. "The B'hai faith is a *universalist* sect. It follows not only Mohammed's teachings, but those of Moses and Jesus as well. Those of the B'hai sect see a continuum in the prophets, not a discontinuity, and they don't just give it lip service, but follow their faith as a truly peaceful means to righteousness. They are not militant. It would eliminate Arab terrorist groups as suspect for they would avoid a holy shrine, especially a mosque. No, the message here is different. They want the world to know that this isn't about Moslems attacking western targets with improvised bombs; this is a truly different war they are waging, and we'd better understand it soon."

"How do you know so much about B'hai, Alan? You sound like a convert."

"Before I'd met Oskar in Graz, I had another roommate, Hamid, who was B'hai. We became friends while studying German our first summer in Graz. He was from Teheran and taught me about his faith. After that summer, he had to leave because his mother died back in Iran. I never saw him again."

"So, what can you make of all of this?"

"The B'hai faith can be traced back to Persia and its Golden Age when it was an empire. The Persians have always been proud of their empire under kings like Darius and Xerxes. Their empire fell to Alexander the Great and the Greeks. Like Hitler's armies, they had to limp back home in disgrace. I think the Haifa terrorists are trying to tell us that empires may be destroyed, but with new vision, pride, and weaponry, they can rise again."

"You mean with this poison gas?"

"In the case of Persia, present-day Iran, I think the analogy for their weaponry is more along the lines of nuclear weapons. Teheran seeks to reestablish its former glory, sending its bombs and insurgents to Iraq, for their future annexation. Seems a lot like Germany's annexation of Austria. Political power comes from fear. Our terrorists in Haifa know that we fear nuclear weapons in Iran's hands. Now we might need to fear this toxic gas in *The Circle's* hands. I'm certain they are behind this. They know fear worked for Hitler. Remember how many countries were ceded to Hitler without a shot from Britain or Roosevelt? Hitler just had to promise to stop annexations if they gave him enough land. *The Circle* will achieve its goals through fear among the people it wants to dominate. Like

Israelis. Like Jews. Like freedom-seeking people anywhere, for that matter." Alexa was sickened by this.

"Alan," she said. "We've sold Ciguatera antiserums to the Israelis already. Do they have enough?"

"I don't think it will work." She was shocked by this.

"How can it not work?" she asked.

"Because *this* Ciguatera is different. It's *weaponized*. The symptoms they're having are developing too fast for my antiserum to work. The victims' immune systems can't build an immunity with my Manchineel sap extract fast enough to be consistent with survival. They will die long before my antidote would kick in. The sensation reversal symptom you mentioned should never have developed this quickly. It is a sign of *chronic* or long-term type Ciguatera, not the more common *acute*, short and mild form of the disease. No, someone has weaponized a toxin that we were combating, but we dealt with its natural form, found in the intestines of unsuspecting fish. That's why the Israelis, Sanger and Yorel, were on your case. They had evidence that someone was altering naturally occurring Ciguatera for purposes that could only mean weaponizing and that meant, terrorism. They must suspect either Father or I am behind this. Since I wouldn't admit Father was alive, they went to you. They knew the key was the IVb Sabourad's medium for growing advanced strains of new variants of the disease. They followed the medium, and it led to my father. This, despite his death twenty years ago, was the source of the order from Grabel's lab."

"Don't you think they'd suspect Grabel as well?" Alexa asked.

"I've no doubt they have investigated his lab thoroughly, as he said, and satisfied themselves that he's just an aging Austrian professor. Whether they know his true identity or think that his assumed name, Sobotta, is truly his own, I can't be certain. But Mosad, Israeli's Secret Service is good. I suspect they need to get their hands on my father's medical records. It would confirm Grabel's identity. If he could be the inventor of Zyklon B, Ciguatera toxin wouldn't be a stretch to figure out."

"Alan, I think you're right. Their nation is too vulnerable to an attack like this not to nip it in the bud."

"Alexa, you must find alternative lodging. Don't tell me where on the phone, just find it. Stay away from the office and away from my lab. Trust me, you are in danger."

"I'm smarter than you think." She was getting sassy and I admired her for that.

"I know you are."

"You probably didn't think I noticed the scar on Herr Lobel's back. I know you're trying to avoid scaring the hell out of me, but I feel more secure when my clients give me the facts, Dr. Becker. By the way, your father can't have been using his real name all these years. What is his alias?"

"Langer. Dr. Fritz Langer. It's on his shingle at the clinic, the Bougainvillea Clinic on Morningside Heights." I wondered about her question, but just chalked it up to what she'd said. She needed complete information to feel secure. I'd hope she would take my advice about finding another place to live. She said she would, and that they would talk again tomorrow.

Alexa knew she'd have to keep her plans secret for now.

****

I turned on the radio for the news reports. I hoped Alexa was safe. I had some breakfast with Dregs. He agreed to contact his parents by the end of the week to make plans about his future. At least they'd know where he was. I would miss him.

I finished my orange juice and croissant he'd brought from the galley and took my medications. The sailboat next to us was blessed with two most admirable females, Anna and Inga, who lived aboard their vessel, *Liquid Assets*. A better name would have been *Silicone Assets*. Dregs couldn't have been happier. He'd learned what I'd known for years about harbor life. Every morning, these naturally platinum blond, Amazonian, shapely Swedish cousins showered on the swim platform of their sailboat. This alone would have been enough, but they showered *au natural*, not even wearing their string bikinis.

They were waving with their broad, white smiles at me or Dregs, or both of us, and Dregs loved it. It made mornings better for me too, I must admit. We waved back at the beauties, then my eye strayed to the water just astern of their swim platform. Anna, or was it Inga, let out a scream echoed by the other. A body floated in the ripples of the harbor water. It bobbed, head down, arms spread-eagled, lifelessly upon the waves. I turned the VHF radio on channel 12 and alerted the harbor patrol.

Anna and Inga wrapped themselves in towels and scurried to the center cockpit of their sailboat. They looked towards *Vanity Fare*, and pointed at the body. I yelled, "I see it." Then they saw the Boston Whaler and heard its sirens. They nodded that they understood. Germaine Caldwell and Alexander Wooster, both in V.I. Police uniforms, nodded to me in thanks for the call. With a gaff hook and much effort, they pulled the waterlogged body aboard their boat.

The next day Vernon called. He asked, "Remember the name of the FBI agent in charge of your case?"

"Hobson, yes?"

"She had an assistant, Special Agent Fielding. Heard you reported a floater near your boat. Thought you might like to know, Hobson no longer has an assistant."

"And the C.O.D.?"

"Drowning is the official cause of death, but between you and me, he had a little cyanide cocktail before that, the autopsy said. It wasn't with a little umbrella either; it was intravenous, very professional. He wasn't breathing when he went for his swim. No seawater in the lungs, so the assailant didn't know, or care, that it would clearly be a homicide. There were signs he was interrogated aggressively. Also, very professional. He suffered. They must have had a lot to discuss."

"Thanks, Vern."

"Got any suspects, Doc? I could use a promotion. My brother just got one, and Mama's disappointed in me."

"Yes, I have several and their crimes are U.S.-based. You'd endanger your Mama and kids if you rubbed these guys the wrong way. They have real sensitive skin and not a lot to lose. Remember, it was a special FBI agent they fished from the harbor."

"Sharks didn't even nibble him."

"They can sense cyanide. Leaves a scent of burnt almonds in the skin and seawater that they don't like."

"Like the Japanese blowfish; either cooked perfectly and you have a delicacy, or you checkout early from life." Vernon liked this analogy.

I thought about what he'd just said; it gave me another clue to this whole affair. "Thanks, Vern, for the tip on the floater, but I wouldn't be doing you any favors with my list of suspects. I couldn't forgive myself if anything happened to your family. Tell Mama I'll come by for some of her sour sop next week."

"Keep your head down, Doc. Watch out for Amy and Pop, too." He clicked his radio off.

What was it that Vern had said that seemed to help me make sense of this...this enigma? It was truly a *puzzlement*, as the King of Siam said to Anna in *The King and I*.

Why is it human nature to seek out that which can destroy oneself? Like the Japanese blowfish, so valued for its delicate, even sensual quality, yet extremely toxic, having been responsible for hundreds of deaths. Is it really the allure of its taste, or is it the *machismo* of eating it for men to prove they are fit lovers? Or is it something else?

I sipped lemonade in *Vanity Fare's* cockpit, petting Eleanor and Rita, who were on nap number seven. Anna and Inga waved to me from their cockpit. They seemed less exuberant and vivacious during happy hour than usual, having spotted Special Agent Fielding off their stern.

My girls raised their heads when a seagull squawked to alert his fellow flyers to a school of fish near the surface. The sun was just setting behind Morningside Heights. I thought of Dad and Amy. She was about twenty years younger. Her family was German, Bavarian; the Luger family came from the mountains in the Garmisch Mountain Region. Amy was a good surgical nurse. She accompanied them to the islands and worked in the clinic. Amy cared for him, I could see that, but he treated her more like, well, a daughter than a companion.

Whatever their relationship, she had known and loved Mom. After Mom died, she grew closer to Dad during the years I was away at school, or on training or work assignments. Amy Luger kept Dad going. These days, he and I had our alone time about once a week on board *Vanity Fare*.

My thoughts returned to things that were developing, most of which seemed ominous. I didn't like the people visiting the island and worried about Amy, Dad, and Alexa. Why was everyone connected with this affair at cross-purposes? The FBI had been alerted to my keel number on a mysterious vessel hanging from a tanker it locked horns with. No crew, though, so no crime. The probable time for *Vanity Fare* to have had a keel *transplant* would have been during her lay-up on the blocks, for her annual bottom paint job.

The newspapers revealed that Homeland Security could not account for the hollowed-out keel. This sounded like a far-fetched plan for smuggling contraband into the country, according to FBI Chief Derek Sweeney in Houston. It would be a lot easier to simply redo the ID numbers in the lead, a relatively simple task with today's easy access to lead casting imprinters and lasers. Thousands of pounds of lead isn't easy or inconspicuous to transport. Sweeney was quoted as saying the owner of record was a *Monsieur Champignon* or *Herr Pilzen*. This had the hand of the sly Sobotta, née Grabel, behind it. Was he setting me up? Why? Was it the files he was after? Or something or someone else? Grabel was a master of deceit. Labeling the gas chambers at Dachau as *showers* was brilliant. Who would not calmly walk to a shower? The suggestion that young, Jewish, girls needed fertilization treatments when they were actually guinea pigs for cruel sterilization experiments was also pure Grabel. Was he responsible for Special Agent Fielding's death?

Vern said it was professionally done with IVs. Cyanide was Grabel's designer poison; Zyklon B was his patent and claim to fame, or shame.

What the papers didn't mention, and what Sanger and Yorel asserted in their conversation with Alexa, was that *IVb was found in trace amounts on the mystery vessel's keel*. This had to be the touch of the *sly fox*. Placing his own lab under the scrutiny of the Austrian authorities was sheer genius. Like the people who dine upon poisonous blowfish, Grabel liked to tease his adversaries, drawing them in dangerously close to him. A clean bill of health from Austrian police after auditing his lab would certify his innocence. Bring the hens to your coop, just to show to the world how safe the fox really is. Which police force wanted to admit they missed the clues that could have prevented a terrorist attack?

I could see his delight in incriminating himself first as the sole manufacturer of IVb and, when pressed, having to reveal the name of its only buyer, with invoices and an address to prove it: Dr. Fritz Langer of Triton Pharmaceuticals, Bougainvillea Clinic, Morningside Heights, St. Thomas, and U.S.V.I. The FBI had been handed my father, or at least Dr. Langer, and Nurse Amy Luger, on a platter. No wonder Hobson was on the island. But Fielding's torture and murder could only be attributed to the fact he might have seen through the gambit. Or worse, *he found something far more sinister*.

With the Jews, Grabel must have reveled in playing with his mice like a cat, before devouring them whole. Fear of him would ultimately serve to panic the vermin and flush them out. He had learned this as a common Gestapo technique. Their fear and resultant panic, faced with the rumors of the so-called *Endloesung*, or Final Solution, would bring them to the railroads and harbors, seeking safe passage from Hitler's net. It was not enough to simply kill his vermin.

No, Grabel was at the Wannsee Conference during the planning of the death camp system. His Zyklon B was integral to mass murder on a level unheard of in history. He wanted state policy under

Himmler to eradicate the *untermenschen*, as Hesse called them, more efficiently, objectively, military-like, and in the wholesale numbers the Wannsee planners and the Fuehrer foresaw. Fear of the Final Solution did indeed send the Jews scurrying. Foreseeing this, the SS troops had requisitioned all rail transport and passenger ships, and closed the borders. In flight, those not already found by the Gestapo had revealed themselves.

The State's plan was no longer vague; it was carefully planned right down to the last efficiency, to the harvesting of the last gold tooth, to the humiliation of shaving from head to toe of both sexes by men in public, and the tattooing of the numbers on their forearms if they were lucky enough to be selected for slave labor. The protocols of the camps involved selection for work now, die later, if you were fit, or if you were under fourteen and over sixty, shower and die now with Zyklon B. Then there were the medical experiments. The doctors who'd conducted these could only be considered sadists by any measure.

Grabel had certainly been actively engaged in human research on Jewish subjects. The effectiveness of his hydrogen cyanide canisters had to be verified as to proper dose and method of delivery. Simply adding water to the canister and depositing it in a receptacle at the top of the *showers* proved that the gas produced was heavier than air. In only a couple of minutes, following howls and screams from the chamber, a pile of corpses accumulated. Just one canister could deliver enough gas for over *twelve hundred bathers*.

I had a handle on part of Grabel's gambit. Without doubt, he was the mysterious Swiss Doctor of Mushrooms or Fungi. So many post-War Nazis claimed to be Swiss that Post-War Switzerland's *native* population doubled. After Germany's surrender, you couldn't find a Nazi in Germany or Austria with a flashlight.

Grabel had managed to participate in *The Circle*, a new Order for an old idea: A new Reich: the Fourth, presumably.

The Israelis were less interested in uncovering elderly Nazis. Their purpose was to keep another deadly toxin from gassing their people. Grabel's fondness for gasses made him a prime suspect for the Haifa tragedy. This could also account for the American FBI presence. Homeland Security would follow any lead in the post-911 world that could net a terrorist with a weapon. They had neither the resources nor the interest in tracking down old Nazis or their medical records. Now that the custodian of these records might be tied to the IVb medium: *I might be their terrorist.*

Hobson and the late Fielding were following the evidence to uncover the cause for the Ciguatera attack. The Israelis were aligned with them and were Hobson's only support team; that is, if they knew of each other. Mosad and the FBI probably shared intelligence, for the FBI probably needed the Israelis for their mideast location and undercover expertise in certain hostile countries. Israel's friendly association with the U.S. assured Israel of not being bullied by their hostile neighbors.

What Lobel wanted with me was the real puzzler. Here was this quiet, gentle man of good manners and grace, somewhat frail, almost feeble, motivated by something that went beyond *The Circle's* agenda; I didn't see him as political. Although he had been a valet with an infamous client, his relationship with a Jewish prisoner excluded him from the Nazi mentality. His homosexual relationship with Gustav at Dachau *should* have kept him out of *The Circle.* His presence here concerned me more than anything, and I had no idea why. I needed to discuss this with Alexa. How had he gained admission, even indoctrination, into the back corner of *The Circle's* chamber? Lobel must have had something special, something that *The Circle* needed. The other explanation was simply that the Nazis were not aware of his background or proclivities? Or did they ignore these because of his privileged position as Hitler's valet? Or were they using him for a special purpose? The duplicity of the Nazi mentality was something I'd understood from Father's stories, but distasteful, nonetheless.

My cell phone rang. The girls jumped. I was sure it was Alexa. She hadn't answered her phone all day and I was getting worried.

It was a female voice. "My name is Kelly Hobson with the FBI and we need to talk."

"I'm sorry to hear about Special Agent Fielding." She must have wondered how I knew his name, but said nothing.

"I'll get right to the point. IVb has been attributed to an order destined for a Dr. Langer's clinic up the hill. Dr. Langer seems to be close to you; in fact, close enough that I decided to research his past. Guess what?"

I let the silence be my answer and hoped the next statement would be different than it was.

"Dr. Langer *has no past*. Pre-War, according to the International Red Cross in Geneva, he's listed as missing from the camp at Dachau. I believe your father was a physician of some note there. You can see where this is going, and I'm sure my intel could be wrong but..."

"You said you'd get right to the point." I sounded more impolite than I wanted.

"Your phone records indicate the word *crisis* dozens of times. Our software surveillance selectors look for words that help us locate terrorist cells. Dr. Becker, I don't care about your family history or your father's body temperature. But, when I hear the key word *crisis* spoken internationally as often as you said it, it's my job to investigate, especially when a terrorist crisis *has* developed, as in Israel. We can talk over the phone or in person, as you wish." I thought about what she said, and couldn't explain myself at all. I didn't remember ever using the word. Crisis suggests panic and, with Alexa around so much, the panic I was feeling was the last thing I wanted to reveal. Then I understood.

"Your software, I assume it involves voice recognition? It selects words spoken and digitizes them in written form after scanning a pre-selected *hot list* you and your associates select as cues?"

"That's classified, but correct essentially." She recognized a bright mind. She wondered if he could also be the Doctor Mushroom, or Champignon, or Pilzen.

"Do you, by chance, speak German?" I said. The solution became clear.

Hobson realized the solution, for she *did* speak German. "You *do* speak German, Dr. Becker. Your *crisis* referred to a German homonym, *kreis* or *kreise*."

I acknowledged her solution to the riddle, but this raised another inquiry from agent Hobson.

"I can go with that. So why mention the word *circle* so many times? Makes no sense in the context of the transcript I'm looking at."

"I guess you don't think I'm trafficking in hula hoops?" She didn't laugh.

"I've got a nasty situation in Haifa that has resulted in fifty-six deaths with more sure to develop over the next twenty-four hours. We've got a gas or powder that my Israeli colleagues can't identify. It's new, unique, and highly effective in paralyzing. It eventually paralyzes the diaphragm. Its death is painful. The bodies lock in a type of tetanus, a muscular knot, for several hours. They can't talk, can't drink, can barely breathe. We've no treatment so far. It's a Ciguatera family toxin, but you knew that. I'm talking about children, Doctor, who were in the mosque at the time. If there's a next site to be attacked, that's *crisis* enough for me. Now what does *The Circle* mean?"

She had shocked me back to reality. The obvious connection between IVb medium for Ciguatera toxin growth and for this new use made me look awfully suspicious. "But agent Hobson, I thought you'd know about *The Circle*." I told her of the cryptic Austrian fencing club, its location, some members who might be staying at Blackbeard's, and how my keel's ID numbers wound up on Wet Dream's keel.

"This information is helpful, Doctor. I can understand your reluctance to call us. The question is whether I believe you. And if I do, does Dr. Langer's research threaten American and Israeli interests? His work *is*, after all, lung-related and we're facing a pulmonary paralytic agent."

"My father owes his life to the U.S. I guess I can trust you with the truth of his identity."

Hobson appreciated the small confidence, but I hadn't answered her question.

"Have you ever heard of the blowfish delicacy in Japan?" Now I knew why this example was relevant. Hobson said she had not.

After I explained the Japanese culture concerning the blowfish, Hobson said, "the Western philosophy is something like *that which doesn't kill us, serves to make us stronger.*"

"Then we agree Dr. Langer's research in pulmonary disorders utilizing IVb might be therapeutic, not sinister." I'd hoped this would explain Dad's inexplicable IVb orders. I needed to talk to him. Hobson's concerns were probably assuaged for now, I hoped.

"That remains to be seen. I'll be in touch." She hung up.

I dialed Alexa for the tenth time. No answer. She'd turned the phone off. Was she exhausted and sleeping off the nightmare I'd put her through or...? I didn't want to consider the *or*. Sanger and Yorel would be intent on her trail. Why wouldn't they be? It seemed to lead to me, my father, the lab, and most importantly, to the IVb medium.

Frustrated and worried, I had to talk to someone. I called Amy.

"Hello, Alan. He's resting, but awake." She put him on the phone.

"Dad, we need to visit the eye doctor."

"No, forget that. My cataracts are not a problem right now."

I knew Hobson would be listening, so I chose my words carefully, so as not to alert her nosy intel services.

"The eye doctor is not for you. I need him." My father understood, and that was enough.

CHAPTER 22

The Wicked Winch

It was long past midnight when Alexa visited her office. She put her key in the deadbolt lock: *the door was already unlocked.* The palpitations started and her breathing was audible. At first, she cursed her paralegal Peggy, for not using the deadbolt, but after peering inside realized her office had been tossed and turned upside down. The intruder had ripped open files. Papers were strewn on the desk, sofa and coffee table, and the floor. It would be impossible to determine if anything, much less what, had been taken. The lock had been expertly picked and her security locks on the cabinets showed no signs of force. It was Saturday; her assistants wouldn't be in.

The sofa had been slashed with a knife, vases cracked open, even ceiling tiles dislodged in the lattice above. Every one of her desk drawers had been emptied. She thought of calling the police, but couldn't rule them out as the perpetrators. There was no search warrant attached to the door, but that didn't mean anything if it was Homeland Security. With the Haifa tragedy dominating the news, all leads needed to be followed in haste.

Then she thought, "What if it's not the authorities, but *The Circle?*"

She considered calling Alan, then reconsidered. Why worry him? He'd had enough after yesterday. He was emotionally drained after visiting his mother, seeing the Callaways, learning of Fielding's demise, and worrying about evidence leading to his father and Amy. His parents' history was re-emerging, coming to a head. Peace in the clinic on the hill had been irrevocably disturbed.

No, she would not add to his worry. She'd chosen to be a part of it because... She didn't want to think about her feelings right now. It was for Alan, and she was going to aid in his rescue, to find his peace by finding his family's legacy in their history, their bravery, and clear the clouds approaching them. *The Circle* and the authorities, American, European, even Middle Eastern, were drawing closer. Would the implied threats become realized?

What she knew for certain: Beck was a good man. That was her anchor in these indecisive, murky waters she was treading. She resolved to help. She contemplated her next move. Her own contracts and licensing documents for Alan's lab were in disarray. She needed more information and she knew where to look.

****

As the Drs. Becker rode in the taxi, I explained the problem to Father.

"I began seeing bubbles, or floaters and now I'm developing a blind spot off to the lower left of my field of vision."

Dad remembered how, as a teenager, I'd hit my head on the side of a community pool in New York after trying a jackknife off the diving board. Mother rushed me to Dad's clinic. He looked at me and stitched up the wound over my right eye. I complained the next day of floaters and blind spots in my right eye. Mother, Dad, and I visited his friend, ophthalmologist Dr. Abraham Kaminsky, who diagnosed the problem as a detached retina. Back in those days, eye surgery was just coming to the frontiers of more advanced optic care and surgery. Dad had picked Kaminsky for a reason. Back in Moscow, they'd known each other at the Medical School Hospital and also in the camps. The Russians had been pioneering laser research, as were their counterparts in the U.S., but mainly for military ambitions. Kaminsky was able to use one for his medical research when the generals didn't need it.

"How do you want me to proceed?" Abraham asked Dad.

"I trust in your research," was Dad's answer, knowing what it would mean.

They explained to me that a relatively new treatment for this involved enhanced light waves that could be projected through my damaged eye. Part of my retina had been knocked loose from back of the eye, making me blind in one corner of my otherwise perfectly round retina. Abraham had had some success with pigs and lambs, using the laser to re-affix the section by fusing it to the back of the eyeball. It was done under a local, and was less invasive than surgery under general anesthetic. It was 1958, and this procedure had not yet been sanctioned by the American Medical Association nor approved by the Federal Food and Drug Administration.

Dad nodded that he advocated it. I agreed. The drops of anesthetic were instilled in my eye after my pupils were dilated. I couldn't see once the pupils stopped constricting. Then Mother came in. She had known Abraham as well, but from another place: Dachau. He had the numbers tattooed on his right arm. It was a bond from a club no one ever wanted to join.

Dad left the room for a few moments, leaving Mother with me and Dr. Kaminsky. I could hear Mother talking and I heard her writing on a piece of paper. The nurses wheeled heavy equipment into the room so the conversation was difficult to discern. They talked a little longer, and both cried.

"Is the blind spot in the same place?" Dad asked.

"Exactly. I hit my head on a bulkhead in the galley of the boat when it rocked suddenly in the harbor. I didn't think anything about it. I'd had a headache anyway from those rum punches with the Callaways." That I was under a lot of stress and not sleeping much, I didn't need to tell Dad. Hobson's phone call was on my mind. He probably was hiding many of the same fears and worries as I, and didn't want to burden me.

Dr. Louis Sherman of the V.I. Medical Clinic for Eye, Ear, Nose and Throat Disorders, examined my eye with his refracting instruments. A native-born Virgin Islander who'd trained in Miami, he was young, lanky, and affable. He jumped back while peering into my eyes. Dad and I were startled by his reaction, and more than a little concerned.

"You know, doctors, I'd heard about the early days of laser eye surgery with primitive equipment. There were a handful of pioneers who have given us so much technology. Some of them were, well, how should I say it, Lone Rangers in the Wild West of medicine. Rebels. There was a medical establishment who felt they had to preserve the status quo that was traditional eye surgery. Some of them felt threatened when these renegades experimented with their laser *toys*. It was too easy, too non-medical. Maybe, *too effective*. Ironically, with laser and other refractive eye surgery, it was the single greatest boost to their profession ever, not to mention to their pocketbooks."

"Why the history lesson?" I asked.

"Well, you have a slight detachment of the retina in its upper right corner. Looks like you had some prior repair using a laser. As I was saying, some of these pioneering laser doctors had to stand up to the establishment and, well, their egos sometimes got the better of them."

"Meaning?" Dad interrupted.

"Some of these loose-cannon laser doctors flaunted their abilities and let vanity get the better of them," Sherman said. "They actually signed their work. They would put their initials, or even a happy face icon, on the back of the patient's eye. It was placed outside the outer rim of the circular retina, in a non-visual corner of the eye. Of course, the patient would be unaware of this."

He went on. "By signing their work, they could brag they'd already been there, done that, and fixed eyes by laser long before it caught on with the current doctor. They would inscribe a date to annoy the next examining doctor as a Johnny-come-lately. It was a sort of a trademark or ego scorecard, if you like. Some licenses were lost and some progress in lasers set back. This, despite the fact it really did no medical damage at all, was unprofessional."

"Does my son have Dr. Kaminsky's initials?" Father asked.

"Not exactly. I'll shoot an optic photo of the retina."

Dad and I looked at the photo. It was a large, white moon with blood vessels. The upper right corner hung down like a sagging curtain. In the circular rim of my visual field was inscribed the words, *ewig u. immer*. Dr. Sherman said, "That's it. Mean anything to you?" Dad and I looked at each other; Dr. Sherman could see we understood its significance. Sherman asked if I was ready? I nodded, and with a blinding flash of light and sound of an exploding shutter, my retina was *zapped* back up. He put a patch on my eye, making me feel like a pirate, and I thanked him. Quietly, Dad and I thanked Mother.

****

Alexa returned to her office building the next night. The garage was empty, except for her car. The rain started, heavy sheets like only the tropical latitudes have. Some birds in the recesses above her car ruffled their feathers dry, and their sounds made her think someone was shaking out an umbrella. It startled her. She scanned the garage to make sure she was alone.

She had a black flashlight and a large empty canvas sack she'd brought from home. The building was too small to justify full-time security. There was a security service that did periodic drive-bys. The halls were vacant.

She came to the door of Triton Pharmaceuticals. The name now had more significance. Did the name have any other meaning? If Alan's mother had named it, there would be little doubt. His mother couldn't resist an opportunity at a *double entendre*. Was Alan the mythic merman Triton sounding a trumpet warning with his work?

Alexa couldn't make sense of this line of thought. Maybe it would be clearer on the other side of the door. She examined it for alarms, and then peered through the glass door. Her flashlight revealed no key code panel near the door, just the receptionist's office. She tried to turn the knob, but it was locked. She thought she'd heard something moving inside, but chalked it up to the sound of the rain.

She took a screwdriver from her bag. The air conditioning kicked on and masked some of the noise she was making. Since her office was already broken into, another office break-in would absolve her from involvement.

She jammed the screwdriver with the force of her palm, between the door and its frame. Using her body for force against its handle, she pried the door from its lock. The door flung open faster than she'd anticipated, slamming into the doorstop behind it. The noise announced that she was no cat burglar. It was surprising that Alan had only one lock. She could see industrial espionage was not his concern.

Using her flashlight, she wandered the reception area. The reception desk was neat with a computer and telephone. There was only one line for the phone. The computer was not the most modern type, and the desk, an inexpensive screw-together. A plastic plant hung from the ceiling and a dusty silk plant stood on the floor next to the waiting room chair, looking deader than it actually was. When she'd first visited Alan's lab, she hadn't realized how flimsy it was. Alan certainly wasn't trying to impress anyone.

The file cabinets were unlocked. She opened a drawer and saw a file of invoices and shipping statements. Some had letterhead from Oesterreichisches Zeugnisse, Grabel's company. The invoices were for fungal media. She noted types I, II, IVa, but no type IVb. She didn't know if this was significant, but put them in her sack anyway. There was another file with utility and rent bills. Very few business forms relating to Alan's research were in evidence.

Alexa sought the real files that this international lab must have. She expected to find incubating equipment, microscopes, culture dishes, employee locker rooms, bathrooms, and various testing rooms with chemicals and testing equipment. Storage for his fungi and algae would require cabinets at certain temperatures, and that meant incubation. She opened the door from the reception area, and it led to Alan's private office. A large desk with a modest chair behind it looked pretty basic. Not even a library to impress his clients and staff. There were no signs anyone worked here. This bare office must lead to a more impressive facility through the door to the right of the desk.

She opened the door and peered into a large empty room with commercial carpeting, bare walls, no electric outlets, and a tiled acoustical ceiling. The space was exactly as Alan rented it. This was no lab; this was a front. She felt like a patsy in a dangerous charade. People, maybe hundreds in Haifa, were dying.

Where was Alan manufacturing his pharmaceuticals? It had to be a sizable facility. True, she'd seen vials of Manchineel Alan had on *Vanity Fare*; they were small. But packaging for transport around the world involved a minimal lab and some employees to run it.

Had Alan's company been illegally producing toxins all this time? Was she just a convenient attorney who could be duped by his clandestine operation? And for what purpose? Was it a coincidence that *she* found him?

Was she part of a terrorist cell that was involved in the Middle East? Why did an FBI agent turn up floating near Alan's sailboat? Why were Sanger and Yorel so suspicious of Alan? What was Lobel really doing in St. Thomas, and what did Alan really know about *The Circle*? Had his visits to that restaurant in Graz been just for paprika shish kabob, or for the meetings?

A light flashed into Alexa's eyes, blinding her. Its beam seemed to pierce past her eyes into her brain. She couldn't make out a figure. There was a folding chair in the room's far corner and she presumed someone was quietly sitting in it watching her all this time. A fire appeared within the beam of the light.

"Please turn off your torch." A deep voice said. She didn't recognize it. The fire was a match to light a cigar. She turned her flashlight off; torch was British for flashlight. His accent was British, but didn't sound native. He turned his torch off giving her eyes a chance to adjust to the darkness.

"While I did not expect to meet you so soon, I am glad for this opportunity to discuss things with you." He inhaled the cigar smoke; she was getting lightheaded from both fear and smoke. Fortunately, the air conditioning came on. Alexa stood there, unable to adjust her eyes to see to whom the voice belonged.

"As you have discovered, our Dr. Becker has little activity at his laboratory, don't you agree?" The cigar's embers provided a faint light for Alexa to try and discern the identity of the man seated before her. He might be wearing a dark suit and white-collar shirt, but the gathering smoke obscured her view. She *did* notice the umbrella on the floor beside him. His leather shoes were either highly polished or wet; they reflected a little of the streetlight making it through the rain rushing at the tinted windows to his right.

"There is much about Dr. Becker you don't know. I don't know him well at all. I have often wondered if anyone really does know him. But, Ms. Grey, my concerns are with what is here now. There is an item that you are aware of. This item is the reason for my visit. I couldn't find it in your offices or in Dr. Becker's. You wouldn't know its location, would you?"

Alexa assumed he meant the medical records and photos. "I don't know what you're talking about."

"That is not a true statement. You made a distinct effort to *pretend* to have them and they were taken by one of my associates."

Alexa had to think, but it didn't take her long. The Rastafarian. She could see the connection now, and she felt very threatened by this man in the dark. She was trying to buy time to think.

"He took that file illegally from my hotel room. I should report him; and you, if you don't leave here immediately." It was a stupid threat. She didn't need to see his face to know he must have been amused. But, she had to continue saying *something*.

"I was not aware of the contents of the case. I was only following my client's explicit instructions." Alexa was sweating. She fished in her pockets for her key chain. On it, she had pepper spray attached in a leather pouch.

She ran for the door with her canvas sack slung over her shoulder and through Alan's office. He was upon her in the dark; tall and powerful. Her purse was still on her left arm. She tried to hit him with the flashlight, but missed and he broke it free from her right hand, hurting her. She fumbled with her left hand, desperate to find the pepper spray. He struggled to get her away from the glass front door.

She broke free and fell to the floor. She pulled her left hand from her pocket. Her keys jingled as she freed them from her pocket. He was upon her with his full weight. She couldn't get her spray free of his grip, and he managed to tear it from her aching hand. He tossed it aside with her keys, jingling to the floor. Then he stood up behind her and tried to drag her towards the inner office. Alexa's neck and ankles hurt. He reeked of cigar smoke. Where was the cigar? It was a potential weapon.

The screwdriver in her sack would work. But she had lost her sack. As her assailant tried to lift and drag her deeper into the office for privacy, she swung her feet around searching for the sack. She felt it and its contents. Deep inside she reached at the last chance she'd have to get it with her free right arm. She felt for the screwdriver, but found something better.

She let the man lift her, appearing to cooperate with him. Once on her feet, she swung around. It connected with his head, on the right side of his temple, sending him flying with a howl, to her left. She was strong enough to overcome his grip, once the winch handle cracked his skull. Alan was right about one thing: A sailor's best friend is the always-available winch handle; it was a heavy, solid piece of chromed stainless steel. When swung with just a little speed, enough centrifugal force was created to dent a tank. It had the additional advantage of being a familiar object in the islands, so customs officials easily overlooked it.

The assailant's blood had sprayed her face and chest. He lay motionless. She fumbled around the floor to find her purse and the sack, her lost shoe, and her keys, and then fled. She limped to the front door. There was a flashlight in the hall.

The light moved as if searching for something. Was this security or was this an *associate* of her assailant? She couldn't be sure, so she stayed inside. The security guard must have noticed her car in the garage. This had to be the guard. She peered down the hall through the lab's front glass door, and saw the light in her office turn on.

If she ran to the elevator, she'd alert him when the motor started to move the elevator car. Was he coming back to take the elevator himself, or did he take the stairs? She hadn't heard the elevator motor, but she was defending herself in a brawl at the time. She opened the door to the lab and quietly, but quickly, moved to the stairs at the other end of the hall.

She made it to the garage. She opened the steel door that echoed a screeching sound. Where was her assailant's car? Had she killed him? Should she report this right now to the police? To not have checked his status, or at least notify the police after she was safe, would look guilty as hell.

The D.A.'s question would be, "So, Ms. Grey, you assaulted the mysterious person in the head, his blood all over you, he falls to the ground, he isn't moving, you fled the scene of the attack. You had a cell phone. Yet you didn't call the police, scream for help, find the security guard, honk your car horn. Why, why, why? Were you hiding something? Please explain to the judge and jury what you were doing in Dr. Becker's office. Did it not appear to you to be a front for something other than what it was? Aren't you his attorney for his business affairs? Does he or doesn't he make fungal materials for terrorist attacks? Didn't you know what he was doing? Was the man alive or dead when you left?"

Decisions had to be made. She jumped into her car and locked the doors. She felt safer. She turned the car on. As she shifted into drive, the staircase door flung open. A man, her assailant, staggered into the garage. His face was crimson with blood from head to neck. He limped in her direction. Thank God, she thought. Now she had an alibi of why she needed to run. He was alone, and, she checked her rearview mirror. There was no security guard in sight. She changed the gear to reverse and revved the vehicle in the opposite direction. The tires smoked; the birds scattered, flying out into the thunderstorm.

He had something in his hand: her screwdriver. He grasped it like a knife. The only part of his face not covered in blood were his eyes. They were fixed on her and determined. She continued revving the tires, creating a horrible smelling smoke that engulfed him. Before she slammed the gearshift into drive, she realized something.

She scanned the eaves and corners of the garage. There wasn't a bird left. Alexa wasn't looking for birds, though; she was looking for cameras. She didn't see any. What she'd done up to now was deniable, defensible, reasonable. The presence of her fingerprints in the lab was of no concern; she was, after all, Dr. Becker's attorney and should have visited there frequently. Why she hadn't, she couldn't answer.

The man left a trail of blood. He was alive and wouldn't want to identify himself to the police. He was desperate, foreign, and probably with a suspicious record. No, he had a mission, an obsession. This was a snag he hadn't foreseen. He'd toss the screwdriver and make good his escape.

She had no idea *who* Alan was. Were his father and Amy, who seemed so admirable, complicit in his affairs and deceptions? Was the OZ lab producing for Triton?

Her apartment was off limits, as Alan had suggested. She'd turned her phone back on. She would tell Alan what had happened here, but only when the time was right, when she could catch him vulnerable and off guard. Information in this affair was like peeling the layers off an onion, like her mother used to say: It smells worse with each layer. Alexa added: and each layer makes you want to cry more.

****

"Hobson, Alan Becker here." I had her phone number from my cell phone's caller ID.

"Yes, Dr. Becker."

"Your partner, Fielding, have you determined where he might have died yet?"

"Why do you ask?"

Ever the cop. No answers, just questions.

She continued, "He was on an assignment for me involving this case. I can't be more exact."

"Could you tell me where you had sent him?"

"You already know he was poisoned, don't you, from your friends in the British Virgins. It was medically done, intravenously. Cyanide. There were signs of torture prior to death, by someone with a solid knowledge of human anatomy. He was tortured by a doctor."

"You still haven't said where you think he died, or where you sent him to investigate."

"Both were the same place." I knew and feared what she was about to say. "The Bougainvillea Clinic. But you already knew that, didn't you, Doctor?"

CHAPTER 23

Diplomatic Philosophy

Alexa had bedded down at the local Hyatt; she slept a troubled sleep. She had been dreaming of Alan, his family, their history, and their secrets. She was afraid of what the next layer would reveal. She awoke at sunrise, in a sweat, and headed for the shower. After she dressed, she called me.

"Where have you been? I've been worried sick." I said.

"I am at a hotel, as you instructed."

"I've moved Dr. Langer and Amy to a safe place. Are you all right?"

"I had a surprise visitor at Triton last night. I'm in better shape than he is, thanks to your universal sailor's weapon. He ransacked my office. Yours, too. How are you?"

I wondered how far she went into my offices. "I'm fine. Are you okay? You sound distant."

"You've been *less than candid* with me," she said.

"Look, I know a half-truth is just a lie. You're in enough danger without getting in any deeper."

"I'm scared, confused, but essentially, okay. Any news on your end?"

"I've talked to Hobson of the FBI, and pieces are beginning to fit together. Our European friends will press us for the records. They are becoming violent. Oh, by the way, I have discovered that my true value in life to Mother may have been as treasure map. Can't be certain, but I'll be investigating this soon. Just thought you'd like to know."

Alexa was smart enough to place the call by landline to Alan's cell phone.

She resolved to meet Alan half way, figuratively, giving him a lot more leeway than he deserved.

"Okay, let's say for a minute that what you have been telling me is true, although I'm not convinced of that. Then I need to know what we're dealing with. Right now, it looks like your main goal should be to stay alive," Alexa said.

She felt better extending him a modicum of trust. After all, he did warn her away from their offices.

"Alan, you seem to have become a lightning rod this last week for air wrecks, floating bodies, maritime crashes, a mysterious fungal toxin dispersal in the Middle East, former SS Nazis, and medical war criminals with a streak of sadism. Did I tell you that the party I met last night during my encounter in your lab was an associate of my hotel visitor on St. Croix? He got your message, and didn't like what it said, or what it didn't say. Tried to take me somewhere, maybe to dinner or a morgue. I wasn't going to wait around to find out which."

"Hence, the winch handle. Right tool for the right job." She was lightening up a bit. "Did you recognize him?"

"No, it was too dark. He tried to escort me to my car, but he was covered in blood so I couldn't see his face. He had some curious questions about you and family relations."

"You forgot to mention one thing that could identify him."

"The DNA from his blood?"

"No."

"I can't think of what else could identify him, considering we were in the dark?"

"You didn't mention he smoked a cigar." Her silence confirmed it. A shiver traveled through my body. For years I had buried these suspicions. I was just another Jew who had been duped into a shower.

****

Alexa felt better after talking to Alan. She had more questions about the source of his income, activities with fungi and toxins, and where he produced his antitoxins. Why did he need a front of an office, if he was legitimate? Alan knew Alexa was only pacified for now. It would have to do.

"Stay where you are. You're safer there. Don't talk to anyone. I'm only a phone call away." Alan said before disconnecting.

The onion peeling was a little less painful for Alexa. Not a tear today. She took a couple of aspirin and decided to walk to the Bayfront Harborside area for a fresh breeze.

She bought an ice cream cone. After she paid for it, two men approached her. They looked like they belonged in Miami with their splashy print shirts, shorts, and sandals. Their sunglasses were less fashionable, but they weren't teenagers.

"Nice wind," Sanger opened, as he noted her scarf fluttering in the breeze.

She nodded and licked her ice cream. Where was her pepper spray? Or her winch handle?

"We have a conversation that you will find interesting, and provide you with answers. We are offering this, because we need you to help us. Dr. Becker has been less than candid with you."

Alexa noted his use of the expression less than candid, so she knew they'd just been listening to this morning's telephone conversation with Alan. How did this Israeli know where her safe house was and be able to tap her landline so fast? She wondered if the FBI was this good.

BBC news reported that Haifa suffered over two hundred and fifty deaths; Israel had declared a state of martial law. This dominated the news until another bulletin followed. Six Italian nationals were detained in Lod Airport, Tel Aviv, under suspicion of involvement in the Haifa attack. The Red Brigade formed in the sixties was funded by international leftist interests, allegedly by Kaddafi in Libya. Interrogation would provide some clues; they like to tell their stories for recognition and publicity. Murder charges were of little concern to them, nor was a firing squad.

"I'll go with you under the condition that the site be public and have cocktails. I am armed, you should know, and dangerous." She was bluffing, but they agreed, feigning fear.

"Your visitor last night can attest to that. You, how do you say it, *crowned him*, pretty good. He looked a mess when we spotted him in the garage. You did the right thing. We sent help to you from one of our staff, but he mistakenly looked in *your* office, not Dr. Becker's. He was a young fellow, dressed as a security guard, and was well armed. Say, was that a club you hit him with or what?"

Alexa knew she was in their debt. They seemed to be more on top of things than anyone else, including Alan.

"We have arrived," Yorel said. They stood in front of the patio of a Cuban restaurant with a view of the harbor, its boats, a Salsa band issuing lively music, and young people in their minimal sports wear. Two gentlemen were already seated. They also wore horn-rimmed sunglasses, but were older, more formal looking. They even wore ties that made them look like salesmen, in casual south Florida.

Yorel helped Alexa to her seat.

She finished her ice cream cone and sat, acknowledging Yorel's help. Sanger joined Yorel on the other side of the table. The other two gentlemen smiled at her.

"We are glad you assented to this conversation, Ms. Grey. I am Director General Levi Herschel of the Israeli Embassy here in Miami. To my left is Dr. Elie Corso, of the Corso Institute."

She acknowledged them, "*Shalom.*"

Yorel and Sanger ordered iced tea, as did Alexa. The two elderly gentlemen were already sipping tea, but hot lemon tea, like in the old country. She wondered what the Corso Institute stood for, but decided to listen instead of talk.

"You are an attorney, are you not?" the diplomat asked.

She nodded, as if this were new information to him.

"You are from Kansas, are you not?" Again, Alexa nodded.

"It is ironic, don't you agree, that we have a factory in Graz called OZ under surveillance?"

He didn't see her laugh, so he guessed she already made this connection.

"Now." His tone was far more grave. "Have you ever wondered about the source of your Dr. Becker's wealth?"

"I'm listening."

"You're clearly very bright, so I won't patronize you with the obvious. If he distributes his antitoxin serum for fish poisoning to the countries that need it the most, and, of course, these equatorial regions are invariably third world countries that can't afford the luxury of curing their sick children from food poisoning, then from where is the money coming, I ask you, Ms. Grey?" His tone was almost accusatory. This was a public place. She was satisfied she was safe knowing the professions of these men. Where they were going with this line of questioning, however, she wasn't certain.

"You have an American expression, no? Always to follow the money to find your answers."

"I've heard it," she said. Corso nodded like a sycophant, always bobbing his head in agreement with the ambassador or counsel general, or whoever he alleged he was.

"The money, in this case, is arriving from outside sources of untraceable origins. Switzerland is a source that always arouses a degree of suspicion. Of course, this situation is usually of no concern to Israel's policies and resources. Two things are of tantamount concern, however, with regards to Dr. Becker's activities. His research involves new and unique fungal toxins that seem to be spreading from a mosque in Haifa. More than two hundred and fifty people have died, and two thousand more are showing respiratory and neurological symptoms. They are expected to lose their battle within the next three days." He let this sink in, looking to Dr. Corso for confirmation of his accuracy in relating this. Alexa assumed the doctor was of the Israeli Medical Corps in some way.

"Also, Dr. Becker's source of income is cloaked in considerable secrecy. Millions arrive in Swiss bank accounts every week, and the deposits are not related to exporting any product. This is the most surprising fact of all." Alexa could see his point. He continued.

"As you can imagine, our intelligence put two and two together, but four never comes up, you see. Dr. Becker is our question mark. Is he somehow responsible for the attack? I can't say no. Motive? I don't know. Source of his bank accounts? Don't know. Where the product is manufactured, as you can now concur, is certainly not his Miami laboratory." He was sweating, but appeared sincere.

Alexa took a moment to think of some plausible explanation. She believed Alan was not responsible for the poison gas dispersal in Haifa. She told them exactly that.

The diplomat responded, "And you know this because..." His voice dropped off. He took his palms off the table and lifted them upwards, as if to heaven. The quizzical look on his face was almost comical. In some ways, Herschel reminded her of Alan's father, warm and wise, with manners and wit. But the diplomat could bare his cold side when the situation warranted; she wondered if Alan's father had the same ability to turn to ice in a second.

"Because of women's intuition." She knew how ridiculous this sounded. It was certainly not something these Israelis could rely on to keep their homeland safe. They spoke to each other in Hebrew, trying to translate *women's intuition* into Hebrew. Apparently, they caucused and had a consensus of opinion on the matter.

"This sixth sense you women assert you have, can often be wrong, can it not?" Dr. Corso spoke for the first time. He was short and rotund, well manicured, and smelled as if he'd bathed in cologne. His line of a mustache and bleached teeth made him look a little glamorous, like a movie producer.

Alexa was an attorney; she could turn icy, too. "I agree, but let's stick to the facts. One, Dr. Becker has little motive for disgracing his faith and his people by supplying terrorists in any form. His history should clarify that, no intuition is needed. He loves the freedom few can appreciate having come from the same background as you, Doctor, judging by the numbers on your right forearm."

The diplomat and the doctor made no effort to hide their camp numbers.

"Two, Dr. Becker is devoted and brilliant, but doesn't have a political mind. Although his father taught him never to forget the past, resurrecting that mass treachery you allude to with this poison attack is not compatible with his beliefs. One Holocaust is enough for any lifetime, as only its victims could know firsthand. Dr. Becker's father drove this message home so well, it affected his son so much, that the young man became tormented to the point of illness from emotionally reliving the horror that was Dachau." She had made the desired impression on her inquisitors. "No, he is a man of peace. That is not women's intuition; those are the facts."

The men spoke Hebrew again. Alexa couldn't believe that, after being so mad at Alan, she had defended him. Well, she was his attorney, after all.

Herschel spoke first. "We agree that his products have been effective, free of charge, and have rendered the equatorial food fish supply safe for the children of third world countries. The record shows that. Yet, we must be wary of people and how they can change. We told you: large amounts of funds go in and out of his Swiss accounts; accounts that you are apparently not aware of." She had to agree, but tried not to show that what he said was true. "Where did Dr. Becker get the money? We must also consider that money in such large quantities can corrupt even the most ethical of men, wouldn't you agree?" He didn't wait for her reply.

Dr. Corso spoke Hebrew to the diplomat. With a wave of his hand, his superior cleared him to speak freely to me.

"Ms. Alexa, your name has Greek background, does it not?"

Alexa nodded. Her family had immigrated from Greece. They worked as cooks on a chuck wagon train, to pay their way to the Midwest seeking farmland to grow corn.

"Do you know of Triton?"

"Yes, the mythical half man, half fish. Poseidon's son."

"He blew his conch shell to warn all the fish in Poseidon's realm of his coming. But he instilled fear in his subjects, not love. This was an effective way to rule, don't think?"

"Apparently it worked for him, but he was only a myth."

"It worked for the Nazis, and, I assure you, they were no myth. They have recently announced their daring and resolve. With the European Union's elections coming in three months time among seven of the twenty-one NATO nations, they feel the time has come. They seek to link with their past before the old guard passes on. Old names and faces that we thought were buried were surgically altered and have new identities."

Dr. Corso looked serious now, like a multimillion-dollar movie he produced had just flopped. "I am not a doctor in the same sense as your Dr. Becker. My doctorate is in philosophy, political especially, and strategies to combat philosophies in politics than are anti-human, anti-freedom, anti-Jewish. There is a group that is guilty of all three of these crimes of political thought and action. I believe you know its name."

"Der Kreis or *The Circle*," Alexa said. It was then she began to understand these people's fears for their people and their land.

"This terrorist attack in Haifa, is there something pointing you towards Dr. Becker? Something that's not in the news reports, something that I am not privy to?"

"Yes." Again, Hebrew chatter. Then silence settled on the table. Yorel and Sanger handed a paper to the diplomat.

He, in turn, handed it to Alexa to read for herself. It was obviously in English, but deciphered, for it was a privileged communiqué of diplomatic status. She was impressed with its format.

> Haifa task force report 22:26 Zulu time. Att: priority 1, clearance; sig: data Steiner, S. Det. CDI, authorization, alpha RE: gas source, determ from interrog. Red Brigade subj. #3, confirms source as St. Tho. U.S. Virgin Isl. Dr. Fritz Langer/Amy Luger. Corroborated witness #6 and verified, authenticity code high probability. Admits Kreis, #3 #6 also, Icon on back both subjects, circle scar, corner missing; action immed. Needed report to follow. #3 #6 confirm, <u>No treatment available</u>, subsequent attacks expected soon, site unknown,

repeat, unknown, according to #3 #6
confirmed. Recordings to follow.
Conclusion: Target: Put Source One
in Pot, Stop, Beta source evaporate.
Nightingale evaporate, Venus to be
in Pot. Act priority, Tel Aviv, send:
Abraham #3342 verified. Received.
End/////

Alexa must have looked faint. What concerned her was the source of the message. Why were Alan's father and Amy involved in this? She hated to confirm their fears and theories, but this did ring true. *Alan's lab was not the source.* This she had confirmed firsthand. Could it be that his father was using the IVb medium, via Alan's lab address, to settle his own bitter, if not misguided, scores? But then why the Haifa mosque? Certainly a man of medicine could no sooner perpetrate a mass murder like his Nazi masters in the camps, than slay his own child or wife. Was there a misguided madness in the father, and was Alan's mental depression somehow running in his genes?

She had more questions than answers for the four men.

"I will be perfectly frank. I think the intelligence that you've shared with me is accurate. I know that took risks showing it to a civilian with no security clearance. I don't have the same vested interest in your nation's welfare, not like a Jewish person or an Israeli citizen would." She needed them to believe her sincerity, to buy time.

"As for the source of the toxin, I don't know. I've never been to the clinic. I see no motive for Dr. Langer and Amy to conduct such a crime against humanity, do you?" She wished she hadn't asked that rhetorical question, for she wanted to control this cordial conversation, but there it was.

Dr. Corso responded. "Who knows the mind of the aged doctor? Is he bitter about being robbed of his hospital teaching position in

Moscow, or robbed of his youth? Perhaps he's enraged at the horrible things he'd been compelled to do during the War? This is no ordinary doctor, Ms. Alexa, this is the famous Dr. Georg Becker, as you well know. His wife is gone, his son suffers from schizophrenia. I know, as a survivor myself, that we suffer the guilt of the living. Why us, why do we live, while thousands died?"

He was getting emotional and knew it was out of order here. "Ms. Alexa, Dr. Georg Becker has anger enough to last more than one lifetime. Maybe he thinks about suicide one day, instead of making believe. He is a man of passion. Sometimes, in the Middle East, we see such men of extreme passions become the terrorists we must defend ourselves against." Alexa believed Dr. Corso was more than a political philosopher; he was a humanist.

Alexa could see that Dr. Corso had a lot of questions to answer. These Israelis might need to be radical, even violent, to achieve their ends. *They needed to act upon the intelligence they had.* The cipher transmission made it clear that a subsequent attack was imminent, but *the site unknown.* Alexa broke the silence that hung over the patio table. She was worried about the future. She was alarmed by their desperation in revealing a top-secret communiqué from the embassy.

Alexa tried to analyze the message. "The cipher refers to *Source One* which commander S. Steiner recommends to *Pot.* I assume that means to kidnap, control, and interrogate Dr. Langer, who is also known as Dr. Georg Becker. He must be the source of the toxic material. The IVb was consigned to him and confirmed by the interrogation of captured Red Brigade men." No one answered. She knew she was right.

"The Beta source sounds like Alan Becker and the associate Amy Luger is Nightingale, as in Nurse Florence, to be evaporated." She didn't like that recommendation. Judging by their lack of response, she wasn't certain if they would take the cipher's advice. She knew she had to help Alan, Amy, and his father clear their names.

By letting her read the cipher, were they hoping she would act on their behalf? Their strategy involved a degree of trust. Back in

Israel, deaths were mounting. The clinic was on U.S. territorial soil making it difficult to assault. That was it! She'd convinced them of her sincerity, and introduced enough doubt that they would give these people a chance to either clear or hang themselves.

"You didn't mention the other name in the cipher, Ms. Grey," the diplomat noted.

"Venus would be the Greek Goddess and the code name for me." Turning to Dr. Corso with a smile, she said, "And thank you for the compliment."

He smiled. She hoped these guys weren't planning to *pot* or *evaporate* her anytime soon.

CHAPTER 24

Birds

Station Chief Derek Sweeney, along with Fielding's replacement, Special Agent Jameson, received the call from Washington to drive down to the hangar at Scholes Airfield, Galveston for a closed briefing. The National Transportation and Safety Board report on the *Hirotu–Wet Dream* encounter was complete.

The six members of the NTSB sat in the hangar, with the parts of the disassembled sailboat and keel to their left. A large projection screen was rolled up above their heads; coffee and rolls were on a long table to their right. All wore their departmental uniforms indicating their ranks and affiliations with various bureaus. They faced over thirty agents and bureaucrats of various state and federal agencies who needed to add the final facts of the investigation's findings to their own files for closure. Everyone entering the hangar was handed a security badge by armed National Guardsmen.

Three official photographers from the Defense Department finished their pictures for release to the media. A speaker convened the meeting. Jameson and Sweeney drank their coffee, and read through the summary of the briefing in their folders. Not until thirty minutes into the program, did one of the speakers finally address something of relevance to the FBI.

This new speaker came from somewhere offstage, not part of NTSB He tapped the microphone, waking his audience. He was young, handsome, with a dark complexion, a mustache, and sideburns a little longer than regulation. He reminded Sweeney of the singer Marc Anthony. There was no sign of a Puerto Rican accent when he spoke, but Sweeney suspected it was there somewhere when he let his guard down.

"Good morning," Hector LeBron said. "I'm a surveillance specialist in the Helix department of the NSA. We have come to the reason for this briefing of the investigation of this affair on such short notice. In light of events in Haifa, Israel, special facts of this case have made it necessary to accelerate what might be the communication of new information to our security departments at FBI, Homeland, and the Coast Guard."

"Sure took him a lot of words to say that," Jameson said to Sweeney. For the first time in two years, Sweeney had a phone call from his daughter Kelly. She revealed that she'd recently had a baby with her boyfriend, and they were coming to town. Sweeney didn't know whether to be grateful or angry. They agreed to meet in Galveston, since he was heading there on business anyway. When they'd met at the restaurant down the pier from the airport in Galveston, he couldn't let go of her and his new grandson. He'd brought a camera just in case she disappeared again.

Sweeney put them up at the Galvez Hotel, with an ocean view. The boyfriend had not arrived, but would be coming tomorrow with the U-Haul. The hotel was overbooked with hundreds of college kids celebrating some college sport championship. He felt a little more whole now that Kelly had returned. He didn't look forward to explaining all this to her mother, who'd finally left him from the stress and guilt associated with her disappearance. She partially blamed Sweeney for Kelly's disappearance and his inability to find her, dead or alive. He'd deal with the boyfriend another time.

LeBron continued, "I have been asked to coordinate certain phone conversations that I've been monitoring at Helix with aerial surveillance intel collected yesterday. I flew here a couple of hours ago, and we're still receiving real-time data." He nodded to his assistant in the back of the hangar, who dimmed the lights. A giant projection screen rolled down next to him from the ceiling, with the hum of a servomotor.

A media projector illuminated the first image. It was live action. The numbers at the bottom right had times and dates and he recognized this type of photo as many he'd seen in Quantico, Virginia, at the FBI Academy. It was a surveillance satellite transmission, recently recorded. It reminded him of the live action photos taken from Fighting Falcons, Tomcats, and Stealth fighters during bombing runs in the Gulf Wars, showing smart bombs surgically destroying enemy targets with minimal collateral damage. These pictures had a video game feel to them. They showed neither blood nor death. One watched them dispassionately, secure in the illusion that only the bad guys were being incinerated. No one else would be hurt, maimed, incinerated, or orphaned.

LeBron pointed his red laser at a picture of the keel of Wet Dream lying unguarded in the security yard at this airfield. Sweeney relived his anger of a week ago when Fielding told him that the keel had gone missing. Now he felt a little guilty at having shouted in a rage at Fielding, whose funeral he'd just attended two days ago. The autopsy showed Fielding had suffered multiple facial fractures, electrocution burns, non-surgical skin tearing, and ultimately, the asphyxiation of cyanide poisoning. Sweeney knew he had to focus on the trail he had before him to find the person or persons who committed such atrocities on his agent. He consciously forced his interest to the live action spy satellite, or *bird*, feeding them a Peeping Tom's view of the keel.

Everyone watched the video of the hollowed out mystery keel sitting in the security holding lot, and then being moved to scanning and sniffing by Homeland. It lay there along with some car wrecks, an airplane wing, and many boxes and crates. The keel's central cavity was sealed and caulked shut. There wasn't anything visible, coming out or going inside. Then a flatbed truck, the type that the Coast Guard used to move heavy loads, and two men used its heavy crane to lift the keel from its dock site, lower it onto the flatbed, and drive away.

"Our bird was focused on the two subjects. Watch now." The keel was moved to a remote end of the airfield, near a small motel. Both men wore large caps concealing their identities, parked the truck, and got out. Then they did something very odd. They walked away from the keel, to the motel. Jameson had heard about Sweeney blasting Fielding about the lost keel. Seemed like it was all about nothing. Maybe whatever they thought they'd hide in that keel's secret compartment didn't show up, or was confiscated.

The next video was taken from the motel's security camera. The images taken from behind the check-in counter were clearer. The two men approached the motel. They were wearing olive green workmen's uniforms and oversized caps. No company name or logo was visible on the uniforms.

One subject was tall and dark-skinned, the other shorter and perhaps Asian. The tall man was carrying a large, silvery-steel piece of luggage, like a professional cameraman would use, larger than a brief case and appeared to be heavy. The other man carried a small black metal lunch box. The next segment showed the two men walking to a white Ford Taurus in the front of the motel, as seen through the glass front doors. Then they drove away, both in the front seat.

LeBron said, "What you've just seen was taken one hour ago, and I now have live feed coming from a bird in thirty seconds as it passes over our target area for scanning, so be patient." The wait was brief. Static noise, then the empty screen came alive with snowy pictures that abruptly cleared to show the roofs of the Island of Galveston with Scholes Field in the center. Jameson wanted to go outside to smoke a cigarette, but knew Sweeney would see him on the surveillance pictures now feeding here. He could see both of their cars parked in the hangar parking area for VIPs.

LeBron used his laser pointer as he spoke. With the joystick on his lectern, he could move the satellite's camera. Jameson was impressed by the technology that empowered LeBron to move a camera instantaneously, sixty-five miles high in space. From what he could see, LeBron's earpiece was giving him real-time information from a third party, about where he should direct the bird's eye in the sky. Then, everyone saw where the director of the operation was; the bird's view revealed a helicopter tracking a white Ford Taurus on the Historic Strand's main street in the Old Warehouse district of Galveston. The car turned right off the Strand, towards the three mega-cruise ships docked there. All three ships were receiving throngs of passengers for an evening departure to the Caribbean.

The car stopped at the docks just ahead of the bow of the first ship.

"Why don't they just go and arrest these two and search that metal case right now?" Sweeney asked Jameson. The unauthorized removal and transport of government property like a keel from a security zone is probable cause in my book. Maybe they thought that these two would lead them to other members of the operation. Sweeney hoped the director in the helicopter would make an attack decision sooner rather than later. Sweeney would have gone in already.

Then something occurred to him. What if this keel was a diversion? There wasn't any evidence of anyone or anything inside. It might have been moved to complete the illusion that we were to look for a person or contraband. Maybe the person or thing was already here, and we were supposed to focus on the keel, rather than the real target of the operation. Hobson did a terrific job of following the evidence, but maybe it was a trail actually laid out to keep us busy. She said this mastermind was clever and playful.

Sweeney learned a lot from Hobson's insights and thoughtful, maybe feminine, angles on the case. He was grateful: she made him look good. This was a difficult case, especially for a first-time field agent, and he didn't want her getting cold feet and transferring back to a desk job. Sweeney turned his attention back to the video game of cops and suspects.

Why would someone want to make it obvious that an operation is underway? Who the hell was Mushroom, and why was he playing games with the FBI?

Suddenly, the two targets of the bird's eye in the sky were spooked as they walked to the docks near the bow of the first cruise ship. The silver case glistened in the sunlight as it was carried by one suspect. They burst into full speed, up steps leading to a docked museum ship; the restored, wooden square-rigger, *Elissa*. She was dwarfed by the cruise ships. The men jumped the turnstile, ignoring the ticket taker's shouts, and ran down a steel gangway to board the *Elissa*. Upon jumping on the deck from the ship's rails, they started climbing up her masts. The taller suspect seemed to be the more experienced climber, but either could have picked coconuts off a tree with ease.

Two dozen officers on the ground reacted as the two targets bolted for the *Elissa*.

LeBron switched his sound-feed to the speakers so we could all hear the conversation from the director of the operation. The director was in the chopper. She shouted, "Go! Go! Go! Blue Bonnet team apprehend both suspects. Hazmat and Bomb, Go Now! Alpha Tangos, back up and contain. Sea Guard orange to waterside *Elissa* ship, seal dock access."

A dozen officers at the base of the masts, their weapons aimed aloft, were shouting at the climbers. The two suspects almost reached the top and were now waving their hands in surrender. They were saying something inaudible. Jameson guessed, "Don't shoot," in whatever language they spoke.

Other officers were clearing the area around the *Elissa* of rubberneckers, should bullets start flying. The bomb squad pulled up to the scene in its black armored truck. The suspects were climbing down to the ship's deck. The silver luggage case was found in a locker near the main mast by two bomb squad technicians in Hazmat garb. The police hurried everyone away from the scene. The suspects were surrounded by police and FBI agents and handcuffed. Both were escorted off the ship.

The helicopter landed nearby. The area was being cleared of tourists who'd gathered to watch what they assumed was the filming of a movie. The report from the sniffers came back negative for toxins, explosives, biologicals, and isotopes. The director declared the site yellow, standing down from orange. The contents of the case were electronic equipment, which might be used to make a bomb. They were being analyzed, and updates would be reported. The director declared the site a *no* threat. There was a smattering of applause from the hangar.

Jameson and Sweeney looked at one another relieved. "Like a cop and robber T.V. show, huh?" Jameson said.

"With all this news coming out of Israel about toxic gas, I'm glad this just turned out to be a T.V. show," Sweeney said.

Sweeney felt better having his missing keel leading to these two suspects. They'd be interrogated and would be a source of new leads. This whole case was about bluff, cat and mouse, false leads, dead ends, fungi, and making the authorities, in general, look where Dr. Fungus, or Mr. Mushroom, wanted them to look. He or she was always one step ahead, maybe two.

Sweeney helped himself to a second cup of coffee and a roll. The first bite revealed some kind of sausage hidden within it. He hated rolls with meat in them. He turned to Jameson. "How is anyone supposed to tell if this is a plain roll or a kolache stuffed with meat? I hate the meat. I hate kolaches. I mean, what are kolaches except rolls with a frank hidden inside. If I'd wanted a frank, I'd order a frank. If I wanted a roll, I'd order a roll."

Jameson added, "I'm from New York City. We just assume anyone who wants a frank also wants a roll. They go together. Don't even have kolaches up there. Chicago does, though. Me, I like...."

Sweeney knew something wasn't quite right, he could feel it inside, and it didn't feel like his usual acid reflux. Then it came to him! He hoped he wasn't too late. He ran over to LeBron, who was still watching the screen. Agents were at the docks packing up their equipment. The helicopter was revving up, getting ready to take off.

"Stop them, stop them now, LeBron," Sweeney said, checking the speaker's nametag. "The operation, it's not over." LeBron didn't understand.

Sweeney continued, "The other suspect had a lunch box at the motel."

LeBron thought a moment and his face changed, "You're right. He sure did."

"He didn't have it when he boarded the *Elissa*, so it's gotta still be in the Taurus."

LeBron immediately called the director in the helicopter and advised her of the missing lunch box. The director acknowledged, and then started to issue orders. Sweeney and LeBron watched the screen. The helicopter aborted lift-off as they both saw on the screen.

Sweeney said, "The director needs to understand that whoever is behind this is smarter than we think. They know our operating procedures. What you are seeing is what they want you to see." There was panic in his voice for a veteran field agent.

The bomb squad and Hazmat personnel were still on the docks. The director ordered a robot to scan and sniff the Taurus. LeBron remembered seeing the lunch box. It was a small black lunch box. After twenty minutes, the robot found nothing and was withdrawn.

The bomb squad and Hazmat personnel approached the car. They opened all four doors and the trunk and hood. Seats and doors were dismantled. The lunch box wasn't there. After an hour, the director called the search off. LeBron thanked Sweeney for his good eyes.

"Wish we found it. Maybe he tossed it from the car en route. Might suggest a patrol car re-trace their tracks," Sweeney offered. LeBron was already on the phone talking to the director about that.

Deep in the folds of a canvas sail furled off the yardarm, was a black lunch box. Its contents – powdered Ciguatera fungal toxin – leaking in the wind towards nine thousand tourists boarding three cruise ships and four thousand crew members of all nationalities. No country would be left untouched. International outrage would be directed towards Homeland Security and the FBI. Nothing could revive faith in these government agencies after such an international assault.

There would be worldwide bedlam in America's own backyard. Martial law would be authorized due to political turmoil and instability. Within four hours of departure, one third of the passengers and crew aboard the three cruise ships would be dead at sea. Widespread panic aboard all three ships would cause mass violence. Such scenarios were envisioned by the Center for Disease Control in Atlanta, but no resolution to such a disaster was found. These ships would not be allowed into any port. Respiratory arrests, heart attacks, even mass suicides, could not be controlled by the ships' skeleton crews. The staff would become insubordinate and violent. Many would blame the food and water supply for the disease. Others would seek the ships' weapons for their defense against the mobs organizing on each deck. Derek Sweeney's reunion with his daughter and new grandson would be short-lived.

****

I was back in *Vanity Fare's* cockpit watching the sunset. I'd been in contact with Hobson who hadn't arrested me, but I knew she had me on a short leash. I was the prime suspect for the Haifa tragedy. Grabel hadn't been tailing me, but I knew he had plans for getting the files. The man who invented Zyklon B cyanide gas would have no moral dilemma in killing to achieve his aims. Lobel was, similarly, invisible. I couldn't be certain whether Grabel and Lobel were together or at odds in their agendas. That they both were of *The Circle* was not in question. Yet, from talking to them individually I thought that there must have been some conflict in their interests. What did Lobel seek that Grabel didn't? I reported this to Hobson because I felt this was a key weakness she could possibly exploit. Then there was the third villain, Alexa's assailant.

Hobson must have been using me. To incarcerate me on conspiracy to commit acts of terrorism charges would have prevented me from reeling in her other suspects. She was after Father; I couldn't blame her, considering his orders for IVb medium. Did she have a search warrant for Father's clinic? Was she was only waiting for Fielding's replacement? How much time, and how long a leash, did I really have?

The orange sun was about to disappear as the last of the cruise ships pulled out of the harbor. Tourists were still photographing me and the island, waving to any who could see them on their balconies and decks. The mighty ships' horns made the island shiver as if it had a chill, and the smoke from their engines' funnels trailed behind. The lights of the city to my stern brightened as the island darkened.

The phone rang. Dregs passed it up to the cockpit where I was drying off from a dip in the harbor. "It is time to discuss current affairs and renew matters of historical significance." I froze. I hadn't expected this call so soon. Was I prepared? Were Amy and Dad buried deep enough on this little island to be safe?

"Go ahead."

"The Bougainvillea are so fragrant this time of year, don't you agree?"

"It'll take thirty minutes," I replied.

"My guests would have you come sooner rather than later. Time is a factor, you see." I'd been caught off guard, unprepared, vulnerable.

I hung up. I knew Amy and Dad's captor had the bait he needed. I hoped his head hurt, bled even. I could hear him sucking on his cigar.

CHAPTER 25

The Clinic

I had to think fast. The voice on the other end made my nightmare real. I told Dregs to stay on *Vanity Fare* with the girls. I grabbed a flashlight and hopped into the dinghy. A taxi from the harbor sped me up the hill to the iron gate of the clinic. It looked abandoned in the dark; I knew it wasn't.

The moon was half full, the air thick and heavy with humidity. The pink stucco walls of the main clinic were at the end of the drive next to Dad's old lab. I paid the taxi driver. His lights blinded me for a moment as he backed away. When I pushed the wrought iron gates apart, they complained with a high-pitched whine. The driveway and parking lot were empty. The security lights were off. My hurried steps crunched on the pea gravel of the driveway. The clinic's shades were drawn.

I didn't have time to be evasive. I was expected. What worried me most was something the voice said: time was threatening Dad or Amy. I stepped onto the front porch of the two-story building. The floorboards creaked; a bird or bat startled me as it fled. My grip on my flashlight tightened. I opened the screen door and inspected the waiting room with the flashlight. The ceiling fan droned a low frequency hum. There must have been a ball bearing loose in the fan for an irregular *click* punctuated the motor's noise. I couldn't see light from the lower edge of any of the three doors that led past the waiting area. I headed to Dad's private office.

As I opened the door to the hallway leading to Dad's office, the floorboards creaked behind me. I began to turn the flashlight around. From the blackness came a brief rush of air pressure, followed by sudden impact to my head. I fell to my knees, semiconscious, semi-dazed. I was dragged along the coarse floorboards, my head exploding from the pain.

My head throbbed; blood ran warm down the back of my neck. I must have passed out briefly, for it smelled like I was in a different part of the clinic. There was the smell of disinfectant in the room. I tried to focus. I was in Dad's operating room in the back of the clinic. The ceiling fluorescents were not on, but the surgical lamp's six high-intensity bulbs were directed at the chrome-framed operating table in the center of the room. I could see a body on the operating table covered in a green surgical drape as if ready for surgery.

I couldn't stand. There were pulsations in my head. I tried to crawl along the floor. My left ankle was shackled to the steel surgical table, which was screwed to the floor. I could lie there, but couldn't reach very far.

The surgical lamp bolted to the ceiling did not scatter enough light to illuminate the room. Then I smelled it; cigar smoke. I could see the smoke hanging in the loom of the lamp. The air-conditioning was shut down. The room was quiet enough to hear breathing from the person on the operating table. It was rapid, shallow, and very irregular.

"Nice to see you again, Alan." The voice was deep, drier and raspier than I remembered. Excellent English, without a trace of German. Then I saw his shadow on the floor. He placed his surgically gloved hand under the light's beam and gently ran it over a face. As my eyes adjusted, I recognized the patient; a terrified Amy. Her breathing accelerated to hyperventilation as he caressed her forehead. Tears ran down her cheeks. The figure in the shadows revealed the two leather belts across her torso restraining her. He used both hands to unbuckle both restraints.

"You see, she has already been anesthetized." Her arms and legs lay still. She didn't turn her head. I could hear her panting. Her forehead glistened with perspiration. The cigar's embers glowed, but his face was still obscured. What did he look like after all these years?

"The Arawak Indians used the toxin of *Gambierdiscus toxicus*, our little fish algae, to dip their arrowheads in, to assure paralysis and death to their game or enemies. I find it an amusing anesthetic, don't you?"

I managed to stand. My left leg was painfully linked to the steel table normally used for instruments and gowns. "It's not an anesthetic at all. It's a paralytic agent. But, you know that. She can feel; she just can't move," I said. The pulses in my brain now riveting me like a jackhammer.

"That's true, Alan. What you are seeing is the newest incarnation of IVb cultured Ciguatera toxin. It causes a rapid, progressive paralytic tetanus of all the body's muscles. Of course, it's not a real anesthetic, Alan, but they never complain either, so who's to say?"

Amy was becoming paralyzed from head to toe. Her extremities appeared to already have succumbed to the toxin, her torso would follow. One by one, each skeletal muscle would become knotted in permanent spasm. Only her heart muscle and, I prayed, her diaphragm, would function. They are a different kind of muscle tissue, not affected by Ciguatera poisoning, at least not nature's version. But I couldn't predict the course of this mutated version grown in IVb.

"Why are you doing this?" I noticed I was blind in the upper right quadrant of my visual field. The floaters were starting to bubble across the darkness.

"Alan," the voice was moving around the room. Something in his hand glistened: a winch handle. He noticed me spot the chromed object with my blood on it. Your lovely attorney hit me with this when we met in Miami. My blood and your blood, together. Ironic. We're blood brothers, Alan."

He circled the operating table. Amy's sweat had soaked through the entire thickness of the drape. She couldn't move. She was a prisoner of her own body. It must have felt like breathing inside someone else's corpse. All thoughts that instinctually told her to run or flee, or even to strike the captor, were futile. She needed to focus on breathing; it was all she could hope to do.

He put the winch handle down on the counter, and took a silver object from the cabinet I was glad Amy couldn't see it. It was a large, chromed abdominal scalpel. He leaned towards Amy's forehead. She could see the scalpel. Amy couldn't recoil from the blade that was only an inch from her right eyeball. She could only smell the cigar on his breath and see the bloodstained bandages on his head.

"The years have left some undesirable lines on her forehead and cheeks, here and here." He indicated the wrinkle lines in a threatening sweep with the scalpel. Amy was forced to watch the blade coming at her face.

"I propose surgery to rectify this. Don't you agree?"

"You're mad. You don't want to do this, Oskar!"

"Ah, you guessed who the surgeon is today. Seeing you and your father has brought back some fond memories of our college days. But you're right, of course. I don't want to operate. Yet. And here's where we need to be perfectly clear, dead clear, Alan. Our past friendship can not save this woman. You have information I need, and I will have it tonight. To obtain it, I will remove this woman's face, in a surgically correct manner, of course, while she is paralyzed. I assure you *she* will feel every part of its resection. Then I will incinerate the flesh, to render it useless for re-grafting. But, she will be alive! Don't worry; I won't let her bleed to death. Imagine when she looks in the mirror? She'll be a living cadaver!"

"I've got what you want, Oskar. I'll get it for you. But she must go free, immediately. Where's my father, Oskar?" I knew Dad must be nearby, dead or alive.

Oskar bent over Amy, into the lamplight. His hands were large, like a fighter's. He'd filled out, his shoulders broader, his neck thicker, but he had few wrinkles. He still looked as boyish as ever. There was the young, optimistic man I had once known. But his boyish exuberance had been replaced with sadistic menace. With the blood-soaked bandages on his head and the scalpel in his hand, he was a mad hyena on the hunt.

Then I heard weeping. Oskar rotated the lamp in its direction. Strapped and gagged in a folding chair, was Father. I tried to reach him, but the shackle on my ankle held me painfully taught to the steel table.

"Damn you, damn you to hell!" The shout exacerbated my already throbbing head. The blood on the nape of my neck must have clotted; it pulled at my hair as I tried to wrestle myself free. My ankle was swelling.

"Alan, Alan. *Sei ruhig. Aeger dich nicht.* I don't want to hurt your father or his woman. You have something I want, it's true, but I don't think you know what it is."

I assumed the obvious. "My parents' files, the Gasthaus files. You need them for your fencing club. To think I believed your stories about the ridiculousness of these right-wing neo-Nazis. You sounded so convincing. I believed you."

He'd stepped back into the darkness. He lifted his cigar. When he inhaled, its red glow made his eyes look like hot coals. "To have honestly discussed my politics, the politics of my family and friends, my brothers and fellow soldiers, would have divided us. You, the Jew doctor, and me: what a pair! My father *did* try to forget what happened to him during the war. My mother couldn't complain to anyone about what soldiers did to her. The Allies tried to make me ashamed of what my father tried to achieve for the Reich. Former soldiers and party members also tried to forget the war years. Others, like me, *embraced* it and what we tried to do for Germany, for the world. We carry on the fight; our cause is not complete, Alan. The land I told you about, where the club has its duels, you remember?"

"Sonnenschein."

"Ja, Sonnenschein. That's what we named it. Would it surprise you to know it used to belong to a Jew and his family? After the War, my father wanted a farm. The Russian POW camp almost broke him, but he started a new life in a ravaged post-War Austria. He managed to work in town on civil work's projects despite his injuries from the Russians. He worked night and weekend jobs. Finally, he saved enough to buy a piece of Sonnenschein, *his sunshine*, a ray of hope for our family. He worked the land for six years." Oskar circled the operating room.

"Then a town magistrate tells him we must vacate the property. It was Jewish land, he said. A Jewish family had made a legal claim. He said the Nazis confiscated it during the War, and these Jews wanted it back. I had to stop my father from committing suicide. My mother, she went mad. I watched as they took our home and our land. The irony was, the Jews never worked the land at all. They just wanted it back *on principle*. They lived in New York City.

"We moved back to Graz and survived on social welfare. My parents were broken. I was my father's remaining sunshine. I promised him I would not fail. I would honor his life's work, both during the War and after it. I would rectify this injustice to my family and Austria. That was my promise to him before he died. We held *The Circle's* duels on that same land for this reason, Alan."

He continued, with less emotion after composing himself with a puff of his cigar. The room was filling with smoke. "Would it surprise you that I have risen to become Austria's Minister of Health? Soon, I will be the next candidate for President of Austria, the Austria I envision. Coincidentally, Austria will be taking its turn on the General Board of Commissioners for the European Union. I will have control of all twenty-one member nations of the EU from England, France and Germany, to Scandinavia, Turkey and the Eastern Bloc nations. All of this democratically. More nations than the Fuehrer himself governed! But first, there are certain items I require to fulfill my dreams, Alan. Do you understand?"

I pretended to understand. I stalled for more time. *Amy had no time to spare.* "I'll get the items for you. I am on their trail right now. My mother left clues as to their location, which I am about to solve. You must release Amy."

"Why, do you have an antidote for this IVb Ciguatera variant?" Oskar searched my eyes to determine if I really *did* have an antidote for his new toxin.

Father's eyes met mine as Oskar manipulated the lamp. We had to do something. Escape seemed impossible. Oskar moved closer to

Father and removed his gag. Oskar hung it on the green oxygen tank on the floor next to him.

"He doesn't want the medical records. They're of no use to him," Father shouted. He took several deep breaths; the gag had made it hard for him to breathe.

"You should listen to your father. You should know the whole truth of your background, shouldn't he Dr. Langer?"

"What's this about, Father?" I thought we were dangling the medical records as bait. What else could Oskar want?

Father said, "All these years, I've had to keep the worst stories from you. I only told you enough to understand your family's legacy. Hate hadn't died with the gas chambers. I needed you to be aware of the past, never to forget it, never to let it happen again, and most of all, to beware of the re-emergence of this inferno."

While he talked, I was certain that Dad worked to free his hands. The rope was thick like the line used on *Vanity Fare*. Dad knew how to untie *Vanity Fare's* lines, so he might be able to loosen this rope. He sat still when Oskar looked his way.

"How long does she have until respiration ceases?" Dad asked.

"Let's see, one third of those exposed to it die in the first four hours, one third in the next four hours, and the last arrest in the eighth through twelfth hour. No one survives twelve hours, at least no rats or Israelis." There was no remorse in Oskar's voice. "She's been exposed for three hours thus far." Amy's breathing was barely visible. The toxin was spreading and her condition would worsen until her breathing arrested completely.

Father went on. "In doing my work on Jewish prisoners inside the camp, and Germans outside the camp, a man by the name of Lobel came to see me. I had helped him see a patient, Gustav Levitsky, his close friend although Jewish, of course. I did not know of Lobel's role as valet to Hitler or companion to Eva Braun. It was on a particular visit that he brought Eva to me. She was young, sweet, naive. I could understand the tyrant's need for her. She was an emotional refuge from his dark side, his paranoia, and his many extreme moods we'd heard about.

"Levitsky and Lobel visited each other under the auspices of being under my care. The young lady arranged to meet with me in the Gasthaus Clinic. She sought a solution to a problem she'd developed. I immediately suspected she was pregnant and I wanted to abort the fetus. Normally, I would not do such a procedure, but if this was the child of Adolph Hitler, I would consider it an honor.

"She explained that, on one of her weekends with Uncle Lobel, she had met a young man in the nearby town, whom she fancied. A month or so later, she knew she was pregnant. She confessed that Hitler did not have sex with her, or anyone as far as she knew. She was lonely at the Berchtesgaden estate and in the Bunker in Berlin. To start *showing* would be a death sentence for her and for her baby." Father looked to me. He saw nothing but my shock.

"Then she explained: it wasn't an abortion she wanted." Oskar listened, not saying a word. "She had read in a magazine about some hospital in Munich where Nazi doctors were experimenting with surrogate gestational mothers. The Party had determined a need to birth more Aryan youths. They needed future soldiers of the Reich to replace the thousands lost in the War. The ever-expanding Reich demanded a future supply of occupiers to continue its cause and to populate its conquests with *desirables*.

"So, the Munich research pioneered techniques of embryonic transplantation. They had plenty of females in the Fatherland to carry Aryan children, just a shortage of men of suitable stock. Why waste a man's seed for just one woman, when a good German soldier could sire a dozen Aryan sons? The War had produced an abundance of widows, and Hitler sought to put their collective wombs in service to the Fatherland.

"The Order of Women Patriots of the Reich was organized to give birth to the youth of the New Germany. They lined up for this duty that only women could perform."

Oskar corroborated what Father was saying; "Hitler would have killed young Eva Braun if her belly enlarged. Imagine his disgrace in the eyes of the Party elite visiting the Eagle's Nest or the Bunker in Berlin?"

Father continued. "Here was a life, maybe two that could be spared. With the Jewish prisoners, I could only forestall their inevitable end and ease their suffering from diseases. My camp-fungi potions would not help Eva or her baby.

"I considered the possibility of embryo implantation in a surrogate, so I consulted with the doctor who I thought could help me with this. Dr. Neugebauer was in Munich, where the research was being done. I'd heard from the German officers I'd been servicing with surgery at the guesthouse that he was brilliant. He'd survived half a year on the Eastern Front treating German casualties in the bitter cold winter. His sudden reassignment to the Eastern Front was punishment for some offense against a German officer. It had happened right there in Dachau where he had worked in the clinic."

Father looked faint, but went on. "I asked one of the Nazi officers if they would contact Dr. Neugebauer to help the wife of a German officer here at the clinic. It must have sounded like a reasonable request, for he did it.

"A week went by. I received a note from Dr. Neugebauer through the same Nazi officer. He wanted me to find a suitable surrogate for the embryo. I had already found one, an Anna Bronfman.

"I told him she was a young prisoner in the camp. Jewish males and females were separated, but despite her imprisonment, she wanted a child. We didn't tell her that if the experimental procedure was successful, the baby would not have her genes, nor would she be able to keep it.

"Dr. Neugebauer agreed to assist with the procedure himself. This surprised me. I thought he would simply write to me to explain his technique. I did not understand his interest in coming back to Dachau.

"The day of the procedure, Lobel and Eva managed to get away from Berchtesgaden. Hitler and his Field Marshals were more concerned about breaking the Allied lines in the Ardennes Forest in

Belgium in a last effort called the Battle of the Bulge. Upon seeing Anna, Dr. Neugebauer cried, as did Anna. The scene had surprised Lobel and me. Dr. Neugebauer had been treating her for *fertility problems* at the Dachau clinic inside the camp. Party orders from Berlin insisted female Jews of child bearing age be used in the camps for experimentation with radical and inexpensive *sterilization* methods. Excessive X-ray exposures of ovaries and silicone implanted in their Fallopian tubes were tried. These methods would eventually be used all over the Reich to exterminate remaining Jews *humanely*.

"Dr. Neugebauer had used placebo medications on Anna thereby not sterilizing her. He had become emotionally attached to the Jewess, although he had a wife and children. He didn't have the heart to ruin this sweet girl. He risked his own family by falsifying her sterilization."

Father was exhausted. He wanted to wipe the perspiration from his head, but the restraints on his wrists prohibited this. He continued. "Anna kissed Dr. Neugebauer's hand upon their reunion at Dachau. He explained that he'd been punished and was sent to the Front. Nurse Carlson told him of Anna's suffering at the hands of Neugebauer's replacement doctor. She forgave him, and kissed his hand again and again.

"After sentencing Neugebauer to probable death at the hands of the Russians, the Nazi doctor alleged that the Jewess had *bewitched* Neugebauer into sparing her fertility, so she could breed more Jews. To exact the Nazi's revenge on the witch, he drugged and violently raped her."

Father was crying. "After the Nazi officer had left the clinic, I was fetched by Nurse Carlson. She begged me to see Anna. She was an awful sight. Her innocent eyes seemed to ask *why?* Such a beautiful young girl, turned into a mass of dying flesh. She would never be able to look in a mirror again, even with cosmetic surgery. I treated her the best I could, but I was sure she wouldn't live but a few hours more. I even thought death might be merciful, as I was not permitted to have pain medications for Jews, only military personnel.

"She had bled a lot, and we had no fluids to replace what she'd lost. IV bottles were reserved for wounded soldiers of the Reich, as was, of course, cosmetic surgery for officers and their wives. I prayed that I could live up to my name; it would indeed take the magic of a Wizard to sustain this girl. But my prayers were answered: she survived the night.

"Over the next week, with Mother's help and using only fungus-derived preparations, she improved. The guards hadn't hauled her off for execution because I told them she was the Nazi officer's girlfriend and deserved special treatment as his whore.

"Had the Nazi doctor returned and found Anna alive, it would have been the end of my life and my family's. Thank God, the Nazi never did return.

"Two months elapsed. Anna was fit and ready for what she'd always wanted: a child."

Oskar interrupted, "Enough. Herr Doktor, get to the point of your story. The patient has little time to tarry and neither to I. The question is: Did you remove the embryo from Eva Braun?" Oskar spoke firmly, his scalpel still in his hand, threatening Amy, whose breath was barely perceptible. There was no sweat on her forehead. She was going into shock.

"The second question, Doctor: Did you transplant the fetus into the body of the Jewess Anna Bronfman? And, finally, where is it today?" As if to motivate my father and assure the veracity of his next answers, Oskar circled Amy's stiff body, looking into her terrified eyes. Oskar had become a master sadist. Amy's eyes didn't disturb him. In fact, her fear enervated him. Father noticed, too.

This was not the Oskar I'd known and loved. He had evolved, no: regressed, into something inhuman. I thought about Father. He'd surmounted so many challenges in Russia, Dachau, the clinics; he had seen so much death, and made so many moral decisions that had no correct resolution. How could I let him end at the hands of this bastard? Was this why Father had tormented my youth with his tales? Did he know it *was not over* and *was not buried*, no matter how deep you dig?

Father knew Oskar would be suspicious of everything he'd revealed. The penalty would probably be Amy's torture by facial skinning, and likely her painful death.

Father chose his statements carefully. "Yes, the procedure was performed successfully. Anna received special care at the camp, Lobel and Eva saw to that. She was given extra rations and assigned light duty when she became ambulatory. Dr. Neugebauer had his own family and work, so he departed for Munich the same day. I saw Anna every week. Both Eva and Anna got what they wanted.

"Eva lived the next months in hope of surviving the end of the War and having her baby returned to her. She inquired about Anna through Lobel. Anna had no idea who the surrogate mother was. I trusted Eva's story that the baby was from a boy in the local town, and was *not* Hitler's.

"Unfortunately for Eva, the end of the War came sooner than later. The Battle of the Bulge failed, Germany collapsed, and the Bunker was surrounded by the Russian army." Father could cry no more.

He looked at me, and lovingly, I smiled to reassure him. He continued, his voice weakening. Even if we had a chance to escape, I didn't know if Father was capable of killing anyone. I didn't think he could. When Oskar wasn't looking, Dad still tried to wriggle his hands free. A good surgeon's hands have enormous flexibility. Father could tie a suture on a bleeding vessel with two fingers, in a blind sac, under a rib cage with one hand.

"So you wish to know the fate of the child? You must understand the parentage was questionable from the start. Dr. Thiel thinks the child is of Eva and Hitler, a link of the old German Reich to the New Reich that he intends to resurrect with *The Circle's* help. Imagine a continuous blood tie to the Fuehrer. With Hitler and Eva's genes, he can rekindle old sentiments and old ideas, legitimizing his vision of a new Europe. Isn't that correct, Herr Doktor?" Oskar stood in front of me, ignoring Father for a moment.

"Imagine, Alan. I know you can understand. Hitler's blood of our blood, flesh of our flesh, the one my father took the blood oath to protect and defend as leader of the Reich. How glorious! When I learned of the possibility of Hitler's child, I knew my time had come. Herr Lobel was the link and the source. He informed *The Circle* of a child we'd be interested in. He knew we would want to ascertain the child's existence and its whereabouts."

Then it dawned on me, "The medical records are only a nuisance to you and *The Circle*, right? This was never about medical files and photos. You wouldn't let us go if we gave them to you, would you?" Oskar shook his head with an expression of false regret. I also knew he wouldn't let us go even if we produced this Hitler baby.

I tried to deduce the rest of the story. "The key is the DNA of the child?" Father nodded. "On the one hand, Eva Braun was a liar, who feared for her life and her baby's. Even Lobel couldn't be sure his little darling told my father the truth. She was a desperate, pregnant, scared little girl. Her newfound maternal instincts told her to stay alive through the darkest hours of the Reich, and to protect her baby from those who would kill it.

"The father could have been Hitler, in which case she must have known neither Hitler, the baby, nor she could survive the vengefulness of the Russians when they closed in on Berlin. They would have strung up the whole family. It would be payback for thousands of Russian men, women and children Hitler's soldiers had hung from every tree they could find. Her pregnancy would certainly not have been a deterrent: more of a motive, sad to say. This was a war of vengeance and every Russian had a family member's loss to repay. Mercy would be hard to find at war's end.

"If the child were from a young fellow in the town, and Hitler knew it wasn't his, he'd kill her, the baby, and the father since he was paranoid. He would have killed Lobel too, I should think." Oskar nodded. I knew I had offended his Fuehrer by calling him paranoid. I needed to further anger him.

Father was grateful that I understood. I said, "On the other hand, it might have been impossible to implant Anna. There is the possibility she was already with child, right?" Oskar hadn't considered this. He was interested more than ever. He looked to Father for validation of this possibility. None was given.

Suddenly the lights in the whole operating room were switched on. Standing by the entry door were Dr. Grabel and Herr Lobel.

Oskar said, "Ah, Willkommen meinen Kollegen und Kamaraden. Come in please. This concerns you both. We are getting Dr. Alan up to date with his father's story. Whether it's fact or fantasy, I think we need a panel of judges to decide. We will wager this woman's face. Do we agree?" Grabel and Lobel nodded.

The visitors saw me and Father. Without expression, without a word, they sat, Lobel opposite me in the far corner, and Grabel, who smiled at me, on a folding chair near the oxygen tank.

Father blanched at the site of them, like ghosts in his nightmares. Their presence must have taken him back to Dachau, of nameless, gaunt faces with numbers tattooed on their arms, more dead than alive. He called them the walking dead.

Grabel spoke first. "Anna needed disciplining after this hoax, this insult she and Dr. Neugebauer conducted under the eyes of the SS. I sent him to die at the Russian front. I'd heard he'd died in Stalingrad, and his family died of starvation. But what I have overheard here tonight contradicts this. Be that as it may, he is of little concern. What is important is the possibility that the Jewess survived. The young Dr. Becker is about to try and convince us that she carried a child, immigrated to America with it, and that it is my child." Grabel drooled as he talked with heightened emotion. I saw a bulge on the left side of his chest, under his windbreaker. A weapon? He held two electrical wires with a two-pronged plug on one end. He was stripping the insulation off the ends with scissors as he spoke.

He continued in English, "If Anna had carried my child to term; then the child bears no kinship with the Fuehrer and is of little use to Herr Dr. Thiel's political aspirations. I lost both of my children to the post-War polio epidemic. They were very young, and the Allies could not airlift the polio vaccines to Berlin quickly enough during the Russian Cold War blockade. They died almost overnight, in excruciating pain from respiratory paralysis of their diaphragms, much like Fraulein Luger is about to experience. My wife was never the same after the children died. She hung herself." He did not cry, but attacked the insulation on the wires with more ferocity. "I am bitter, jawohl, but if I have another child, I must know. I had never thought this possible, until Herr Lobel announced this story back in Graz. He told of a child of the Jewess, Anna Bronfman that might be alive. He said Anna Bronfman had lived, after all these years."

Lobel stood and spoke. "What I *do* know is Eva could lie about baby's father. For fear of her life or baby's life. She often lie to Fuehrer. She know people like to believe she sweet child. If it be Fuehrer's baby, she was to have it. If they live, he will love and protect it. But, he could not have child, according to Eva's telling me. They have separate bedrooms, and he been at Bunker over one month before she get the morning sickness. This is true. Baby *cannot* be of der Fuehrer." He sat down again, looking away from Father.

Oskar went over to Lobel to shake his hand, and he smiled. "Herr Lobel, you have been most helpful to *The Circle* and our work." He grasped Lobel's right hand with his own. A flash of chromed steel in Oskar's other hand flew across Lobel's larynx, leaving a crimson gaping deep hole across his throat. Oskar had anticipated the gush of blood from Carotid arteries and Jugular veins. He recoiled like a cat to avoid the splatter from Lobel's almost severed neck. I could hear the air surging, gurgling, in and out of Lobel's trachea, as his head, graceful, lifeless, flopped to his left, almost coming off his torso. It stopped only when his spine wouldn't yield anymore flex. Lobel's eyes opened wide with shock. He convulsed as his fluids poured down his chest and onto the operating room floor.

The splatter flew across the room in all directions. Dad and I closed our eyes. Lobel's skin turned pallid, then grey. Air no longer rushed down his windpipe, and the tremors in his hands and legs ceased. Oskar placed the scalpel on the surgical tray next to the operating table, not bothering to wipe it clean of Lobel's blood. Amy's eyes were closing; her breathing was shallow and fading.

Oskar spoke. "The late Herr Lobel forgot to mention that Eva could have, indeed, been intimate with the Fuehrer. Lobel's lie was that Hitler was at the Bunker without Eva. Another member of der Kreis has confirmed that, during the Battle of the Bulge, Hitler had sent for Eva. The two were locked down in the Berlin Bunker for over a month. Herr Lobel put his own personal interests, gaining access to his beloved Eva Braun's child, above *The Circle's* need for a link to the Reich's legacy. This is unforgivable."

Father was getting sick, reliving the bloodshed he'd seen like this at the hands of these monsters.

Pacing around the operating room, Oskar continued, "Imagine being locked up together, sharing a bedroom for over a month. It is possible, likely, this child is the Fuehrer's and Eva's – ours. Lobel was not one of us; he was a homosexual and Jew-lover. He disrespected the Fuehrer who'd given him a position of respect and privilege. His usefulness in uncovering the existence of the child was all he was good for."

Amy, locked in her paralyzed torso, couldn't have seen the murder, but she must have heard the gasps from Father and I, and the Lobel's last gurgled gasps of life. She had to know this madman was making good his threats.

Me, I prayed that Hobson had my message. I called her while coming ashore. Only voice mail answered. Where the hell was she? I hoped she was coming to the clinic loaded with weapons and backup. Amy was near death and I was shackled to the table.

"So, dear Dr. Langer. What happened to the child? As you can see, truth is of paramount importance to your son's future and Ms. Amy's face."

"I can take you down the story's path only as far as I know." As Father spoke, I noticed a shadow in the light from under the hallway door. No one else had noticed. The shadow moved as it was skulking furtively in the hall, perhaps listening in. Father's hands hadn't moved for quite a while now. Was he exhausted? Or, was he free?

Father continued. "I removed the embryo from Eva's womb, and transplanted it into Anna Bronfman's womb. It survived in the womb of Anna, with uninterrupted growth. There was no need for an obstetrician in the camp. Besides Anna, pregnant women were sent to the *showers*. Anna thrived. While her *special treatment* was due to Eva and Lobel, written medical orders could only come from a doctor, a German doctor, of course. Dr. Neugebauer saw to these.

"Anna radiated a future and hope to the other prisoners that had never been seen in a death camp. They were consigned to starvation, slave labor, and the lethal showers. Then, about three months into Anna's pregnancy, the rumors started. We could hear bombs falling on Munich: American bombs falling by day and British bombs by night. All of Bavaria suffered saturation bombing to rubble. There was a new attitude in the camp: we were soon to be liberated. The Nazi guards were frightened of their future on the horizon. Some even apologized to us in advance, with self-recriminations and excuses.

"They knew they'd be hunted. The German officers kept me busy at the clinic day and night, even as the bombs fell. I could demand pretty much anything I wanted in exchange for their new faces. They'd secure new papers once they could look good enough for ID photos. I had the preoperative photos that would prevent them from getting away with their misdeeds. With Lobel's Leica, I photographed every SS and Gestapo officer, every Field Marshal and Camp Commandant I treated." Dad looked at Lobel's corpse. "I knew they'd deny their murders, their pasts, their abuses of common civility. They could only hope the tales were so inhuman that no one would believe anything had happened it the camps at all. Did I have a choice? Of course, but it was clear: I would either perform their facial surgery, or they'd string Mother up from the ceiling right then and there. But first, we would get to watch them set our baby on fire with petrol. Not to kill you, Alan, just to cause disfigurement and pain the remainder of your life." He was crying now, wailing. I couldn't console him, so I cried too.

"*What could I do*? Let them kill my Hanna, the only woman I had ever loved? No, I chose to bide my time, for it would come. The files, the photos, the testimony of others, and my own. Mother insisted on being the custodian of the records. But, we found no international justice agency that wanted to know our secrets. The War Crimes Tribunals at Nuremburg had come and gone. Post-War America and Europe didn't want to hear any more. Their newspapers told of other threats like the Atom Bomb and Communism.

"No agency wanted the medical files of old Nazis. They even threatened to accuse me of complicity with the enemy if I persisted. Me, who kept thousands in the camps alive! This they forgot! Mother had warned me: history would judge my surgical work only in abetting the escape of Nazis. She knew that the moral dilemmas I faced under those horrible circumstances would be ignored. I couldn't let them kill your mother, Alan. You can understand that. They were going to flee and the world was soon to forget all they'd done. The support and testimony of my fellow prisoners at Dachau would have vindicated me from all criminal liability. So many are alive today because I was their Wizard." Oskar relished the old Jew's anger and moral indignation.

Father looked like a drained shell of the man I remembered.

"I asked some of my former patients to write affidavits on my behalf. They wanted only to forget those days and the many loved ones they'd lost. Mother and I couldn't find anyone willing to testify for me. She was my only witness. We isolated ourselves from the world up here on the hill, on this island, where we could help others. Others who didn't care where we'd been."

I noticed that Oskar was getting impatient. The shadows had moved away from the door, perhaps down the corridor. Maybe it was Hobson! Oskar caressed Amy's face; he hadn't forgotten his plan. Amy's eyes showed signs of fading into deep pools of lifelessness; her breathing was no longer perceptible. I knew she would soon arrest. Her nightmare would then be over and maybe she would even avoid the scalpel.

I nodded towards Father to note Amy's condition. He got the message, and then continued, "Your answer, Herr Oskar, is that no one can be certain whether the child is alive. You see, when Dachau was liberated, General Eisenhower and his staff entered the camp, in disgust and utter shock at what they saw. Stacks of human corpses were piled upon each other as far as the eye could see. And the stench: incredible. Eisenhower ordered thousands of these bodies to be properly buried. He even had the German townspeople of the nearby village march through the camp to see what their military units had done. He made movies, so no one could deny it. In the turmoil, I lost Anna Bronfman. I was transported to a Displaced Persons Camps until we arrived in New York City."

"I am certain you looked for her all these years," Oskar stated, impatiently.

"Yes, I did. The International Red Cross had several hundred missing Bronfmans, some dead, some alive, some still unaccounted for. The problem was, and still is; the child probably doesn't even know its true parents. Anna was only the surrogate, and she herself didn't know. Today, one can verify the identity using DNA. However, you do need a potential candidate who can donate their DNA and compare it to Hitler's. Then, you'll have your answer, and can verify it for your future voters."

Oskar was ready for this. "You are wise, Langer. You can play your game of I-don't-know, trying to buy yourself time. But I need the candidate who could be the Hitler-Braun child, and I need the Fuehrer's own DNA. You know that Hitler's DNA was incinerated by our late friend on the chair over there."

I jumped in. "But Oskar, his DNA is available to you. Soviet President Putin unlocked the post-mortem autopsy results and specimens that their generals collected of the purported remains of Eva and Hitler. Lobel himself told me he didn't have the heart to pour petrol on Eva's body before igniting her. While Hitler's corpse was more thoroughly burned to ashes, I'll bet Lobel had reason to be confident he could prove the parentage of Eva's child. That must be why he came to St. Thomas. He knew she was a liar, he said so himself. She was young and scared, and would do anything not to be at the mercy of Hitler or the Russians. No, Lobel had a secret piece of proof no one else could have had. You don't need Hitler's DNA, but Eva's would be sufficient, wouldn't it?"

I could see Oskar thinking it over: Would a child of Eva Braun, Hitler's sole mistress and his short-term wife, put to rest any skepticism about the child's lineage, if DNA could prove at least *Eva's* genes were present? If the Russians had even a tiny piece of Eva's remains, a bone, hair, the root of a toenail, that wasn't burned, he just needed to match up the proof to whoever the child might be. Unfortunately, Oskar didn't have access to such specimens, and the Russians would certainly investigate him if he asked for a specimen. No, he needed an undeniable sample of Eva Braun's DNA to make his case.

Oskar let this possibility simmer for a moment. "Did he tell you what his source of Eva's DNA was, by chance?"

"Yes, inadvertently. He didn't know he was telling me."

"And that is?"

"I need motivation, Oskar. Let my father and Amy go. Then I'll give it to you."

"Alan, you know that's impossible. But I can provide incentive. The time is rapidly approaching when I think Ms. Amy Luger's name may be ready for a headstone. Her respiration is all but gone, and we need to get an antidote for her. Know of any?" Then Oskar did the unexpected. He nodded to Grabel as if there had been a strategy planned at this point in the interrogation.

Grabel acknowledged Oskar and stood up. I figured he had other interests in the Bronfman child. He was less interested in a figurehead for the new Reich; he was too old to benefit from it. That was for Oskar's generation. He wanted to know if he'd fathered a child. Moreover, Grabel was greedy and wanted riches.

Grabel's OZ had developed and distributed the weaponized Ciguatera toxin to its only client, *The Circle*, with Oskar as its Minister. Grabel had the IVb medium to isolate the strain he needed, and the facilities to manufacture it in commercial quantities. *The*

Circle demonstrated its effectiveness in Haifa using Red Brigade mercenaries. The Israelis had nothing to counter it.

Grabel needed to know whether the old Wizard's orders from OZ for IVb were for research in developing treatments for lung diseases or for something else? Could the something else be an antitoxin to Grabel's mutant strain? This would be extremely valuable, financially, to the owner of such an antitoxin, should it exist. It would also render Grabel's discovery valueless. He had to know which was the case. He could sell mountains of the antitoxin, if he could only determine its existence.

Would the elder Dr. Becker let Amy die from the weaponized Ciguatera to keep the secret? His behavior here and now was the acid test. Grabel asked, "Herr Dr. Becker, have you used the IVb media for your research or for developing an antidote to my formula? I think you lie when you say such an antiserum doesn't exist. Herr Oskar, shall we play poker with these Jews? Let's see if the antidote does exist, shall we? In the next few minutes there will be a fifty-fifty chance Ms. Amy Luger will have respiratory arrest. I'll bet there's an antidote, and it is nearby. I would remind the doctors, that her odds are diminishing by the moment." Father and I looked at each, helpless. The air stunk of old cigar smoke, locker-room sweat, and Lobel's body. Amy was immobile on the table. I assumed she had passed quietly into a coma or death. Her muscle paralysis would prohibit any movement. Even a death rattle.

Grabel and Oskar had lost patience. Grabel turned to me, furious. He held the exposed electrical wires in one hand, and put the plug in the wall socket. I knew what was coming.

Sparks jumped between the wires. Grabel grinned at me. Standing clear, he touched the wires to the steel table. It jumped and vibrated, and so did I. My body contorted in an excruciating spasm. I couldn't breathe, couldn't unlock my muscles. He withdrew the wires and grinned again. I could smell the burning hair and skin on my left ankle where the current charred me against the metallic handcuff holding me there. The metallic fillings in my teeth were hot.

He reapplied the wires: again, I convulsed. When he released, I thought my heart almost stopped on that one. I was exhausted, but saw the situation more clearly. It was like shock therapy back in Austin State. My weekly sessions were exhausting, just like this. But they did give me more clarity in my thoughts. The doctors said the depression had caused me to see things and hear voices no one else seemed to see and hear. Oddly, I felt rejuvenated by the torture, and the voices vanished. I was emboldened.

"Let's not cause complete fibrillation of the heart muscle or smoke his eyeballs," Oskar said. Most considerate of him, I thought.

Father couldn't bear any more. He spoke up.

"I have the answers you need. The antidote is nearby; in fact, it's in the basement of the clinic's lab, in the building next door."

Without knowing if Father's story was true, I reacted loudly and abruptly to give him the dramatic credibility he needed. "No, Father, don't help these men. Grabel has been using *The Circle* to sell his weaponized IVb Ciguatera to Italian extremists for money, not politics. Giving him the antitoxin allows him to burn it, making his toxin more valuable. Your antidote will disappear with us."

Grabel punched my head exactly where Oskar had struck me with the winch handle. Grabel had a quick and violent temper as Anna Bronfman and now I had discovered. He didn't like being crossed or deceived. He was a madman, out of control. Father made a futile attempt to help me, but his chair only rattled. Then I saw something in his eyes and it wasn't fear.

I knew what Father wanted me to do. I said, "Okay, Oskar, I'll give you what you want, but you must agree to use the antidote as soon as I've told you the details and given you Lobel's specimen of Eva's DNA. Agreed?"

Oskar smiled and nodded his head. "You see, I can be reasoned with. We all have our wants and wishes, and I'm not going to spoil things for anyone." He was truly a snake. I spoke up.

"Okay, Lobel just wanted Eva's baby as a legacy of his love for her, like a doll. He understood her DNA would certify her parentage.

Eva gave Lobel a unique gift. Country girls kept their baby teeth as a memento. Many made chains to wear as a bracelets or necklaces. Before she died, Eva gave Lobel her chain of baby teeth she'd always kept with her. Dental DNA is long lasting and durable. The incineration of her body is irrelevant, even if the Russians kept any remnants. Heat denatures and ruins the protein of the DNA, as any doctor knows." Oskar nodded in triumph, satisfied that this information had the ring of truth and was certified by the fear of electrocution. He had heard that farm girls saved their baby teeth, but had forgotten this as a possible source of Eva Braun's DNA.

"And where would this chain be now, Alan?" he asked.

"It would be close to him. I suspect the old fellow would not have trusted safes, hotel rooms, or, especially, his cohort Dr. Grabel." Grabel smiled, then sneered. His only solace was knowing that my life expectancy was diminishing by the minute as I gave up my leverage with answers. So did I. I hoped Dad knew that as well. The shadows re-appeared under the exit door. Someone was listening. Hobson? But why wouldn't she just break in? Time was getting tight.

Oskar reacted as I expected, and started to search Lobel's pockets. First his jacket, then his pants. I remembered that Lobel took heart pills when he visited my boat.

"The most likely place would be in his pill box or pill bottles, don't you think? After all, he's not a young or healthy man. An item like this would fit well in a pill bottle and he has plenty of those." I was improvising, but Father couldn't be sure. Oskar was excited to find three plastic pill bottles, as I'd hoped. He fumbled with the childproof tops; he needed both hands to open them.

Oskar threw the opened bottles aside, scattering pills over the wooden floor.

"Pills, Alan. Only pills. Think how you and your father are going to look, dangling from the clinic gates. Ms. Amy, I'm afraid, is comatose. I don't see her breathing, do you?" He walked over to the surgical tray, and saw that the scalpel was gone. He looked at Father, whose hands appeared tied, and at Grabel, who didn't understand the look on Oskar's incredulous face.

With a tremendous gasp of fresh breath, *Amy came alive*! Her arms thrust upwards, her hands grasped the scalpel. Oskar froze. She drove the blade upwards with a fierce grunt, through the drape, gouging just below Oskar's rib cage. Oskar leered at her, his face distorted with disbelief and rage. Shock and pain caused his face to engorge with unholy fire in his eyes. His hands gripped hers, trying to pull the scalpel from his gut. He was using her hands to slowly remove the blade, an inch at a time. As the blade receded, Amy let him overcome her resistance just a little, enough for her to suddenly divert the blade's direction *across* his belly, widening the stab wound into an abdominal slash far larger and far more damaging.

Grabel reached for his gun. Father stood up, his hands free. Reaching for the switch behind him, he turned off all the lights in the room, leaving us in blackness. I stretched to reach Grabel before he bolted away. The shackle on my burnt ankle pulled me back to the floor. Grabel stood up on his right foot, bringing him an inch closer, which was all I needed to grasp his ankles. I jerked his feet towards me. With a thud and a groan, he landed flat on his back. I thrust my right elbow down hard into his abdomen. "Oof," he groaned. I'd found his solar plexus, and I heard more than one rib snap and hoped their sharp edges would start internal bleeding. I had a minute until he could breathe normally. I pulled. He tried to resist, but he couldn't move. I dragged him a foot closer clenching his right wrist just before he withdrew his gun, ripping it out of his hand.

It was a small caliber revolver. Grabel was not able to defend himself. Dad, Amy, and Oskar were somewhere in the room. "Dad," I yelled. "Say something. Lights on!" We squinted under the brilliant lights. There was no sign of Oskar, but a trail of blood led out the front door. Father, with his wrists bloodied and raw from the ropes, went to Amy.

He grabbed her shoulders. She was covered in blood, but breathing.

"I'm okay. You?" We nodded.

Dad examined her eyes and checked her pulse. Then he nodded to me and smiled. "Get Oskar," he yelled. "I can watch him." He tilted his head towards Grabel who was struggling to get up, ignoring the weapon in my hand. I needed to chase down Oskar. The scalpel wasn't on the tray or in Amy's hands. Grabel would kill Dad and Amy the first chance he had.

"Dad, take the gun and shoot him if he moves."

"No, you'll need it to get Oskar. I can handle Grabel." Dad then ran out the door and back into the room with his spear gun. Grabel laughed at the sight of it. Without hesitation, Dad shot Grabel's left thigh, impaled it to the wooden floorboards. The sound of Grabel's thigh bone snapping and his wail were grotesque. "Now go, Alan," he said.

The violent shaking of the table when Grabel had electrocuted me must have loosened its floor screws, because I could lift the table releasing the cuff tethering my ankle. I took the gun and limped out the door after Oskar.

****

"Are you having difficulty breathing?" Father asked Amy.

"I think I'm okay, just scared and sore."

Father went to get the stethoscope on the steel table beside Grabel. That was Grabel's chance. The electrical plug was still hanging from the wall. When Father placed his left hand on the table, Grabel touched both exposed wires to the table leg. Father convulsed from the current. Grabel pulled him to the floor. Grabel's left arm locked his neck, choking him. Amy tried to pull him free from Grabel's strong grip. She tried to pull the spear from Grabel's leg, but it was too deep in the floor. Father wasn't breathing.

Amy grabbed the oxygen tank, opened the valve, and slammed the mask over Grabel's nose and mouth, holding it until his lungs filled with oxygen. She pulled the mask off, grabbed Oskar's still-smoldering cigar from the table and shoved it into Grabel's mouth.

Grabel's body jerked with the explosion of his lungs. Smoke filtered from his nostrils. His body fell limp, his arms falling to

Father's sides. Father gasped for air. Amy had tears in her eyes as she hugged him.

****

The lights in the corridor were off, but the ceiling fan in the waiting room whirred and clinked. Somewhere in the darkness was a madman, bleeding and angry.

My retina had detached again; floaters moved across my field of vision, and I was blind in one quadrant of my right eye. Someone moved in the waiting room. It had to be Oskar. I shot towards him; a window shattered, then silence. I stumbled outside after the shadow bolted out to the porch. He stood in the driveway, blood-soaked, his left hand holding his intestines in. He made no effort to conceal the scalpel in his right hand. He held it like a murderer, not a surgeon. He looked beaten, but I knew better. *Fear and deceit were his weapons.*

"Look at me, Alan." Blood oozed through his left hand. He staggered a step closer. I didn't raise the gun. He lowered the scalpel, but didn't drop it. My right eye was useless. I tilted my head to the right so he was in view of my left eye. He was two steps from the porch, and me. He said, "All those good years we had back at school, where have they gone?" I looked down at the gravel that was soaking up his blood. He looked at his torn abdomen. "What was that word you couldn't think of at the exam?" He looked at his intestines trying to spill out of his abdomen..."Oh, ja."

I said, "Chitlins."

He fell to his knees, as if praying. Dad and Amy stepped out onto the porch. Amy stepped closer to Oskar, removing the blanket covering her shoulders. She moved perilously close. The scalpel dropped from his hands to the gravel. He knelt and looked into Amy's eyes. Oskar's hand was no longer holding his abdomen. In the blood, I saw the grip of a gun. He lifted it in a sudden spasm and pointed it at us. A flash and a shot came from out of the darkness.

Oskar's head shuddered for a second, then a section of his skull sprayed with his ear to the gravel. His body fell. Amy hid her face in Father's chest, and he held her close.

"Everyone okay?"

"Yes, we're fine," I lied. I recognized the voice in the dark. Agent Hobson stepped into the moonlight, while holstering her automatic.

Hobson said, "Grabel? Lobel?"

"Both in the O.R.," I said. "The Minister of Health here killed Lobel with a scalpel."

George, holding onto Amy for support said, "Grabel's dead, too."

Amy looked like she was going to collapse.

"I'll take her inside and take care of her," Dad said.

"Seems like Dad developed an antitoxin for this Ciguatera strain of Grabel's. Amy must have been immunized," I said.

"I know," Hobson said. I was dumbfounded. "Your Dad's not only developed IVb derived antitoxin, his lab over there has been producing large volumes of it for months in anticipation of an attack like the one in Haifa."

"Why didn't I know of this?"

"We told him it must be absolutely secret. You helped us locate the site of the attack by drawing out the planned location of the operation. The medical records and your mother's trail helped us identify the players we needed to have under surveillance. We infiltrated the fencing club, and their board revealed who made the toxin and where the Red Brigade was paid to release it."

"So, I'm your bait?"

"I prefer lightning rod." Hobson went on. "Grabel, or Dr. Mushroom, set the wheels in motion when he heard about a Hitler-child from Lobel. He knew you lived on a boat. He had the financing to concoct a maritime accident, to direct guilt and suspicion at you. The hollowed-out keel with your keel's ID numbers, traces of IVb medium in the hollowed out keel, both pointed towards your father and you. This would get you to work on solving your mother's ciphers and, at the same time, help them determine if your father was dead or alive. Furthermore, if he was alive, could the old Wizard have enough expertise to produce an antitoxin for Grabel's weapon? Most importantly: Did he know the whereabouts of the Hitler child?

"The maritime accident was no accident. Seems *Hirotu* anchored off the coast of Galveston the night before weighing anchor for the Houston ship channel. A Rastafarian friend of Grabel's sails a boat, just like yours, under the bow, while a Philippine cabin boy is innocently fishing from the bow. His bait happens to be a small black lunch box with a plastic bag full of a powdery substance. I put all of this together, about this anchoring, at a briefing in Galveston after the crew was interrogated. I figured the cabin boy let the lunch box down to the Rastafarian who had sailed a boat just like Vanity Fare, the Wet Dream, beneath the bow overhang of *Hirotu*. The Rastafarian uses a line to sling around the *Hirotu's* anchor and Wet Dream's mast. No one can see the relatively small sailboat under the flare of the *Hirotu's* bow. When the anchor is raised, viola, up goes Wet Dream, apparently snarled by its rigging to *Hirotu's* anchor fluke. The Haifa incident was averted successfully thanks to our moles in *The Circle's* planning sessions."

"But I heard the radio reports of hundreds of deaths."

"Fortunately, with cooperation from the Israelis, they had instituted martial law *prior* to the attack, thereby controlling the news media. Haifa had enough of your father's new IVb antiserum at all the local medical facilities. *The Circle's* members in Graz have been arrested on multiple criminal charges associated with their organization's attempt to overthrow governments and for terrorist conspiracy. They will not see the light of day again. It was you who gave us Der Kreis as a lead by your telephone crisis calls."

****

Hobson followed me into the operating room with a man I didn't recognize. He was elderly, well dressed in a suit, bald and a little overweight.

"I brought this gentleman here to identify the real names of the players," Hobson said.

"That's him," the stranger said. "This Felix Grabel, not Sobotta. The other, Werner Lobel. I recognize them. Outside, the Austrian Minister of Health, Oskar Thiel."

"Thank you, doctor," Hobson said.

I looked at this stranger and said, "I'm going to take a guess. Dr. Neugebauer, I presume?" He smiled. Father recognized him, and struggled to his feet. They embraced as tears flowed. It has been over sixty years.

"Let's all go to the waiting room and let the coroner's office clean up here," Hobson said.

Sitting in the waiting room, Dad was looking better.

I turned to Dad. "One day you're going to tell where you met Amy, really."

"You heard the story of Anna Bronfman, didn't you?" he said.

"You're going to tell me, Anna really *did* have a child, aren't you?"

"Amy's last name is Luger, the name of her sister's husband. She was orphaned when Anna died of typhus in a displaced persons camp after Dachau was liberated. Anna saw the baby shortly before her death and entrusted her to me and Mother. We were to bring the baby to New York City with us. We found Anna's sister who accepted the child as her own. The sister had fled the Nazis in 1938, before the borders closed. Many years later, we received a call by the girl's court-appointed guardian. A car accident had taken the lives of the child's parents; Amy was orphaned once more."

Dr. Neugebauer, whose English was marginal, understood the story. He almost fainted. Staring at Amy, he said: "You Miss Anna Bronfman's child, I hear him say? This be true?"

"Yes," she said. Her eyes probed his for a clue.

Dad was still holding onto Amy, who seemed to be coming out of her own shock.

I said, "You couldn't have come from Grabel." Amy couldn't be certain, but she saw no resemblance, and neither did I.

I mused and said, "Amy's real last name could be Braun, Hitler, or even Schickelgruber for that matter. Lobel seemed an unlikely parent and you certainly don't resemble him. Don't think he'd take advantage of Eva anyway. Dad says he transplanted you as a fetus from Eva to Anna. She could be a Hitler or a Braun, or a Braun alone if she did have an affair in town without Adolph." We looked at Dad.

Dad tried to help out with what he knew. "I transplanted a baby, for certain. Since Dr. Neugebauer didn't actually sterilize Anna, there could have been a baby in the womb already, making the transplanted fetus un-implantable. It was so remarkably tiny; Anna could have lost it in the toilet, without noticing. Anna and I assumed the baby was transplanted, but no one could be one hundred percent certain, without DNA.

He turned to Dr. Neugebauer. "Care to donate some of your DNA for a test?"

Dr. Neugebauer said, "If I understand correct, I might be, you think, Amy's father?" Dad nodded. I don't have sex with Anna, Amy. I can't be father. I wish you my daughter, but no." He took her hand and with both of his, pressed them together and with a warm smile, cried. He said, "You come to visit in Salzburg, any time you like." He reached into his pocket. "This be your mother's. Nazis took all Jewish jewelry. But I took it for her before it melt down. I love Anna and glad I not sterilize her. She would be very good mother to you. Me, I have two boys your age and wife." Amy looked down at the necklace of a Star of David he'd given her. He and Dad said a warm farewell.

Amy didn't feel any better narrowing the potential fathers down to Hitler or Grabel.

"No one has Hitler's DNA, as far as we know," I said. "The Russians might have some of Eva's, which is what you really need. As for Neugebauer, I'm not sure I believe him," I said. A German doctor taking advantage of a Jewish prisoner in Hitler's death camp. That's a whole lot for his moral code to swallow, both as a doctor, a German officer, and a former Party member. He must have some guilt, I'm certain. Sure would like some of his DNA, Amy. Wouldn't you?"

"I have some of it." Hobson held up the hat Neugebauer had left in her car on the drive to the clinic. She had put it in a plastic evidence bag. "I think he just lost his hat." She gave it to Amy. His hair that accumulated inside the hat was all that the lab would need. Turning to Amy, "You give me a couple of his hairs if you want, and I'll run a DNA profile on them for you and on yours as well, when you're good and ready." Amy held the hat tight and cried in Dad's arms.

****

Hobson reminded us to come to her office at the local police station for statements, and then she said her *goodbyes*.

"One more thing I need to do," I said. Dad knew what I meant.

We three went to his office. Behind the desk, hanging on the wall, was a shelf with the conch shell Mother had given him decades ago as an anniversary gift. I picked it up. "See it here?" I pointed to the inscription, *Ewig und Immer*, she wrote along its edge. Ever and always.

"That's what was written in your eye, so she is telling you to look here?" Dad said.

We looked at the triton and Amy noticed something unusual about it. "There's no hole! The hole to cut the animal inside out; it's been patched up."

I'd seen it too. "Yes, look. It's been repaired. Unusual but…."

Amy said, "Tell me again what your mother used to say to you down here at the docks facing out to sea. It was something about how you cracked the cloak or mantle of others revealing the secrets inside. Translating from German, a mantle, or cloak is *Eine Schale*. That's also a shell. That was what she was saying, Alan." I had to agree, but instead of throwing the shell on the floor, I took a letter opener from the desk and forced it gently apart. When the thinnest portion of the triton's shell severed in one big shard from the thicker hollow, the inner surface had an additional inscription from Mother.

"Numbers," Dad said.

"You read it. I'm not seeing well right now."

Amy took out a pen and recorded, "174532/644221."

"Mean anything to you, Alan? Maybe a bank account number?"
I shook my head.

CHAPTER 26

Scabs and Scars

Alexa was at the helm as I raised the mainsail. I looked astern over her shoulder at the two range markers in the harbor. Mother loved her hidden word games and ambiguous phrases. I was glad Dad's nightmare of the emerging Circle was over. That the passengers on the cruise ships in Galveston had enough antiserum for the Ciguatera attack to fail was the result of Dad's lab and the Israelis alerting Sweeney and LeBron after the briefing in Galveston.

My lab had relied on his *wizardry* years ago and, apparently, now more than ever. The Israelis, along with U.S. and European governments, had been financing Dad's work the last six months for his new antiserum, hence the Swiss bank accounts neither me nor Alexa knew of. He had convinced Dr. Corso in Israel of the impending threat he perceived by The Circle terrorists. He knew only Grabel could have a mind to develop a strain so evil using IVb medium. He knew Grabel was proud of Zyklon B; weaponized Ciguatera had a natural appeal to him. Only the Wizard of Dachau could defeat it, but he needed financing. This made Grabel suspicious of Father's purported suicide. Hence, Grabel arranged to throw suspicion on me by becoming Dr. Pilzen or Champignon, the fungus clues, further pointing at me. I was to help Grabel ferret out a connection to Father, if he were alive.

Since I wasn't a hands-on operator of the lab, Dad could do his work and I wouldn't know he had modified the antiserum to address Grabel's new version. By distributing it months in advance, all of our regular clients had the updated version in use and on hand in their medical facilities, as in Haifa and the ships in Galveston.

Alexa was reflecting, too. The attorney revisited us. "You know, it's entirely possible your father has not been completely candid with you still."

"Meaning?"

"I was looking through your English-German dictionary below after breakfast and looked up the word *luger*."

"Liar," I said. She nodded. "You think Amy's parentage may be a lie. You think Dad's taken over Mom's word games?" She smiled.

She went on. "It would protect Amy if she was a Hitler, a Braun, even a Grabel or Neugebauer. Her life might be safer with the fog of uncertainty about her parentage shielding her. Clever prospect, don't you agree?" I had to hand it to her, it was plausible. As long as they were looking for medical records of their past, they might come across Amy and threaten her to get Dad or Mom to divulge their location. But if Amy were of personal or political interest to them, they couldn't be certain of her being pursued by a next generation of radicals? I had a feeling this scenario had the touch of Mother's instincts and foresight. Luger might be her cover family name with a hidden agenda.

Alexa went on. "So, who is Amy, really? I have a theory. The end of War comes; your Mom and Dad realize they might live. They knew Anna. She wanted a child very much. They had you already and your life was spared as long as your mother and father provided surgical services to the Nazis. Anna would have perished if she were pregnant, as all mothers were condemned to death."

I added, "Dad had learned the embryonic transplantation method from Dr. Neugebauer. Dad probably met with Eva Braun and Lobel to relieve Eva of her at risk baby, and see to its safer future in Anna's womb. I don't think Dad actually would have aided in propagating Hitler's fetus, even if there was only a remote possibility existed it really was Hitler's baby."

Alexa agreed. "Yet, we know pregnant Jewish women were to be gassed; that was Dachau protocol. Your mother and father were the only Jews to quarter together since they were medical staff in essential positions for the Reich. Anna's womb was protected by Eva Braun's and Neugebauer's *special treatment*. Anna's womb would be a safer haven than your mother's."

"You're saying, Mother was pregnant, aren't you?" I said.

"Maybe she was. Then your mom and dad would have had a larger problem. Your dad may have seen an opportunity in the upcoming embryonic transplantation for Eva Braun." I needed to think this through, as apparently Alexa already had.

"My Dad could have performed the fetal transplantation of *Mother's* fetus to Anna's womb to act as surrogate, instead of implanting *Eva's* fetus!" I had to let this sit a moment. It was entirely possible. The fetus was extremely tiny. Dad did the embryonic removal with Neugebauer in another treatment room doing the actual implantation for which he was more experienced. Switching the minuscule beings during such a delicate procedure was possible. Dad would have been in the examination room next door with Eva Braun. He could remove Eva's embryo, and then remove Mother's in another room nearby. Neugebauer wouldn't suspect a thing, for both fetal specimens would look identical to the naked eye.

"Alan, Amy may be your sister."

I could see Mother's mind behind this, from Dachau to her riddles at the docks here in St. Thomas. Alexa was pleased with her insight.

"Why couldn't he tell me about this before?" I wondered.

"Not until Neugebauer left, satisfying your father that the child was of no interest to him either as a daughter or, in the unlikely case he'd become part of The Circle, a political figurehead. I think your father may be ready to introduce you to your sister now that Amy's life is secure from Oskar, Grabel, Lobel, and even Neugebauer. No potential threats seem to be on the horizon, so it's safe."

We sailed for about an hour. The autopilot gave us time to drink some lemonade and look over some charts of the Virgin Islands I had in the cockpit. Alexa asked some questions about longitude and latitude, and then noticed something familiar about the charts. She took out the paper from her purse with the numbers from the conch shell Amy recorded. We looked at each other, realizing the significance of Mother's numbers. They were the coordinates of a point identified by her longitude and latitude. We located the point on the chart: Buck Island Cove, not an hour's sail from here.

"I feel like Long John Silver with a treasure map," I said.

"Me too, matey," she said.

I turned off the autopilot and swung the helm around, heading Vanity Fare under full sail, north to Mother's fix point.

As we sailed for the spot in the cove on the chart, I said, "I think we'll need snorkels. There's an old steel-hulled wreckage there of a ship that went down about seventy-five years ago. Tourists like to dive on the wreck and it makes a good matrix for new coral reefs."

"Alan, your mother recited her coded words to you saying to crack the mantle of those around you, but also something else. Something about your soul, wasn't it? What's the German word for your?"

I said, "Seine."

"Hmm." She retrieved the dictionary from below. "Seine, but a mother talking to her son wouldn't use *seine* according to this. That's too formal."

"Correct. She'd say *deine*. Then I made the connection. "Guess what the name of the wreck in Buck Island Cove is?"

Alexa guessed, "Ships are often named for women. It couldn't be *Dinah*, could it?" I smiled, as did she.

"But where in the wreck would her hidden treasure of medical records be stashed?" I wondered. It was a big ship. We needed more.

"Did your Mom know nautical language?" she asked.

"She knew enough to get around a boat pretty well. We sailed as a family even back when we first came to the islands and set up the clinic. She liked to be in the galley a lot, but she knew port from starboard."

"She would also have known a bulkhead from a floor, right?" she said.

"It's not the floor, it's the sole," I said, answering my own next question. "She said my soul was good. She was telling me where: in the galley, where she always worked under sail, *under the sole*!"

EPILOGUE

I snorkeled down to the *Dinah*, which was only a dozen feet below the water's surface. I made my way into the cabin's galley, where I strained to find the galley's sole. There was only one hatch cover in the sole. It took me several dives to pry it open with a screwdriver I'd fetched from Vanity Fare. Alexa sat on the deck ready to hoist the file cabinet aboard with a line and winch she'd readied. She wondered what we would do with the medical photos and records now. Georg Becker had been exonerated by all that had happened. Amy was now finally safe from *The Circle's* members. Their crimes of the past, which the medical records would prove, were of historical interest only; their current crimes had put them in prison.

Alexa looked puzzled when I surfaced without a file or box.

I climbed aboard and toweled off. "There is no box. Mother must have destroyed it. Unlike Father with his horror tales, she may have wanted to bury the past and forget it. She looked ahead as a mother worried about her son's future and mental health."

"Did you find anything under the sole of the galley otherwise?" she asked.

"Mother had a message for us. She wrote it on the underside of the hatch cover under the sole. She knew it would be safe for us if we were able to get this far. She knew the rumor of the records would bring old enemies to the island."

"So, what did she write on the hatch cover?" Alexa asked.

It said, "Amy Becker."

We sailed that afternoon back to St. Thomas. The girls took their fifth nap on our laps. There were three of them now. Alexa had bought me a baby Westie, Lucy.

"Why Lucy?" I asked.

"You liked the Beatles back in the Sixties, didn't you?" she said. I nodded for I listened to them all the time.

"How'd you know?" I asked.

"You named the other girls, *Rita* and *Eleanor*. I assumed you were thinking of *Eleanor Rigby* and *Lovely Rita, Meter Maid*, the Beatles' songs. *Lucy in the Sky with Diamonds* just seemed to fit.

"I have more of my mother's sense of word games than I was aware. You saw that connection in their names when I didn't."

"You are your mother's son."

As we came into Charlotte Amalie Harbor, I saw those range markers that always reminded me of Mother. The markers where I had had stood with her pointed directly out to sea to Buck Island Cove where the *Dinah* and her secret rested safely. Mother had coded her map to my sister to always be etched in me even when I couldn't see it with my own eyes.

"I hope Dregs is at the dock to bring the dinghy out right away. I want to visit my new sister on the hill and tell Dad where Mother's trail ended."

"Sounds like a good idea. Just one question I've always meant to ask you. Dad and Amy asked me about it as well. Who is this Dregs person you keep referring to?"

We looked at each other. She was serious. Then we smiled a knowing smile.

"I'll get your pills, Beck."

Ewig und immer

THE END